KT-494-795

LORD JAMES HARRINGTON AND THE CHRISTMAS MYSTERY

It's Christmas, and James and Beth are preparing for Harrington's festive dinner and dance. This year, famous diva Olivia Dupree is singing, a wedding is taking place, and they're hosting a reunion of Pals ex army comrades from the Great War. When Olivia falls ill and claims she's been poisoned, James puts his sleuthing hat on. But things take a sinister turn when a further attack occurs. What links the two victims? James must race against time to stop multiple murders taking place.

Books by Lynn Florkiewicz
in the Linford Mystery Library:

LORD JAMES HARRINGTON
AND THE SPRING MYSTERY

LORD JAMES HARRINGTON
AND THE SUMMER MYSTERY

LORD JAMES HARRINGTON
AND THE CORNISH MYSTERY

LORD JAMES HARRINGTON
AND THE AUTUMN MYSTERY

LYNN FLORKIEWICZ

◆

LORD JAMES
HARRINGTON AND
THE CHRISTMAS MYSTERY

Complete and Unabridged

HIGHLAND
LIBRARIES

18 0 12 49

LINFORD
Leicester

First published in Great Britain

First Linford Edition
published 2018

Copyright © 2015 by Lynn Florkiewicz
All rights reserved

This book is a work of fiction. Names, characters, places and incidents are the product of the
author's imagination or used fictitiously. Any
resemblance to actual events, locales, or persons,
living or dead, is coincidental.

A catalogue record for this book is available
from the British Library.

ISBN 978–1–4448–3920–3

Published by
F. A. Thorpe (Publishing)
Anstey, Leicestershire

Set by Words & Graphics Ltd.
Anstey, Leicestershire
Printed and bound in Great Britain by
T. J. International Ltd., Padstow, Cornwall

This book is printed on acid-free paper

1

Diary note: France April 12th 1917 His orders are vague. There is no preparation — no thinking about the landscape. We should begin further east where there are craters to hide in. This officer is too quick to see it out. He doesn't strike me as someone who's cut out to do this. Why didn't he select his own men? We don't have a hope in hell. Not with enemy lines positioned as they are. Perhaps if the men running this war fought with us they would give more thought to tactics. I don't think we'll make it back. I feel anxious. Perhaps that's why they're sending us in. We're dispensable.

October 1958

'Harrington's! Carlo, what on earth is Harrington's?'

'Issa country hotel in Sussex,' replied Carlo. 'You must have heard of it. Joe

Loss has played there, that famous actress, wassa her name, has stayed there. *Mamma mia*, have you not heard of it?'

'No, I've not heard of it,' replied the lady, showing little interest.

'You wanna sing with my band, you gotta do Harrington's. Take it or leave it; they 'ave connections, Olivia.'

He received a frustrated sigh and a reminder that she was already the hottest big-band singer in the country. Carlo decided against mentioning that he was yet to reach those dizzy heights. He stood by the window of his London flat and studied the traffic. Not worth mentioning because Olivia Dupree only cared about her own career.

'*Si, si*, don't worry, I will ask Kathy: she will sing.'

Olivia purred. He had a vision of her pouting down the phone. 'Oh darling, don't do that. Of course, I'll do it. I couldn't bear the thought of that woman singing for you. Give my agent the dates. But, in return, you must take me to dinner and perhaps for a night cap after. Goodbye my darling.'

He slammed the receiver down. Why did he put up with her? He knew why of course. Was that wrong? Using her to climb the ladder? He shrugged. Thank heavens she didn't live nearby — too much of that pretence would drive him crazy. His gaze followed the shapely legs of a lady as she crossed the road. Sometimes, he could strangle Olivia Dupree.

Sunday November 30th 1958

Lord James Harrington looked on as the Reverend Stephen Merryweather and his wife Anne unbuttoned their coats and took off their scarves and gloves. Their small boys, Luke and Mark, kicked their shoes off and kept a tight hold of Radley's lead as the little dog stood on his hind legs to greet everyone. After hanging his coat on an available hook, Stephen glanced at him.

'St-stir up Sunday? W-what's that when it's home?'

Anne gave James a knowing look as she shrugged her jacket off. 'You're not stirring up another mystery are you?'

He chuckled. 'Nothing like that. Have you not heard of Stir-up Sunday?'

Their blank looks answered his question, as his wife, Beth, went to close the front door.

'Oh look, Bert's on his way,' she said, leaving the door ajar.

'Mummy says me and Luke stir up trouble,' said Mark. 'Is that what we're doing?'

James ruffled the young boy's hair. 'No, that's not it.'

'If it's not a mystery,' said Anne, 'then what is it and why the secrecy?'

'Anne, you really are rather too suspicious of my activities. It's simply an old custom. The last Sunday in November is the traditional day for households to make their Christmas puddings. Stirring the pudding is a ritual and we make a wish. Someone, somewhere down the centuries, named it Stir-Up Sunday.'

'Oi, oi,' said Bert as he peered round the door. 'Collared the Merryweathers, 'ave yer?'

James shook hands with his old friend.

They'd known each other since a chance meeting during a school outing and an unlikely friendship, that crossed the class system, had developed between them. Beth closed the door and motioned for Bert to hand his coat over.

James continued his conversation with the Merryweathers. 'We consider you family, so we thought it'd be nice for you to be a part of it.' Beth led them through to the kitchen where the pudding awaited. Closing her eyes, Anne breathed in through her nose.

'I can tell what you're making without looking. It smells divine.'

An infusion of orange, almonds, fruit, cinnamon and brandy filled the kitchen and the Merryweathers were quick to admire the mixture in the huge bowl.

Bert pushed his flat cap back and did the same. 'Another Nan Harrington special?'

James nodded. His grandmother had so enjoyed cooking and although in those days the family had employed a cook, the young Alice Harrington had relished the opportunity of making her own. She had jotted every successful recipe down in the now-frayed book that had pride of place alongside Beth's own recipe collection. James had inherited his grandmother's love of cooking and the villagers were used to seeing her creations feature in the many events and festivals they held.

Beth reached for the brandy and poured a small drop into the mixture. 'Don't want it to be dry.'

The kitchen door swung open.

'Morning all,' said Oliver and Harry Harrington in unison. They squatted down and made a fuss of Radley who wagged his tail in excitement.

The twins were given a warm welcome by Bert and the Merryweathers, who hadn't seen them for some months. James peered behind his sons to the hall.

'Is George not with you?' His long-standing friend Detective Chief Inspector George Lane didn't normally miss out on stirring the pudding.

Harry explained that George was held up at Lewes police station and had asked that someone make a wish for him.

'We're back for Christmas,' said Oliver

to the Merryweathers, 'or rather Harry is. I'm just off to the West Country to stay with Aunt Fiona for a while. She has a friend in their village who's allowing me try out my teaching skills.' He checked his watch. 'I'm being collected in an hour.'

The twins were on their Christmas break from Oxford. Oliver's calling was to teach and James' sister, Fiona, had mentioned that a friend was happy for him to shadow her for the last week of their school term.

'I'll be back for Christmas,' added Oliver, dipping a finger in the pudding. Beth gave him a playful slap.

'And I think Dad is expecting me to sort out Christmas at Harrington's,' said Harry, giving James an expectant look.

'That's exactly what I'm expecting and I have to say that we have our work cut out.'

The old estate was now a country hotel, nestling at the foot of the South Downs, and making its mark on the wealthy and famous as *the* place to stay. James and Beth had made what had been a millstone around the family's neck, a thriving business. The days of the landed gentry were gone and they had been quick to predict it, years previously. A large number of their peers had clung on to their homes, with dire consequences. James was forever grateful that the family made the decision to move when they did.

'We're hosting GJ's and Catherine's wedding and the first Christmas dinner and dance; all on the same night.'

GJ, an integral contributor to Harrington's summer activities, ran a number of painting workshops in the converted barn. Catherine had enrolled herself on one of his courses and the pair had hit it off immediately. When they announced their wedding date, James and Beth were quick to offer Harrington's as a venue for their reception.

'A little b-bird told me that you've hired C-Carlo Pisani and his band.'

A gasp went round the kitchen. Carlo Pisani was the up-and-coming band leader who had, in the last year, stepped up from ballrooms to a smattering of television appearances. James picked up the bottle of brandy and, winking at Beth, poured another tot into the pudding.

'Yes, we were at a function a few weeks ago where he was playing. The booking he had over Christmas was cancelled so I thought I'd ask.' He picked up a spoon and tasted a small portion of the mixture. 'I say, that's tasty — a great mix of ingredients and, if I'm not mistaken, a dash of black treacle.'

The bottle of stout they'd brought home from the Half Moon added an extra flavour. The raisins were juicy and he detected the tang of molasses. Beth's upbringing in Boston meant that she added an American influence to many of their recipes.

'I thought he'd say no but he seemed really pleased to do it. We have him for the first of December as well as the dinner and dance later in the week before we close.'

Harrington's closed for Christmas and didn't open again until February. It gave everyone a well-deserved rest and enabled James to decorate and refurbish any areas of the house and gardens that needed it.

'Goodness,' said Beth licking her spoon, 'this is wonderful. I think we're ready to make those wishes.'

As if on cue, the presenter on the small radio in the corner announced that the next record would be 'When You Wish upon a Star'.

She dropped half a dozen silver sixpences into the mix. The coins were Victorian and James brought them out every year specifically for the pudding. Not only did they all make a wish on Stir-up Sunday but if you were lucky enough to find a coin in your portion on Christmas Day, your wish would allegedly come true. She stirred the pudding in a figure of eight; it squelched as the spoon waded through the mixture. She closed her eyes and sent up a silent wish and then opened them with a wide smile and invited Oliver to do the same. James watched as everyone, including the children, made their wishes.

The telephone rang. He made his way to the hall and picked up the receiver.

'Cavendish — .'

'Ah, *ciao*, Lord Harrington?'

10

'Mr Pisani, how lovely to hear from you.' He caught his breath. 'I say, you're not cancelling, are you?'

'Carlo Pisani, cancel? No, no, I have good news. I wanted to surprise you but Carlo, he's no good at keeping secrets.'

James raised his eyebrows. 'And what is the secret?'

'Olivia Dupree, she issa my secret.'

'Good Lord. Is she your singer?'

'*Si, si,* she like to sing with my band. I say, Olivia, you wanna sing with my band, you have to come to Harrington's.'

James winced. Harrington's was, by no means, a run of the mill hotel but Olivia Dupree was used to singing at the London Palladium and topping the bill on the BBC variety shows. He cleared his throat.

'Is this going to be expensive?'

The band-leader chuckled. 'She issa part of the band, Lord Harrington, you don't pay any extra.'

After the call, James imparted the news to everyone.

'H-how wonderful!' said Stephen.

Anne's eyes opened wide. 'She sang at

11

Buckingham Palace a few weeks ago. She's a real coup.'

'Oi' said Bert, dropping his spoon in the sink, 'don't let the image fool you; she's as common as muck.' James stared at Bert who shrugged. 'Real name's Diane Brown; born in Shoreditch to a grocer and 'is wife. She's as Cockney as I am.'

'Good Lord, are you sure?'

Beth frowned. 'How do you know?'

'She went to school with a mate's daughter; had ideas above 'er station even back then. Fair play to her, though. She's got what she wants: she's rich and famous, but not without upsetting 'er mum and dad.'

'Oh, how awful to disappoint your parents like that.'

'Do we have a full house, Dad,' Harry put in, 'because if we don't we should advertise and make sure we do.'

'Yes, nothing to worry about in that department. Let's get into the study and I'll go through what's happening. Apart from the wedding party, we've four veterans from the Great War attending.

I've given them a complimentary evening; the majority are in the following week for a proper reunion.'

He felt Harry pat him on the back. 'I hope this is going to run smoothly, Dad.'

'Run smoothly? Why shouldn't it?'

'I mean I hope there'll be no mysteries to solve. You didn't wish for any, did you? Not sure that's my bag.'

He gave his son a sarcastic grin as he nudged him into the study.

'Fingers crossed it'll be a murder-free season.'

2

The church bells rang a merry peal and spontaneous applause broke out in the Church of St Nicholas in Cavendish. James and Beth watched as GJ kissed his bride and gave the congregation a bashful smile. The wedding had been small, but perfect. Beth, Anne and members of the Women's Institute had decorated the church with Christmas garlands and poinsettias. Forest ferns were laid along the aisle to help the church resemble a wooded clearing. Catherine looked resplendent in a simple white gown trimmed with a white fur collar. She held a bouquet of ferns, lilies and roses. GJ struck a handsome pose in a black suit with a red carnation buttonhole.

There were few spare seats among the pews. Along with invited guests, many of the villagers, who had come to know GJ since he had been discovered in the Harrington's barn, had wanted to be involved. As neither GJ nor Catherine had much family to speak of, James was pleased to see so much support and affection being shown for the young couple.

Catherine's widowed mother wept joyful tears. Even her cousin, Carl, such a moody individual when James last saw him in the summer, appeared genuinely happy for her. From GJ's circle, he was pleased to see Gladys from the East End mission and his late mother's sister, Juliet Brooks-Hunter. It was also wonderful to reacquaint himself with Gerald Crabtree, a man who had assisted him during the spring. His access to family records at Somerset House had been of great value.

And now, invited guests were enjoying the reception in an area adjacent to the main dining room at Harrington's. The staff, with instructions from Beth and Anne, had decorated the tables with a selection of vibrant roses, royal blue napkins and tall winter-white candles. They mirrored the forest theme from the church by placing sprays of fresh ferns and holly on the tables and around the door and window frames. Outside, a flurry of snow fell, leaving a dusting of white on the terrace.

Through the arched opening, in the main dining room, the hotel guests enjoyed a sumptuous feast of goose, stuffing and vegetables. Prior to being seated, James and Beth were introduced to Olivia Dupree and her two companions: hairdresser Enid Carmichael and personal assistant, Mandy Billings. Olivia had given Mandy an impatient huff.

'Smooth this material down. Enid, hairspray please, I can't possibly appear in this state. You should be able to see that for yourself.'

He decided, along with Beth, that the wonderful Olivia was a rather egotistical individual who had no respect for those she deemed beneath her.

Earlier in the day, the staff had decorated three huge Christmas trees; one to welcome guests in the reception area; one for the corner of the main dining room and, for this particular year, a smaller tree for the wedding reception.

Their branches sparkled with delicate baubles and vivid wooden toys. White tinsel was draped around the branches and colourful fairy lights twinkled magically. Although most households didn't put their trees up until nearer Christmas, James always remembered his father instructing the gardener to bring them in early. As far as Harrington Senior was concerned, Christmas began on the first of December.

Once the trees had been decorated, the final act was down to Beth. James had held her tight as she reached up from the ladder to secure each of the angels. For decoration purposes, each tree had half a dozen boxes wrapped in Christmas paper under it but, by the following week, there would be gifts from James and Beth to all of their staff by way of a thank you for their hard work.

In the main dining hall Adam, their young but experienced head waiter, organised the flow of food for the hotel guests as the band finished setting up. Meanwhile, the maître d', Paul, took charge of events at the wedding reception. DCI George Lane arrived late with profuse apologies. He waved a quick hello to James and took his seat alongside Dr Jackson and his wife, Helen.

James looked along the top table. Beyond him and Beth were GJ's adoptive parents and Catherine's mother. Further along were Stephen and Anne. Six tables of six guests were finishing their meals of roast pork, potatoes and vegetables. The pork, supplied by local butcher Graham Porter, was the tastiest he'd had in a long time and, as was his habit, James had left the crispy crackling as a treat to have at the end of the meal, with a sprinkling of salt. He noticed his chef, Didier, hovered at the door every so often with a slight air of anxiety. He certainly had his work cut out serving two complete menus in one evening. The smell of goose and pork mingled and sent his taste buds jumping even though he was full.

'Isn't this a wonderful day?' said Beth. She wore a flattering tea-length lavender ballgown with a pleated organza neckline.

James heaved a satisfied sigh and pushed his empty plate away. 'It's all been rather splendid, hasn't it?'

'Are you ready for your speech?'

'As ready as I'll ever be.'

Catherine's cousin, who had stepped in to give her away, tapped a crystal glass with his spoon and the room hushed as he rose; notes in hand. James glanced out of the large windows that, in summer, gave extensive views across the grounds. It was early evening and darkness had long set in but, in the glow of the house lights, he saw Olivia and Carlo in what appeared to be a heated argument. He narrowed his eyes in the false hope that this would help him make out what was happening. Olivia stamped her feet like a child having a tantrum and Carlo waved his arms about theatrically before pushing her to one side and marching back toward the dining room. A ripple of applause broke him from his thoughts.

Paul topped up everyone's glasses with champagne as the speeches came and went. GJ was generous in his thanks to the residents of Cavendish and to James and Beth in particular. James, in his role as best man, delivered a short, eloquent, address to the newly-weds that was both humorous and gracious. He raised his glass. The band began warming up.

'I'm sure that you don't want to listen to me wittering.'

'You'll not be wrong there!' shouted Donovan the pub landlord, in his soft Irish lilt. He received an elbow in the ribs from his wife for interrupting.

James acknowledged the comment with a grin. 'We have an excellent band and singer in tonight so make the most of what has already been a perfect day. To finish off though, please stand and raise your glasses to the bride and groom.'

Chairs scraped on the floor as the guests stood and held their champagne flutes toward the couple.

'The bride and groom,' they chorused.

Paul appeared behind James and leant in. 'Sorry to disturb you, your Lordship. I need to call upon Dr Jackson.'

'Oh? Someone ill?'

'Yes, Olivia Dupree. We've taken her to the office.'

'I'm sure Philip will be more than happy to take a look.' He noted Paul's concerned expression. 'I say, is everything all right?'

Paul lowered his voice. 'She hinted that someone had poisoned her.'

3

He pecked Beth on the cheek, made his excuses and grabbed Harry on the way through to reception. Didier stood in the doorway to the kitchen with the expression of a man on the edge of eruption. Familiar with his chef's temperament, James decided another couple of minutes wouldn't hurt Miss Dupree. He gestured for Didier to return to the kitchen. Didier did so. They followed him through to where his minions scurried around preparing desserts and pouring after-dinner liqueurs. His chef turned on his heels and faced them. He stood no more than five foot six inches and his rotund frame suited him. He placed his hands on his hips.

'Didier, what on earth's the matter? Have you dropped the trifle or something?'

'Trifle? *Non, non,* I 'ave not dropped ze trifle,' he gesticulated. 'The trifle is magnificent, there is nothing wrong with the trifle.'

'Well, what is it?' asked Harry.

Didier thrust a pointed finger toward the wall, behind which was the office. 'Olivia Dupree. Pah! She say she is poisoned.' He flung his chef's hat on the floor. 'I, Didier Le Noir, do not poison my clientele. I do not poison guests at 'arrington's. *Non, non*. I will not serve that woman. You choose a different singer for next week.'

Harry picked up the hat while James put a reassuring hand on Didier's shoulder. 'I say, Didier, no one is accusing you of that. I'm sure she didn't mean *you* personally have poisoned her. I mean to say, if there was something in the food, more people would be ill. And it wouldn't be your fault if there was a bad batch.'

Didier sneered. 'I obtain these ingredients personally. I 'ave never had a *bad batch*.'

Harry placed the hat on Didier's head. 'I've eaten everything in front of me, Didier, and it was all splendid.'

'*Oui, oui*, but you 'ad the pork. She 'ad the goose.'

'Well, no one else is ill, are they?'

The chef reluctantly agreed. He straightened his hat and pulled his shoulders back. 'I will return to my duty but you must speak with that woman.' He clicked his heels. 'I will not 'ave a common singer ruin my reputation.'

Turning quickly, he marched off, muttering about having put a knife in someone before and how he wouldn't hesitate to do it again. James knew he must have looked perplexed. What on earth was he harping on about, putting a knife in someone?

Harry bit his lip. 'I didn't realise he was so temperamental.'

'Mmm. He is a phenomenal cook but he can be a little pretentious with it.' He steered Harry out of the kitchen. 'Come on, let's go and see what Miss Dupree has to say.'

Olivia Dupree was draped across the small couch in the corner of the cramped office. Although physically beautiful, her pomposity and aloof expression made her the most unattractive individual to James. His friend and local doctor, Philip Jackson, was going through the motions of a general check-up. His dark, wavy hair and good looks was normally a magnet for women like Olivia but she seemed intent on playing the part of a lady close to death. The dramatic pose sent a spark of irritation through him. As Philip examined her, she threw out dramatic sighs and whimpers.

Philip put his stethoscope away and got to his feet.

'I don't suppose you have any spare rooms, do you?'

James raised an eyebrow at Paul who was quick to explain that every room was taken. 'This event's always sold out months in advance, especially with the wedding too.'

Olivia Dupree swept her hair back from her forehead and closed her eyes in despair. 'It really is too awful for words. I've been poisoned and no one is doing anything to help.'

James pulled up a chair. 'What did you eat?'

She glared at him. 'I haven't eaten. I don't eat before I sing. How can I eat before a performance? It's far too heavy. I had a light lunch before I arrived.

Poached egg and one slice of toast.'

'Well, it's unlikely that made you ill.'

Philip was quick to agree.

Harry sat down opposite her. 'Perhaps it's because you haven't eaten. That can make you feel a bit queasy.'

'Perhaps she has a bug?' Paul put in.

'I don't have a bug; I was perfectly fine until I drank the wine.'

James bristled at her tone. 'Lots of other people have drunk the wine and they're all fine. What makes you think this is poison?'

'For pity's sake, why so many questions? Just call the police.'

4

James left Harry and Philip to appease Miss Dupree, convinced that, as she was now revelling in their attention, she was prone to dramatics.

In the main dining hall, the tables and chairs had been skilfully rearranged to allow for more room on the dance floor. Waiters and waitresses carrying trays of wine, beer and champagne buzzed among the guests. He negotiated his way around the room, dodging couples who moved gracefully to 'Cherry Pink and Apple Blossom White'. The ladies, looking wonderful in their evening dresses, seemed to glide as their husbands guided them across the floor. Some of the men had loosened their bow ties and discarded their jackets. He skipped to one side to avoid Donovan and Kate as they swished by. He mounted the low-level stage and tapped Carlo on the shoulder who leant toward him.

'I'm afraid your leading lady's been taken ill.'

Carlo motioned for the band to continue and accompanied James to the side of the stage. '*Si, si*, I know. She issa playing the drama queen, *si*? Arching her back and faking the fit.'

James held back a chuckle but Carlo saw through him. 'You agree, *si*? Let her 'ave the attention she seeks on her sick-bed. I 'ave a replacement singer.'

'You do?'

'*Si, si*, Mandy Billings.'

'Her assistant?'

'*Si*. She's a good singer but she no sing for a while. She look after her mamma. But Mamma's dead now so she issa singing again.'

Mandy stood on the other side of the stage wearing a ruby-red ball gown. She'd untied her thick blonde hair; it was dishevelled but in an attractive way. She cast a sultry glance across the room. James couldn't help but stare. She was stunning. He returned his attention to Carlo.

'I presume you've heard her sing?'

'*Si, si*, but not in front of such a crowd. I 'ope she can take the pressure. If she can't, you still have Carlo Pisani.' He held out a hand.

James shook it warmly and weaved his way to the back of the room. Anne scurried up behind him.

'Is it true? Was Olivia Dupree poisoned?'

'Absolutely not, Anne. She's just come down with a bug, that's all.' He gave a look of puzzlement to where Olivia had been sitting. Adam was changing the tablecloth and wiping the floor. 'What's going on there?'

'Oh, the glass of wine she was drinking got knocked over. There's red wine all over the cloth.'

James started. The woman was over-theatrical; everyone had said as much. But if this had been poison, should he hold on to the evidence?

'Are you all right, James?'

He tore himself away from his thoughts and patted her hand. 'Absolutely, old thing. I see the people in the wedding party are all enjoying themselves. Why

29

don't you get young Stephen up on the dance floor?'

Anne didn't need to be asked twice. She dragged her reluctant husband away from his brief rest as the band launched into the classic Charleston. James stepped back as his guests laughed at each's frantic attempts to master the steps. He chuckled as some of the older men left the floor, gesturing that it was far too active for their taste. He made a beeline for Adam who had now reached the reception area with his arms full of stained linen and an empty wine glass.

'I say, Adam, who was sitting at Miss Dupree's table this evening?'

The young man looked up to gather his thoughts.

'The band leader, Mr Pisani; her two assistants, Miss Billings and Miss Carmichael, and the four ex-army gentleman.'

'Did you see who spilt the wine?'

'No I didn't, your Lordship. I was in the area but was listening to the band. Is it important?'

He assured Adam it wasn't and watched the young waiter go on his way. Philip closed the office door and approached him.

'Is George still here?'

'Yes, he's just opted out of the Charleston.' James noted the doctor's expression. 'Is there a problem?'

'Olivia Dupree will be fine but, James, I do believe she was poisoned.'

'What! Are you sure?'

'Well, I spoke with Eddie Simmonds, the old army man who was seated at their table. She showed some odd signs, apparently. She'd been the life and soul of the party, laughing, socialising, behaving rather flamboyantly.' He gave James a knowing look as if he disapproved of such behaviour. 'Then she drank some wine and got agitated, almost paranoid and started complaining of neck ache.'

'And that suggests what?'

'Well the paranoia and neck ache indicate mild strychnine poisoning. I've taken a blood sample to be sure.'

'Right. You get George. I'll ask Adam to bring the glass and tablecloth to the office.'

5

George and Beth joined James in the office where he explained that a couple had allowed Olivia Dupree use of their room for a couple of hours. Fortunately, none of the guests or the wedding party had taken much notice of what happened. They'd simply seen a woman be taken ill. He handed George the blood sample and instructed Harry to go and reassure Didier. As much as he hated the fact that the famous Miss Dupree was ill, he wanted to keep his prized chef happy, especially in the run-up to Christmas.

His friend eased himself into a chair and winced.

'You all right, George?'

George grunted that he was fine; that he probably had eaten too much and was suffering as a result. James studied him as he prepared his pipe. It was almost a meditation, a ritual that put him in the frame of mind required for police work;

the tobacco carefully placed in the bowl, the strike of a match and the considered first puff. Although James didn't smoke a pipe himself, he always loved the aroma as the first waft of its perfume reached him. George grabbed a pen and paper from the desk.

'Right, I need the names and addresses of everyone at the table. From what Adam said, everyone was seated and the wine was served with the dinner. No one approached the table at that time and no one else is ill.'

Beth sat down. 'But wouldn't Adam have been keeping an eye on the service flow?'

'He said he wasn't out of the room,' said James.

'He was watching everything from the main door but distracted a little by the band. But, yes, the wine was served with dinner so there would be no reason for people to move from table to table during that time.'

'And the main door was near where Olivia Dupree was sitting?'

James nodded.

'The people sitting at her table, do you know much about them?'

James held a finger up to indicate that George should wait, nipped out to reception to retrieve the seating plan and returned to his seat to peruse the names.

'Carlo Pisani was next to her. To the other side were Enid Carmichael and Mandy Billings. We put them all together as they know one another.'

'D'you know much about them?'

'Only first impressions.'

'They're sometimes the best. What're your thoughts?'

James allowed Beth to speak first.

'Well, I only met Miss Dupree today but I couldn't warm to her. She has a standoffish approach to most people. Anne was with me and she behaved as if she wasn't there. I found that a little rude.'

'I agree,' said James. 'She likes to be the centre of attention. All this business about being poisoned was taken with a pinch of salt by Carlo. The dramatics were worthy of an award. You might want to have a word with Bert. He has a friend who went

34

to school with her in Shoreditch. Our Olivia is not what she purports to be, George. Acts in a rather pompous manner but her family are working class.' George raised his eyebrows. 'She obviously achieved her dream but not without rubbing people up the wrong way and falsifying her status in life.'

He watched as his friend scribbled a few notes down. 'And what about this Pisani chap?'

'Oh, I like him,' said Beth, 'very gracious and charming.'

'Mmm, seems a decent chap and wise to Miss Dupree's tantrums.' He sat up. 'Speaking of tantrums, the pair of them appeared to be having a rather heated argument on the terrace before dinner was served.'

George leant in. 'About?'

James shrugged. 'No idea. It was somewhat noisy in our room with all the chatting going on and the windows were shut so I can't help there. You'll need to ask them; and Mandy and Enid. I'm sure they can give you their perceptions of Miss Dupree.'

'Who else was at that table?'

'We had our four Pals there.'

'Pals?'

'Yes, you know, the Cavendish men who signed up for the Great War. They added another battalion to the Sussex Regiment, called themselves the Cavendish Pals although men from Charnley and Loxfield were recruited too.'

'Ah, yes, the men who worked and played together.'

'Worked together, born and raised in the area and joined up together. Their actual reunion is later this week but I invited those four tonight as they've been organising events for their little gang.' He checked the guest list. 'Here we are, Eddie and Billy Simmonds, Walter Anderson and Scotty Bull. All Cavendish men.'

George scratched his head and puffed on his pipe. 'Right, I want to have a word with all of those people before the end of the evening. Can I use your telephone?'

James pushed it toward him. George began dialling as Harry knocked and came in.

'Hello, thought you'd like to know that Miss Dupree is feeling better. She's in room 15 and has been flirting with Dr Jackson and me.'

Beth groaned. 'Oh, sweetie, don't get involved with her, please.'

'Mother, I'm wounded that you'd think she was my type. It's all quite amusing really. She's really quite pretentious. I'll tell you something though, that Mandy Billings has the most fantastic voice. I think she's better than her ladyship upstairs.'

'Really?' said James.

'Go out and listen for yourself. Her version of 'Let it Snow' was spot on.'

George replaced the receiver. 'An apt song, I think. It's been snowing quite heavily over at Lewes and I can't get any constables over here. It's stopped now but I'll have to speak to these people tonight.'

'Do you need help?' James said, aware of a twinge of excitement in his stomach.

'If you don't mind.' He jutted his chin at Harry. 'What was that about Mandy Billings?'

'Great voice, better than when I saw Olivia on the television recently.' He looked at James. 'I'll make sure the evening carries on as normal if you like.'

'We all need to be there, we'll be notable by our absence. We should be circulating.'

Beth agreed. She turned to George. 'Who do want to see first?'

'I'll start with the infamous Miss Dupree. I want all of you to keep this evening running to your usual standards. James, get chatting to a few people, that's what you're good at. See what you can glean.'

James followed Beth and Harry through to the dining room to join their guests. The music stomped and the air was thick with laughter and chatter. Some ladies had wrapped tinsel around their necks and secured pieces of mistletoe in their hair. He could hardly see the dance floor for people. The guests applauded as Carlo Pisani led his band into Cool Yule. The bandleader didn't let up; one tune after another for the whole evening with only the occasional break for the musicians to catch their breath.

James grinned at Bert who had linked up with Gladys, his old friend from the East End Mission. What a couple they'd make. He'd never seen Bert in a dinner jacket and this one was borrowed from a friend for the evening so he looked a little clumsy. Even if he'd had one especially made, James was sure he'd still have looked a mess. He knew his friend felt uncomfortable and had even asked if he could still wear his cap. Beth, thankfully, had talked him out of it. Gladys, although from the East End, had no qualms about joining in. She wore a gaudy orange and lemon dress and her hair, tied up for the wedding, had become bedraggled — indeed she looked as if she'd fallen out of a washing machine. But still she laughed and danced with Bert, oblivious to her lofty surroundings. He grinned; how wonderful to see them here and enjoying themselves.

The Merryweathers jived like professionals and GJ and Catherine sat to one side of the dance floor whispering to each other and smiling. Outside, the snow had settled although he was relieved to see that it hadn't fallen as heavily here. People would, at least, be able to go home.

He caught himself listening to Mandy Billings. 'He'll come a-flying from a higher place, and fill the stocking by the fireplace.'

My word, she is *good*; and strikingly attractive, he thought. Carlo seemed to like her too, glancing across and giving her the occasional nod of encouragement. What were he and Olivia arguing about earlier? Did Mandy Billings poison Olivia to gain her place in the spotlight?

Juliet Brooks-Hunter waved and he returned it with a playful salute. He really wanted to sit down and have a chat with her and the rest of the wedding guests. He'd managed to do that during the reception but, since Olivia's illness, he hadn't had a chance. Fortunately, Juliet had booked in for a few days so that GJ and Catherine could use her house in Cornwall for their honeymoon. He checked his watch. George had entrusted him with digging deeper and that's what he must do. He grabbed a flute of champagne from a passing waitress.

'Do you want a hand?' said Harry.

'I didn't think you wanted a mystery.'

'I didn't think I did but it's intriguing, isn't it?'

James grinned and steered him toward a table.

'Let's start with young Enid Carmichael.'

6

James and Harry drew up their chairs to join Enid.

'I don't really know her that well,' said Enid staring at her nails. 'I trained to be a hairdresser; sort of fell into this position. In the right place at the right time, that's what people say, isn't it?'

James put Enid in her early twenties, with shoulder-length brown hair, hazel eyes and a homely expression. She was someone you'd easily pass in a crowd without noticing and he felt that she probably believed that herself. She wore a navy blue shift dress and a minimal amount of make-up. He let Harry lead the questioning as Enid appeared attracted to him.

'I'll bet it's a treat working for her, isn't it? All those famous people you mix with? The concerts?'

Enid gave an uninterested shrug. 'I'm leaving soon.' She shot them a look. 'I haven't told her so don't go saying anything.'

James detected an element of alarm. If Olivia were to discover her intentions, he felt Enid would receive the brunt of the singer's rage. 'Do you really not enjoy it?'

She made a face. 'I can't stand her. She's too full of herself and has absolutely no consideration for anyone else. Can't even fill her own wine glass up; fawning all over Carlo and getting him to bow to her every whim.'

'Did Carlo serve the wine?' said Harry.

'We all did; even the men from the Pals. All that drama at the table earlier was typical of her. We'd started listening to those lovely men and how they fought in the war together. They were so interesting to listen to but, of course, no one was paying her any attention so off she goes, having a fit.'

Harry started. 'Oh but she was — '

James stopped his son from contradicting her.

'Does she do that a lot, Enid?'

'She'll always have a reason for getting attention if that's what you mean. I must admit this one really was good. She should take up acting, she'd get an Oscar.'

'Where will you go,' asked Harry. 'When you leave her employ?'

'My family live in Devon and I miss them and that part of the world. I'm setting up my own hairdressing business back in the village where I was born. Me and Mandy get on well but now her mum's gone she'll probably want to make something of herself.'

'Did she lose her mum recently?'

'A couple of weeks ago. I was with her last week helping her clear the house out. Right state it is. Looks like her mum kept everything she could lay her hands on. You should see the amount of rubbish she had. Old Victorian bottles and ornaments.'

'That must have taken up some space.'

'Yeah, I'd imagine so. Used to go to junk shops and markets. Some of 'em are really old.'

James added that they could be valuable, to which Enid explained that Mandy just wanted rid of them.

'Understandable,' he said, pleased that they didn't have such clutter in their house.

'But, like I say, if I've got to work with Olivia, then it really isn't worth it. One hair out of place and you'd think I'd killed her.' She sipped her cocktail. 'I'm walking out with a lovely man called Derek and he's proposed.'

James and Harry congratulated her.

'He comes from Torquay and works for a merchant bank. But he said he'd come back to Devon and work in one of the local banks or even do something different. We prefer it down there. We're not really city people.'

James empathised with her and agreed that he loved the sense of community in a village. 'Did you see anything happen before Olivia became ill?'

Enid's apathetic shake of the head answered his question. 'Like I say, I was chatting to the old men. My father fought in the Great War and was with the Sussex Regiment. He was in the regular army though, not the Pals. He doesn't talk about it much. I suppose most of them don't, do they?'

James left Harry to continue the conversation. He didn't like to be scathing about his guests but Enid Carmichael was a bit of a wet weekend and he could quite understand why she wouldn't like working for Olivia. He could imagine the diva tormenting Enid over the least little thing. But, to be fair to Enid, she clearly intended to walk out and leave her employer without an immediate replacement. That took some degree of spirit.

Carlo stepped up to the microphone. 'Ladies and gentleman. Issa time for my boys to 'ave a last break. We'll be right back for the last 'alf-an-hour in a few minutes.'

James picked up a cocktail from Adam and threaded his way through the crowd to speak with the bandleader. Carlo was a striking figure with classic Italian features, an olive complexion and seductive smile. The guests loved him and he made a point of spending time with them as they asked for autographs and enquired as to whether Olivia Dupree would be singing.

'Olivia? I'm so sorry but she issa not well. But Mandy, you like her?'

The guests eagerly agreed that Mandy

was an excellent replacement. James looked at Mandy who stood nearby looking pleased with herself. Charlie Hawkins, the librarian, walked toward him. It wasn't often he saw the librarian in this environment but he didn't look out of place.

'She's spectacular.'

'Yes, she certainly appears to have made her mark on the evening.'

'And Olivia Dupree won't be singing at all tonight?'

'No, Mandy has the evening in which to impress and impress she appears to be doing.'

Carlo spotted him and made his excuses to join James. Charlie made a beeline for Mandy as James steered the bandleader out of the dining room.

'Thought you might like a bit of peace and quiet,' he said.

Carlo bowed and strolled around the reception area, examining the photographs. Although the theme and decor was Christmassy, the portraits depicting the village and its residents during the Great War took up one wall of the room.

Charlie had supplied them with a number of photographs from the library. With the Pals reunion later that week, they wanted to pay tribute to the community by having those memories on show. Amid the colourful decorations, sprigs of holly and red-leaved poinsettias Beth, together with Anne, had framed some wonderful photographs and added an artistic display with handwritten notes depicting names and places.

'A little unusual to put such pictures up at Christmas, *si?*'

James explained their reasons for doing so. 'We didn't want to be sombre or anything but the men tonight, and those attending later in the week, will appreciate the effort.'

'They are an interesting group.' Carlo went on to outline how much he had enjoyed the small amount of time he had speaking with the Pals quartet and the amusing stories they told. 'They speak little of the fighting but the, 'ow you say-ah, camaraderie, was good, *si?*'

'You're absolutely right and there is a tremendous fondness for the Pals. They were part of the community and didn't initially join up. But I believe our forces were almost non-existent at one point; so the call was put out for communities to serve with the assurance they'd fight alongside one another.'

After a polite interval, James steered the conversation to Olivia. He opened his cigarette case and proffered it. Carlo accepted a cigarette and, using his own stylish leather-cased lighter, lit both his and James'.

'She issa a diva, you know that?'

'You know her better than I.' James shuffled on his feet, unsure how to go about the next question. In the end, he thought it best just to come out with it. 'I couldn't help noticing the pair of you having words earlier this evening.'

Carlo laughed. 'We are always fighting, Lord Harrington. I'm Italian, it's in my nature. She wants me to be her lover.'

James baulked at his directness.

He held his hand open. '*Si*, all the time she tells me she wants me, she loves me, she want to marry me.' He looked somewhat forlorn about the whole affair and shook his head. 'I want to get married, *si*; but I want a wife who wants children and cooks like my mother. I'm a typical Italian boy, Lord Harrington.'

'You're an old-fashioned man at heart.'

'*Si*. And I want a woman who will make a home.' He jutted his chin toward the dining area. 'Women like Olivia want what will suit them. She hassa no respect.'

The conversation was an enlightening one for James. He thought Carlo Pisani, the up and coming bandleader, was driven by his career. The man was in constant demand around the country, on the radio and, now, the television and here he was talking about settling down with a wife and family. His comments about Olivia were not for sensitive ears. He admired her as a singer but, as a person, there was an underlying animosity; he tolerated her. The bandleader confirmed what many others had said: Olivia was a manipulating individual whose sole goal was to reach the top and fiddlesticks to anyone who stood in her way.

'She wants me because I am the man of

the moment; handsome, famous band-leader. I look good as her escort.' His face turned to thunder. 'I will not be used, Lord 'arrington. She will parade me like a puppet and drop me when issa convenient for her.'

The band began playing. Carlo's face brightened. 'Ah, issa time to play again. You come — dance with your beautiful wife.'

James followed the bandleader through and watched as he jogged back to his band and smiled warmly at the audience.

Beth sidled up to him. 'Isn't he a dream?' she said as she led him to the dance floor.

James held back his thoughts. He'd witnessed a flash of Carlo's temper during their chat. And not once did he ask how Olivia was. Did he not believe she was ill? Did he simply dislike her or did he actually hate her? Had he tried to kill her tonight? As he led Beth around the dance floor, James saw Harry gesturing him over. He held up a hand to indicate they'd be over once this dance was finished. He'd hardly had a chance to enjoy a waltz with Beth and he wasn't going to see this evening out without paying her some attention.

Five minutes later, they'd joined George and Harry in the office. Paul delivered a trolley of drinks.

James poured a whisky and ginger for the men while Beth opted for a gin and tonic.

'So, George old chap, what news?'

George let out an exasperated sigh and explained how difficult it was speaking with Olivia Dupree. 'I can see why people don't like her. She spoke to me as if I should be cleaning her shoes. It's a wonder someone hasn't tried to poison her before.'

James agreed and outlined his chat with Carlo. 'No love lost there. His account of the argument outside is that he was trying to convince Miss Dupree that he is not interested in being her lover.'

'Oh heavens,' said Beth. 'She has designs on him?'

'She has designs on everyone, darling, but where Carlo is concerned it is not reciprocated.' He went through his conversation with Carlo, then sipped his drink and regarded Harry curiously. 'Did you glean any more from Enid Carmichael?'

Harry made a face to suggest that he hadn't. 'Only that she can't stand Miss Dupree but she's settled on a future down in Devon with her chap. She's got it all planned out. If she's doing that, then why would she try to poison her employer?'

'Fair comment,' James put in and shifted to face George. 'What about Mandy Billings? She's making a name for herself out there. D'you think she's incapacitated her employer to grab the limelight?'

George swirled the drink around in his tumbler.

'Strychnine is a dangerous and volatile way to encourage your employer to have a night off. She could have just emptied a load of laxatives into her meal last night — that would have done it.'

'Have you spoken to Mandy?'

'Briefly. She seemed shocked, swears blind she didn't see anything untoward. She's worked with Miss Dupree for three years now and never had a problem. Miss Dupree said the same thing. I don't think there's any love lost between them but that appears to be par for the course where Miss Dupree is concerned. I'd be surprised to find anyone in her circle that does actually like her.'

'Enid,' said Harry, 'indicated that she and Mandy had been chatting to the Pals throughout most of the dinner. They were talking about The Royal Sussex Convalescent Home, the one down on the coast. It appears that many of their comrades and forerunners went there. Not just men from the Pals — Mandy and Enid had heard of it too.'

James knew the one he was speaking of. It was situated a few miles along the coast from Hove and stood in its own grounds. A magnificent building where they had looked after many of the soldiers from the war and which now operated as a general convalescent home. 'So you're no further forward.'

'It's difficult to pin down who had means and opportunity and, more importantly, a motive. I know she wasn't well liked but that's not enough.'

'Who would have benefited if she'd been killed?'

George explained that no one present would. Although she never spoke to her family, the bulk of her estate would have gone to her parents. Beth expressed her surprise. 'She must have a soft side after all.'

Harry topped up everyone's glasses. 'Do you need to speak with anyone else?'

'The Pals.'

James started. 'Surely, you don't–'

'I want to see if they saw anything, not if they did anything. As far as I know, they have no connection with Miss Dupree. She certainly indicated she'd never met or heard of any of them. Let's get them in and have a chat.'

7

Beth finished her gin and tonic. 'I'll leave you to it. Don't be too long, James, you are the host of Harrington's and best man at this wedding.'

James assured her that he would be through shortly and asked Harry to gather the four Pals together. His son gave him a mock salute and marched off. In two minutes, he'd returned with the four men. George arranged chairs in a circle to make the interview less formal. James, meanwhile, distributed more drinks.

'Thank you, your Lordship,' said Billy Simmonds, the older brother by three years of Eddie who sat alongside him.

Now in their fifties, they were alike in many ways. Same build and similar mannerisms. They were dressed in their best suits although it was likely these were the only suits they owned.

'It's good of you to let us come tonight,' added Eddie. 'Our little gang are all looking forward to the dance next week. We've been saving up regular for the last couple of years and, if it's anything like tonight, it'll be grand.'

James assured him they would have a wonderful time. He knew that Harrington's was beyond their means and this year was the first that all the Pals who were still in contact with one another would be together since leaving the army. A number of them had emigrated to Australia and a few had married and moved out of the county. But they had vowed to have one reunion where they were all together and this coming Saturday would be that day. On learning of their desire to celebrate in style at Harrington's, James had offered a considerable discount for them as a thank you from the village for their sacrifice.

Walter Anderson, a bulky man, loosened his collar and grimaced at its tightness. Scotty Bull, an equally large man, filled the room with his presence. With everyone comfortable, George went through the events of the evening, describing how Miss Dupree fell ill and that they suspected someone meant her harm.

'Correct me if I'm wrong, gentleman, I'm assuming that you have no connection with Miss Dupree, but I wondered if you'd seen anything at all?'

The four men looked at one another and shook their heads.

'I'll be honest with you,' said Eddie. 'I didn't like her very much. Bit hoity-toity for my liking.'

Walter agreed. 'New money. That's what they call it, isn't it. I mean, his Lordship here is a gent. Treats everyone equally, whereas that Dupree woman . . . '

'Stuck up madam,' added Scotty Bull. 'Don't mind speaking as I think.'

Billy reminded them of their place and they quickly apologised. James held his hands up to dismiss the apology.

'So you didn't see anything?'

The men, between them, explained that they'd had a few drinks, were enjoying chatting to the two young ladies and that Adam kept the wine flowing. Eddie put in that he only noticed what happened when the wine was spilt.

'Did she knock the glass over?'

Eddie shrugged. 'We were listening to Scotty and one of his anecdotes so I wasn't looking. Sorry we can't help. Is it serious then?'

George advised that it wasn't and that Miss Dupree would be quite well. Walter scratched his head. 'It's a bit funny though, isn't it? Someone putting stuff in a drink.' He turned to James. 'You didn't do it to get another mystery going, did you?'

In spite of the inappropriate remark, a giggle went round the room and James chuckled along with the group, assuring them that he was not that desperate. With nothing to add to proceedings, the men checked their watches and decided that it was time to wander home.

'Are you walking back to the village?' James asked.

Billy insisted it was only a mile and they had their overcoats. He turned to James. 'Is it true that there's a Mummers' play at the next dance?'

James confirmed that there was. 'I was contacted in the summer by a touring

Morris-dancing team and they wondered if we'd like a traditional Mummers' play. I couldn't resist so, yes, we have that plus the wonderful Carlo Pisani back again.'

The men's eyes lit up and Billy said the party couldn't wait for the next evening to come round. They shook hands with George. James led them out to Reception and indicated for Paul to collect their coats. 'Are you sure you don't want a lift?' he asked. 'I have the Jaguar parked outside, it wouldn't take long.'

A united 'no' was the answer along with the insistence that James join the wedding party and the regular guests.

James did so. Carlo had slowed the pace down to draw the evening to a close and most of those remaining were on the dance floor shuffling in each others' arms.

Many of the villagers from the wedding reception had long since disappeared, as they had to work the next day or needed to get back to their children. Those remaining were slipping their coats on and saying a fond farewell to GJ and Catherine who were getting ready to leave. James joined Beth as they said their goodbyes to the newlyweds. 'I'm so sorry we've not been on hand much tonight.'

GJ held a hand up. 'Please don't apologise after everything you've done for me. You got me on my feet and you've provided this wonderful celebration. How is Miss Dupree?'

Knowing that the singer would thrive on people talking about her, he delivered a quick one-line update. Beth hugged them both.

'You're not going to Cornwall tonight, surely?'

'No, no,' said Catherine. 'We're back to GJ's, sorry, our cottage tonight and getting a train tomorrow.'

GJ explained that Juliet could stay at their cottage while they were making use of her house.

'How long are you away for?'

'Two weeks. Back in time for Christmas.'

'Well, you have a wonderful time. We'll look after Juliet.'

Beth, together with those villagers remaining, waved the taxi off before returning to the dance floor.

A movement caught James' eye as he stood in Reception. Miss Dupree descended the stairs using Adam's arm for support. He dashed across to help her negotiate the last two steps.

'I say, Miss Dupree, how are you feeling?'

'I'm fine. Or I will be when I find out who did this.'

'Yes, it's a rather unpleasant thing to have happened.'

He walked with her toward the dining room where Mandy Billings was singing 'Every Time We Say Goodbye'. Olivia's eyes narrowed. 'How dare she! The moment my back is turned! She won't get away with it. And Carlo; how could he betray me like this?' She snatched her coat from Adam and marched through the front doors. James turned to his waiter.

'Where's she going?'

'There's a taxi waiting, your Lordship. She asked me to call for one a while back.'

Beth appeared beside him and pulled his sleeve. 'Come on, one final dance.'

With a last glance at Olivia, he took

Beth's hand and led her back to the dining room. Carlo and his band announced the last tune, the more up-beat 'In The Mood'. James swung Beth on to the dance floor and the pair of them jived in and around the remaining couples.

As the band hit the last note, enthusiastic applause broke out around the room with encouraging shouts of 'Splendid!' and 'Magnificent!' Carlo signalled for the band to stand and take a bow. Anne and Stephen came toward James and Beth.

'W-what a wonderful day.'

'Would there be room for us next week when he's back?' said Anne.

James beamed. 'Of course.' He called across to the Jacksons. 'I say, Philip, Helen, would you like to join us on Saturday? We could squeeze another table in if you'd like to attend.'

The doctor and his wife didn't need asking twice.

'That would be lovely,' said Philip. 'Don't often get to do this sort of thing. Do you think Mr Chrichton will babysit again?'

Beth tilted her head. 'You know how

much he loves children. Unless he has other plans, I'm sure he'd love to.'

'S-surprised he hasn't children of his own.'

James explained that the teacher had planned to marry quite some time previously but everything fell through. 'Unfortunately, he's never found the right lady. He did have someone in tow earlier in the year but she seems to have flown.'

The band began packing their instruments and music stands. The guests, exhausted by all the dancing, slowly made their way upstairs to their rooms, stopping on the way to thank James and Beth for another first of December success. Many of the ladies had taken their shoes off and walked in stockinged feet. All of the men had undone their top shirt-buttons and taken their jackets off as they plodded wearily to their beds.

Anne, Stephen, Philip and Helen said their goodbyes with the reminder that everyone was meeting in the Half Moon the following day to discuss the Christmas festivities.

Paul opened the doors leading to the

terrace and a paved area where the band's driver had parked a small coach.

James excused himself and strolled over to meet Mandy. 'I wanted to say how magnificent we all thought you were. To step up and sing so wonderfully was incredibly brave of you and we did appreciate it.'

She positively beamed. 'I loved every minute of it, I really did. It's so good of Carlo to give me a go. I didn't think he'd ask.'

'It's a pity about your employer becoming ill.'

She shrugged and, not for the first time, James received confirmation that Olivia was prone to dramatics.

'Did you enjoy the meal?'

'Oh yes. I can't remember ever having such a feast. I probably ate too much. Olivia doesn't eat anything before singing. I loved the old men at the table too. Real sweethearts.'

Carlo strode across with an outstretched hand and beckoned Beth to him. He bowed and kissed her hand and took James' hand.

'I have had the most splendid time and we do the same on Saturday, *si*?'

'*Si*,' said James. 'It's been an absolute joy, Carlo. Will Miss Dupree be singing next week?'

'I 'ave the replacement if she does not. But she will come round. She is like a child, Lord Harrington. She has the tantrum and she pouts the lips for forgiveness. She will be here. But I may not forgive her. Mandy hassa talent, a natural talent and she issa respectful. That issa what puts her above Olivia. Perhaps someone make her ill again, *si*?' He smiled.

Beth scanned the room. 'Where is Miss Carmichael? And Miss Dupree, is she still here?'

'Flown the nest, darling.'

Mandy froze, her lips curled with disgust. 'That bloody woman didn't even ask me if I wanted a lift. My God, she's something else. Shame that poison didn't kill her.'

Carlo looked sheepish as he wrapped an arm around Mandy. '*Si*, she snap her fingers and Enid go running. I would not

66

leave you on your own, Mandy. You come with me.'

She shrugged him off and, with a face like thunder, stormed out to the coach.

'*Mamma mia*,' he muttered. He smiled at James and Beth. '*Ciao*. Till Saturday, Lord Harrington, Lady Harrington.'

He bowed and joined his fellow musicians on the bus.

Paul closed and locked the doors. Adam, along with fellow waiters and waitresses poured in and began cleaning the room. James witnessed this every year and was constantly amazed at their efficiency; he likened them to a row of starlings picking up every last scrap from the lawn. They separated into groups; some cleaning, some dusting and vacuuming. As each section of floor was covered, others came in with clean tablecloths and cutlery to prepare the tables for breakfast. He clapped his hands to attract their attention and put an arm around Beth.

'We just wanted to say thank you for everything you did tonight. You had your work cut out this evening and you did your job without fuss or complaint. We'll be sure to recognise that nearer to Christmas.'

They received nods of appreciation. He and Beth returned to reception to retrieve their coats. Harry emerged from the office with the guest book.

'Harry! We thought you'd gone home.'

'I put my feet up. I did a jive with Kate Delaney and she ran me ragged. I've been taking a look at the books and the guest list. We have a war hero at the dinner on Saturday, did you know?'

'No I didn't. I don't tend to examine the next intake until the current one is over.'

Harry flicked open the pages. 'A Captain William Carlton, DSO, retired. I'm presuming he's a hero. You don't get a DSO for any old punch up.'

'Sussex regiment?'

'Their address is Pulborough so he could be.' Harry helped Beth on with her coat. 'Mother, you manage to look stunning even after dancing and hosting two functions on one night — not to mention the poisoning of the walking ego.'

She thanked him and stepped up between them. 'Shall we go home? I could really do with a nice cup of hot chocolate.'

James patted her hand. 'Good idea.'

'What do you make of this poisoning, Dad?'

James explained he didn't know what to make of it and was pleased to leave George to investigate. Truth be told, he didn't like anything untoward happening at Harrington's. The sooner it was resolved, the better.

As he and Harry brushed the snow from the Jaguar's windscreen, he couldn't help but recall the look on Carlo's face when he'd suggested that Olivia might become ill again. The smile was a playful one but that playfulness hadn't reached his eyes. And Mandy's reaction on being stranded by Olivia seemed steeped in animosity. This coming Saturday might prove to be an eventful one.

8

The following lunchtime, James and Beth joined the Merryweathers, Bert and Charlie in the Half Moon. The Delaneys had added a festive feel to the bar with plenty of tinsel and fairy lights draped over pictures and along oak beams. A small tree stood in the corner and a roaring log fire spat out a warm welcome. Most people were at work but a few farmhands and retired villagers sat at the bar discussing Christmas, the wedding and events in the news.

Donovan waved a cheery hello. 'Is it being too early for the Christmas ale?'

His wife, Kate, who was hanging tinsel around the bar, looked down from the chair she was standing on. 'And we've Christmas mead too.'

James examined the brewer's label depicting a jolly Santa Claus skimming across the rooftops against a midnight blue backdrop; he was holding a pint of the said Christmas ale. He didn't like judging the quality of a beer by the picture but he'd not been let down on previous years so he ordered a pint. Beth settled for a large schooner of mead.

'You won't be disappointed,' said Kate to Beth.

'It's made on a farm near Brighton using honey from their own bees kept on the South Downs.'

Donovan gently allowed the ale to flow into a dimpled pint-jug. He placed the beer on the ancient oak bar. A white head formed on the top. James held it up to the light. Dark ale, fruity, he suspected. He leant in and took a sip. Undeniably, a Christmas ale with, he remarked, a hint of cinnamon if he wasn't mistaken.

Kate grinned. 'You know your ale, your Lordship.' She stepped down from the chair and picked up a card from under the counter. 'Honey, chocolate, ginger, oranges, cinnamon, nutmeg, cloves; along with all the normal malt and hops.'

Beth sipped her mead. 'And this is delicious.'

Drinks in hand, they wandered across

to join the others who had taken up residence in the booth overlooking the village green.

'Any news on Miss Dupree?' asked Anne. 'Was someone trying to kill her?'

Stephen rolled his eyes. 'A-Anne, you are b-becoming far too eager to learn of someone's demise. R-Remember your position, please.'

Charlie put in. 'I didn't even realise she was ill until her replacement got up.' His face softened. 'She was a wonderful replacement though.'

Bert prepared a roll-up. 'Don't surprise me that someone wanted to knock 'er off.'

James blinked with surprise. He shrugged.

'I'm just saying, that's all. I spoke to my mate this morning; the one whose daughter went to school with 'er. A conniving cow, that's what he described 'er as — even back then.'

'I guess,' said Beth, 'if you're like that as a child, unless someone takes it out of you, you'll continue like that as an adult.'

James agreed and suggested that she'd probably upset a few people on her road to success.

'Someone once said that you were to be nice to those people on the way up because you might meet them on the way down.'

'That's right, Jimmy-boy,' said Bert, 'and she's gonna find out the 'ard way; trampling over people's feelings to get wha' she wants. Not right.'

'Well, we're not here to judge. Providing she turns up and sings on Saturday, I'll be happy. Now, what's happening this week?'

Charlie held up a piece of paper. 'Dorothy's given me the list. She's up in London today visiting a sick relative.'

Dorothy Forbes was the chief organiser of village events. Although James and a handful of others knew the local folklore and traditions, Dorothy could be relied upon to whip everyone into shape and actually make things happen. Even in her absence, she didn't disappoint.

'Well,' continued Charlie, 'the Cavendish Players are more or less word perfect for the pantomime. Still a couple of rehearsals to go but that's all coming on nicely. The nativity play is being performed this Saturday and next Friday afternoon. The

Saturday performance is at the old people's home down the road. The Friday performance is at the church at four o'clock.' He looked up. 'I take it everyone will be there.'

They agreed that those who were able to attend would be there.

'Who is pl-playing Father Christmas this year? Is he handing out presents after the nativity or at a separate time?'

'St Nicholas Day falls on Sunday so we thought we'd do it after the church service if that's all right with you.'

Stephen's eyes opened wide with delight. 'Of course, the sixth of D-December. St Nicholas Day at St Nicholas Ch-church.'

Anne beamed. 'Oh that will be wonderful. That's this Sunday.' She turned to Beth. 'Shall we get together and try and encourage everyone to attend? I know we have a relatively full house at church but, if they know Santa's coming too, we can make sure all the families are there. I have to muck in a little more at the moment because Stephen is doubling up on things.'

Stephen explained that the vicar at Loxfield had succumbed to a nasty flu virus. 'I-I'm afraid I shan't be a-about as much as normal.'

'Me neither,' Bert put in. 'It's Christmas, I've go' orders to get in and you lot 'ave put 'em in so don't give me filthy looks.'

James bit back a grin and silently hoped that the likes of Bert Briggs would remain in our society for years to come. He knew his friend was a rogue and his goods and wares were probably obtained down a dark alley somewhere but he turned a blind eye. On more than one occasion, Bert had helped James resolve an issue and, although he felt incredibly guilty for doing so, he put an order in for a few presents.

Beth confirmed that she was more than happy to help Anne gather a congregation. 'The Snoop Sisters have all the presents locked up in their front room. They've wrapped them up and coded them.'

Rose and Lilac Crumb, nicknamed by James as the Snoop Sisters because they were so nosy, integrated better when they had something important to do. This was their role for the Christmas period. The Women's Institute, throughout the year, put a percentage of its takings from village events into a kitty to purchase toys for the children in December.

Bert frowned. 'Coded 'em.'

James explained that they had around thirty young children in the village aged between two and ten. Each present was coded to suit a boy or a girl and the approximate age it would suit.

'They're generally pretty spot on because it's normally jigsaws, annuals, toys, that sort of thing.'

'That reminds me,' said Bert taking out a scrap of paper and a small pencil. 'I've got some children's books and annuals coming in the next few days. Let me know if you want any. Half price.'

Anne immediately asked if he was able to get a copy of *Tom's Midnight Garden*. 'The story sounds wonderful and I'm sure Luke and Mark will love it. I adore children's books.'

The next ten minutes were taken up with orders being placed. James smirked at Beth, knowing she was thinking the same. All of these items would have fallen off the back of a lorry; but, people can't resist a bargain. Suffice to say, he had to accept that Bert would be unavailable for most of the lead-up to Christmas. He sipped his ale.

'So, we have a nativity play on Saturday. Is everyone walking to the old people's home or are we ferrying the children?'

'Walking,' said Charlie. 'Even if it snows, it's only just outside the village. Has anyone heard the forecast?'

'Yes, we did,' said Beth. 'We had the radio on before we left — the odd flurry of snow most days.'

'P-perfect,' said Stephen. 'I do like a frosty and snowy Christmas season; i-it makes it jolly special.'

Instinctively, they all peered through the window to the village green where about an inch of snow had settled overnight. Immediately outside the pub they could see footprints across the green with the occasional paw print of a dog or fox. The branches on the trees glistened white and wispy smoke swirled from the chimneys of the surrounding cottages. It was a Christmas card scene, no doubt about it, thought James.

A sturdy rat-a-tat on the table brought them out of their musing. Donovan stood there with his arms folded. 'Christmas dinner for the regulars — what're you thinking?'

James and the rest of the people seated with him looked at one another with some confusion. He met Donovan's eye and questioned what he meant.

'It's something we were doing back in Ireland. Gather the locals, you know, those who come regular like; have Christmas dinner. Not on Christmas Day; we thought about a couple of weeks' time. Bob Tanner and the Taverners said they'd do the singing. What're yer thinking?' James felt Beth's rush of excitement. 'Oh what a wonderful idea.' She turned to James. 'You could do the Yule Log ceremony too.'

The burning of the Yule log was a tradition that went back centuries and the Harringtons had carried it out for several decades. It stemmed from an old pagan tradition. At the end of each Christmas, a part of the old Yule log was held back and formed a part of the lighting of the new log the following Christmas Eve. James said that, although it would be earlier than it should be, he would happily bring a piece of log for that evening. Anne suggested they gather those invited to plan the menu and delegate preparation of the food. James gave Charlie a knowing looked as he envisaged another tradition in the making.

Kate interrupted them. 'Sorry to disturb you but there's a young girl outside wanting to talk to you, Lord Harrington. Carol, her name is.'

James knew he must have looked blank but he couldn't think who Carol could be. He slipped out of the booth and wandered through the bar and out on to the cobbles where a girl of around fifteen stood in a brown coat with a wool scarf pulled around her neck. Her face registered.

'Ah, Carol, you volunteered to help out at Harrington's this morning.'

With the traditional first of December dance and the wedding party on the same day, Beth had organised some help to cover the breakfast roster. Carol, from the nearby village of Loxfield, was one of those volunteers. James hid his amusement as the young girl curtseyed.

'What can I do for you, Carol?'

'Well, your Lordship, I've just come from Harrington's see and Paul said I was to come and give this to you straight away. I went to give it to him but he said he wouldn't be seeing you until later if at all. I cycled here as quick as I could. Paul called your house and your son said you were here.'

'And what is this thing you need to be showing me?'

She gave a start of surprise. 'Oh, sorry.' She fumbled in the pocket of her woollen coat and brought out an envelope. 'I found it when I was bundling the napkins up for the cleaners. It fell on the floor.' She opened her eyes wide. 'I didn't read it. Paul read it and told me I was to find you. He said it obviously belongs to one of the guests and wanted it kept safe but he wondered if you might know who it belonged to.'

James took the piece of paper and gave Carol half a crown.

'Ooh, thank you, your Lordship.'

'Thank you, Carol. Are you helping out again this weekend?'

She assured him she was and James thanked her for her efforts and for taking the time to deliver the note. She climbed on her bicycle and pedalled away. James cleared a sprinkling of snow from the wooden bench, sat down and opened the envelope. He pulled out a small piece of, flimsy paper but, before he could read it, a young man in his mid-twenties sat down beside him.

'Hello, I just popped into the pub and they said you were out here. I'm John Carlton, one of the Mummers' team. You booked us over the telephone — you spoke with me.'

'Of course. We're not expecting you until Saturday. Is there a problem?'

'No, no, we're performing in Loxfield tonight so I thought I'd cycle over and introduce myself. I called at the manor house and the maître d' told me you were here.' He rubbed his hands together. 'I thought I'd confirm everything and assure you that we'll be at Harrington's around six-ish to perform for seven thirty. Is that right?'

'That's right. We're starting dinner around seven and we thought that would be a nice break before the main course.'

'My mum and dad are stopping at Harrington's this weekend.'

'Oh?'

John went on to explain that they'd never seen him perform the Mummers' play and that his mother had heard many good things about Christmas at Harrington's. 'I saw all the pictures of the Pals up in reception. Is the house connected to the war?'

James told him about the reunion and expressed his realisation that John Carlton was related to the retired Major, William Carlton. 'He fought, I presume.'

The young man confirmed that he did. 'Doesn't talk about it much. He was a Captain at the time and I think he saw too much. A lot of them did, I suppose.'

'I say, did you want to join us for dinner while you're there? I know you'll have all your costume on and all but it would be a nice surprise for your parents.'

John beamed. 'Well..yes, I'd love to, if it's not too much trouble.'

'Olivia Dupree is singing with the Carlo Pisani band.'

'Olivia Dupree? I thought she only deigned to be appear on television and at palaces?'

'You know her?'

John shrugged and stood up. 'Just what I read, that's all.' He held his hand out and thanked James for the invitation. 'See you Saturday.'

James' gaze followed him until he cycled out of sight, then he returned his attention to the piece of paper. It was a diary entry. The writing was tiny and he struggled to see through some of the marks and stains. He crossed his legs and began reading: *France April 12th 1917: His orders are vague. There is no preparation — no thinking about the landscape. We should begin further east where there are craters to hide in. This officer is too quick to see it out. He doesn't strike me as someone who's cut* *out to do this. Why didn't he select his own men? We don't have a hope in hell. Not with enemy lines positioned as they are. Perhaps if the men running this war fought with us they would give more thought to tactics. I don't think we'll make it back. I feel anxious. Perhaps that's why they're sending us in. We're dispensable.*

He turned the paper over.

France April 14 1917: This isn't war; it's slaughter. What's the point? These generals are miles away, telling us where to fight. The plan is set up to fail. He's leading us to our deaths.

James sat back and gazed at a robin sitting on the old stocks. The diary must belong to one of the Pals. My word, that man, whoever he was, had taken a risk writing this in the trenches. If he'd been found out, he would have risked the firing squad. He took out his wallet and carefully placed the paper inside. Perhaps one of the men wanted to share it with his comrades. He rapped the wallet with a silent reminder to return it to its owner, whoever that was, on Saturday.

Saturday. The attack on Olivia Dupree was a shock. He hoped there weren't more on the horizon. As he entered the warmth of the pub, a sense of unease welled up inside him.

★   ★   ★

Major William Carlton, retired, grumbled over his soft boiled egg. 'Blast it, Cynthia, do we have to attend this dinner at Harrington's? And why do we have to stay the weekend? We could drive back.'

Cynthia, unseen by William, pursed her lips. How often had she refused invitations and declared false illness to those polite enough to request their company? These last few years, their social functions had fallen dramatically and all because of William's pomposity and inability to trust anyone. But for once Cynthia had stood up to her husband. Tired of the ever-increasing excuses for not attending dinners and celebrations, she'd insisted that they spend the night at Harrington's to see their son perform the Mummers' play.

'Good God, woman, it's not as if we haven't seen a Mummers' play,' William growled as he straightened out his copy of the *Times* over the dining table.

She threw the tea towel down on the draining board. 'This is not about seeing the Mummers' play; this is about seeing our *son*. This is about getting out and socialising; being with other people instead of being cooped up in this godforsaken house every weekend.'

She watched him bristle.

'Godforsaken house? We're in the middle of the Sussex countryside — this is an estate that people look on in envy. Not many people can afford a house like this.'

She slammed the cutlery drawer shut. 'You're right there. People look through the gates and wonder who lives there. They don't wander up the drive and knock on the door. They don't enter these empty rooms and fill them with life. No. Because you won't have anyone set foot inside the place.'

She knew he'd heard her but he chose to ignore the comment and focus on his newspaper. She untied her apron and cast it aside.

'Well, I'm not making excuses any more. Harrington's has a wonderful reputation and Carlo Pisani is playing. Lord and Lady Harrington will be there — or are they not deemed worthy of your time either?'

'Cynthia, for goodness' sake woman.'

'I'm going to the village. I'm meeting the ladies from the bridge club for tea.'

At the front door, she picked up an envelope from the doormat and brought it through to him. 'Another of those cheap brown envelopes; that's the third one in as many months.'

She observed him falter. The bluster had disappeared. She'd seen it the first time he'd opened one of these envelopes.

William waved a dismissive hand. 'No one you know.'

Later that evening, Cynthia peeked inside the envelope. It was the same as before. She knew where he kept them and she'd made a point of seeing what it was that had rattled him. It had sent her on her own journey of discovery and, oh my, the secrets she'd uncovered. They were composed of letters cut out from newspapers and glued on cheap paper; they accused the Major of something dreadful. The enclosures were as alarming as the notes. She read this latest letter, knowing it would be similar to those that had come before.

I KNOW WHAT YOU DID.

She had discovered what it meant but William knew nothing of her probing into his past. Her eyes narrowed. Secrets could ultimately lead to the downfall of Major William Carlton. She stared out of the window. Dark clouds gathered and cast shadows across the snow. Was the sender of these awful letters out there now, watching?

9

Saturday arrived in the blink of an eye and the first event of the day was the nativity play at the old people's home.

The Grange, on the outskirts of Cavendish, was a rambling old house with around forty elderly residents calling it their home. Standing in its own grounds, it made an impressive sight, with its large Georgian sash windows and a wide oak-panelled front door. Majestic evergreen trees stood guard around the property and a gravel drive led visitors from the main road through the snowy landscaped gardens to a parking area by a small fountain.

Stephen Merryweather and Mr Chrichton, the primary school teacher, had led the children from the village along a country lane and into The Grange's main dining hall. Staff, with help from the WI, had served gammon with vegetables while the Charnley choir sang popular carols.

A bushy Christmas tree stood to one side of the makeshift stage. Elsie Taylor, the owner of James' favourite local café, brought out some individual Christmas puddings and set them on the tables.

Mr Chrichton ushered the children on to the stage.

With everyone comfortable, the nativity play began and James and Beth settled on chairs to one side of the room to watch. James particularly enjoyed this time of the year. His own father had been a huge traditionalist where Christmas was concerned and any custom he could find to celebrate, he'd follow. Of course, the nativity was something that all schools performed. Beth leant in.

'It only seems like five minutes ago when Oliver and Harry were in this play.'

'Yes. Oliver hated being a shepherd, do you remember?'

Beth chuckled. 'I do. And Harry wanted to be the star in the heavens.'

James reminisced. How the time had flown. Now Oliver was a couple of years away from pursuing his teaching career and Harry had made a start on following in James' footsteps. He scanned the room.

'I say, where is Harry?'

'He's up at the manor house organising things. Sit back and enjoy your time off.'

The children did themselves proud as they presented the story of Christmas. As always, a few hiccups occurred; one of the wise men dropped his gold; a shepherd had a sneezing fit and Charlie Hawkins' son, Tommy, picked a fight with a fellow wise man over who stood closest to the donkeys.

Sebastian and Delphine, the donkeys from the Harrington estate, behaved themselves with the exception of a slight accident toward the end of the play. With a good deal of chuckling from the audience, Stephen shuffled onto the stage with a brush and pan to clean up.

The residents were delighted with the show and joined in with the children as they sang 'The Holly and the Ivy'. After around an hour, the play and carols came to an end and Mr Chrichton and parents led their charges back to the village. James and Beth remained behind to chat with the residents. Harry joined James in the kitchen to help the staff with afternoon tea.

'Ah, Harry, everything all right?'

'Rather.' Harry arranged cups and saucers on a tea trolley. 'The leader of the Morris-dancing team popped in — John Carlton. Nice chap; they sound like a merry bunch of Mummers.'

'Yes, I met him a few days ago.'

'So he said. They perform the traditional play, with people dressing up as a dragon and as Saint George. I think it'll go down well.'

James agreed and commented that he hadn't seen a Mummers' play for several years. 'I'm pleased to be reacquainting it with Cavendish again. And what time are the Pals arriving?'

'The first is due in around an hour, I think. It's a bit full on today, isn't it? This John Carlton is the son of that retired Major. Be interesting to know if he's familiar with the men organising the reunion.'

James pinched a couple of mince pies from Elsie. She motioned him to put them on to a plate where she topped them with brandy butter.

'Can't have them dry,' she said with a hint of a Sussex accent. 'If you're going to have them, you have to have them proper.'

He thanked her and bit into the melt-in-the-mouth shortcrust pastry. James swept his tongue across his teeth. 'Mmm, they're tasty.' He turned to his son. 'Yes, William Carlton. His wife's name is Cynthia — I think she made the reservation.'

'Were the Pals all from Cavendish, Dad?'

James explained that they were made up of the cricket and football teams from the three villages in the area; Cavendish, Charnley and Loxfield. Beth joined them.

'Are you talking about the Pals?'

'I was just explaining it all to Harry.'

'You should speak with Charlie Hawkins. His father was in the Pals. He has quite a selection of photographs at the library. Anne and I are going there later — we thought we'd display a few more for tonight's dinner.'

'By the way,' said Harry, 'that Carlo

Pisani chap called to confirm that they're arriving around six o'clock to set the band up. He's intrigued about the Mummers play.'

James put his plate down and brushed some stray crumbs from his sweater. 'Did he confirm that Olivia Dupree was singing?'

'Ye-es, he did.'

James couldn't help but notice the slight hesitancy in his son's response. Harry grimaced.

'He hinted that he couldn't tell her not to come but he really wanted Mandy. Less trouble, he said. We may have some jealousy between the two ladies.'

James raised an eyebrow. He couldn't disagree with Carlo.

Beth reached across for a tea towel. 'I don't mind them all coming but I sincerely hope we won't have anyone else taken ill.'

Harry frowned. 'You don't think there'll be any trouble do you, Dad?'

'I hope not.' And he couldn't think of a reason why there would be; but something nagged deep inside him. The diary entry that had been found; on the surface it appeared to have little to do with the events that unfolded earlier that week; yet, somehow, he felt it was connected.

10

James stood by the reception desk observing the activity. Beth held a picture in place as Anne stepped back and judged whether or not it was level. Charlie stood by with hammer and nails to secure the photographs. Mrs Jepson finished the dusting and began packing her polish and cloths away. Paul was preparing a roster for the evening, while Adam and his fellow waiters and waitresses fussed around the tables, ensuring everything was pristine for the evening.

He made his way toward Beth. Anne tilted her head to one side. 'I didn't realise so many men from the village fought.'

'Me neither,' said Beth. 'I knew there was a Pals regiment but I didn't realise so many signed up. I believe around fifty went in total.'

Charlie pointed to a photograph of a group of young men in uniform. It had been taken in the warm sunshine by the edge of the cricket field in Charnley. Although the men had their uniforms on, they'd discarded their jackets and undone their top buttons. Their youthful faces were full of excitement and laughter.

'That's my dad there. We named our Tommy after him. And that bloke there is Paul's father.'

'What, our Paul?' said Beth, 'the maître d'?'

'That's right and that's Adam's grand-dad and your gardener's brother.'

Anne put her hand to her chest. 'I didn't realise your staff had so many ties.'

James reminded them that it was a close community so it made sense that many of the staff would have those links. The noise of a car drawing up caught their attention. An elderly couple emerged from a large Daimler, gathered their coats and a small suitcase each and came in to Reception. One of the temporary staff rushed forward to take their belongings.

'Ah,' said James, walking toward them, 'you must be Major and Mrs William Carlton. I'm Lord Harrington, welcome to Harrington's.'

The Major was an upright man, a little shorter than James, with some weight around his middle and a no-nonsense expression. He judged the man would not suffer fools gladly. James' welcome handshake was not reciprocated by the Major but by his wife; a thin, elegant woman with shoulder-length greying hair.

'So lovely to meet you, Lord Harrington. I'm Cynthia.'

James gestured for Beth to join him and he introduced her. 'We've been preparing the reception area for a reunion.'

'Oh, how exciting,' Cynthia replied. 'Our son said something about this but I confess I wasn't taking too much notice.'

'Well, some of our party are a reunion of Pals from the Sussex Regiment.' He faced the Major. 'I say, Major, weren't you a Captain in the Great War? Was that with the Sussex?'

The Major's face paled and James was quick to ask if everything was all right. Beth suggested that it would have been a tiring drive through the snowy country lanes. 'Perhaps a lie down would restore you before the evening,' she said tactfully.

Paul joined them and steered the Major to a chair to complete the check-in formalities before ringing the desk bell. A young bell-boy, hired for the weekend, appeared.

'Luggage to Number Eleven,' Paul said to the boy and then turned to the Carltons. 'Would you like some tea delivered to your room?'

'That would be lovely,' Cynthia said. She commented on the festive decorations. 'I'm really quite excited about tonight, Lord and Lady Harrington. We rarely attend such functions these days and the ambience here is most welcoming. Reminds me of the big functions we used to attend when William was in the army, don't you think, William?'

William grunted and followed the bell-boy up the stairs. James raised his eyebrows at Beth. 'He doesn't seem to think so.'

'Perhaps he'll be better after a lie-down.'

Half an hour later, a loud Italian accent interrupted them as they put the final touches to the arrangement of photographs.

'Lord Harrington; Lady Harrington.' The man bowed. 'Carlo Pisani issa back to play in your beautiful house.'

James couldn't help but grin. The man was so friendly, he felt he'd known him for years. He shook his hand. 'Mr Pisani, lovely to see you. Has your band parked round the side?'

'*Si, si,* the staff 'ave opened the doors and we can set up. Olivia has arrived, *si?*'

'It appears not,' Paul put in. 'Is she driving down? The roads are a little icy. Perhaps she's taking her time.'

'Mandy is driving. She issa good driver, a good singer.' He leant in towards Anne as she came across to greet him. 'Maybe she's a good lover?'

Anne flushed. Beth suppressed a grin and James motioned for him to go straight through to the dining room.

As if on cue, Olivia Dupree entered the reception area as if she'd been announced to the Queen. Mandy Billings and Enid Carmichael followed, carrying vanity cases. Olivia flung her gloves on the centre table. She spoke aloud but not to any one in particular.

'This weather is too awful to drive in.' She mumbled to herself. 'What on earth possessed Carlo to take this appointment?'

'I think you're being terribly ungracious,' Anne said with some asperity. 'Lord and Lady Harrington are your hosts and employed you to perform in this wonderful setting. You really are terribly rude.'

Olivia glared at her. James put an arm around Anne. 'I'm sure we'll be able to live up to expectations, Miss Dupree.'

Didier emerged from the kitchen and locked eyes with the singer. He put his shoulders back, sneered and returned to the kitchen. Miss Dupree chuckled. 'What an odd little fellow.'

Beth guided her through to the dining hall to meet up with Carlo. James scrutinised Anne.

'Anne, is everything all right?'

Anne heaved a sigh and put her hand to her forehead. 'I'm so sorry, James, but you and Beth have given her such a warm welcome and Harrington's is not some grubby bed and breakfast. She really is the most infuriating snob.'

James chuckled and gave her a reassuring squeeze.

'You really mustn't let her get to you. She'll get her comeuppance one day.' He suddenly hoped it wouldn't be that day though.

Anne let out a frustrated sigh and went to help Mrs Jepson refresh the floral display.

A taxi drew up and a man in his fifties stepped out holding a battered suitcase with a number of travel stickers affixed to it. He surveyed the country hotel and brushed the toes of his shoes on the back of each trouser leg. Then he straightened himself up and smoothed his hair back. James dashed out to welcome him.

'Hello, I'm Lord Harrington; welcome to Harrington's. Have you come far?'

The man looked a little startled and made a half bow as James ushered him through to Reception. His eyes darted around the exquisite interior and through to the dining room. He puffed his cheeks out.

'Crikey, I know the blokes said it was a

nice gaff but that's an understatement.' He checked himself and put out a hand. 'Sorry, I'm Alfie Stone and, yes, I have come quite a way. Australia.'

'Ah, you're one of the Pals. You're not Cavendish though, are you? I don't recognise the name.'

Alfie confirmed that he was part of the Loxfield cricket team. 'Joined up with everyone else. Most of the Loxfield team were killed and I couldn't face coming back so I went to Australia. A few of us ended up over there. When I heard from the Simmonds boys, I couldn't believe it. We've been trying to get together for a few years and this is the first time we've all been able to make it.'

'How long are you staying for?'

'Just the night here. Thought I'd treat myself and the rest of the Pals are doing the same. But, tomorrow, I'm going to see my cousin in Cambridge.' He studied the photographs. 'These are of us, aren't they?'

James suggested he leave his bag at Reception and take a look around. 'Paul will get you checked in and you can reacquaint yourself with your memories.'

Didier came through from the kitchen and handed Paul a sheet of paper before returning to his area of expertise. Alfie followed his every move with intense concentration. James couldn't help but ask if he'd seen a ghost. The ex-army man frowned and jabbed a finger at the kitchen door.

'He reminds me of a lad that worked in France, sort of résistance fighter-type — like a runner, passing messages and bringing food in. Only a young man then but there's something about the way he holds himself.' He snapped his finger and thumb to try to bring back lost memories. 'Didier something or other . . . '

'Didier le Noir?'

Alfie swung round. 'That's it. Is that him?'

'It most certainly is. Did you say he was in the resistance?'

Alfie nodded enthusiastically and gave James a quick rundown on Didier's actions during the many battles in France. He and a number of the villagers from small villages in the Artois region passed messages to the allied commanders about German movements along the front line. They helped wounded soldiers back on their feet and provided food and shelter in farmhouses and barns. James was aware that he must have looked stunned. He couldn't imagine his rotund chef doing anything but prepare beautiful food. He made a mental note to have a chat with him and perhaps encourage him to take a place at one of the Pals tables tonight.

The afternoon soon went by and guests from all over the country trickled in for the evening event. The Christmas dinner-dances had proved to be popular among the socially elite and, over the last few years, were fully booked by the end of the summer. Many returned year after year and James found they now had to say no to a good number of enquiries. They'd already increased the dances to two during December and he wondered if, next year, he should hold three. He discussed the idea with Beth while they were getting changed. He looked in the mirror as he tied his bow tie.

Beth agreed that they should. 'It's a wonderful evening and festive too. Last year, a few of our regulars said it wasn't Christmas until they'd attended our dance. Perhaps we could have a theme for each one.'

'A theme?'

'Yes.' She fastened her earrings. 'Well most of our events follow custom and folklore. Perhaps we could do the same for the dinners. Christmas isn't short on tradition.'

Satisfied with his bow tie, James slipped his dinner jacket on. 'What a splendid idea. We could have the Christmas Mummers at one, perhaps a carol service or something on another and the burning of the Yule Log at a third.'

'We could combine that with the Lord of Misrule. Didn't you say that was a Christmas feast of some sort?'

'Good Lord, yes. That would fit in perfectly. I'd have to research it a little but I believe it's a festival for dressing up and I don't mean evening dress, I mean something colourful and gregarious.' James stood behind Beth to fasten a diamond necklace round her neck and suggested they had a good chat about it once everything had quietened down.

Beth turned to face him. She looked glorious in a long midnight-blue satin dress. She wore kitten-heeled shoes of the same colour and a beautiful matching bolero jacket. Her make-up was subtle and her chestnut hair shone in the light.

'Beth, darling, you look beautiful.'

She looked at him coyly. 'And you, my Lord, look handsome and debonair.'

He smoothed his hair back. A man couldn't fail to look good in a well-cut dinner-jacket and, although not a vain individual, he did feel as if he had stepped up for the evening. There was a knock on the bedroom door.

'You decent?' Harry entered and took a step back.

'Well, look at you two! You look like you're attending dinner at Buckingham Palace.'

Beth plucked a stray hair from Harry's own dinner-jacket. 'I think we all look grand.' She checked her watch. 'We've time for a sherry before we leave.'

107

James said that would be wonderful. Beth snatched her evening bag and went. Harry commented on the number of people attending the dinner. He added that he hoped Olivia Dupree wouldn't be ill again. James groaned.

'I have to say, I couldn't care less if she was. I find her incredibly rude and, truth be told, I rather prefer Mandy Billings.'

'Me too.' He sat on the corner of the bed. 'Do you think someone intentionally poisoned Olivia?'

'You can't mistakenly take strychnine, Harry. Someone was either wanting to make her ill or trying to kill her.'

'Well, I know who I'd put my money on. There's only two people who would do that. Carlo has motive and opportunity. He wants Mandy singing for him now but doesn't have the guts to tell Olivia. And Olivia is lusting after him and he wants nothing to do with her. And Mandy is being told by all and sundry that she's better than Olivia. She wants her place in the spotlight and who better to do it with than Carlo? He could open doors for her.'

James reminded his son of his reluctance to be involved in any mysteries. 'Not my bag, I think you said.'

Harry grinned. 'I can see why you do it. It's interesting isn't it?'

They wandered downstairs and into the lounge which they had earlier transformed for the season. Christmas had emerged from the cupboard in the form of a wonderfully decorated tree, and festive tinsel was draped artistically over paintings and mirrors. A set of red candles flickered on a corner table. Harry accepted his sherry from Beth.

'Who is Olivia sitting with tonight?'

'The same group as last time plus a couple of others. We have an extra Pal on the table; Alfie Stone. A few are on the next table with Stephen and Anne. Oh, and Didier has a place laid.'

Harry and Beth stared at him. He took a quick swig of sherry and picked up a white silk scarf.

'Yes, it appears our chef was quite something in the French résistance during the Great War. Alfie Stone recognised him when he arrived. I had a chat with Didier afterwards and, of course, he played everything down but I insisted he join the table for at least one course. He has plenty of help in the kitchen so he's joining us for the soup and then returning to his domain.'

'How wonderful,' said Beth who went on to say how surprised she was to find so many descendants from the Pals working at Harrington's. 'Remind me who we're entertaining?'

'We have the Major and his wife, their son, John, Juliet Brooks-Hunter and a couple who are celebrating a wedding anniversary.'

Beth let out a satisfied sigh and emphasised how much she enjoyed Miss Brooks-Hunter's company. 'I think it's because she is so like her sister. And although I didn't know Delphine that well, she's someone I warmed to immediately.'

Delphine had been the subject of James' investigation during the spring and he had to agree with Beth. Juliet not only mirrored Delphine in looks but personality too; assertive with a wicked sense of humour beneath the surface.

James slipped an overcoat on and draped a fur coat over Beth's shoulders. 'Right, come along. Let's get ourselves over to Harrington's. Adam and his team are serving cocktails in around half an hour.'

'Is Dr Jackson coming?' said Harry.

'Yes he is. Why?'

'Thought you might want to have him on standby just in case someone falls ill.'

His son laughed and Beth chuckled along with him.

'Harry, don't tempt fate.'

Outside, James locked the front door and they strolled toward the Jaguar. He hoped things would go smoothly that night. There were some odd personalities attending; the standoffish Major Carlton, for one, who appeared none too pleased about the reunion. Then again, perhaps he simply didn't want a reminder of those days. There were the ambitious Mandy Billings, the flirtatious Carlo Pisani and the infuriatingly dismissive Olivia.

Although Harry had joked that Dr Jackson should be on standby, James

111

hadn't told them that he'd already had that discussion with Philip who, himself, had raised concerns. Indeed, he and Philip would be searching for anything untoward during the evening. DCI George Lane, although off duty, had arranged to meet Charlie for a drink in the Half Moon should he be needed.

James swung the passenger door open for Beth and silently prayed to the heavens that the evening would run to plan.

11

Carlo Pisani started as he meant to go on. The bandleader had promised a festive evening and he'd planned that every number played and sung that night would be Christmas-themed. True to his word, the band's first three numbers, while guests tucked into their entrée, were a medley of hits from the wonderful film White Christmas.

Ten tables, each seating up to eight guests, surrounded the dance floor and, to James' delight, not one person had failed to arrive, even though light snow continued to fall. The entrée of French Onion soup was light and warming and James sensed an air of anticipation. The majority of guests had attended this particular dinner for several years running and made a purpose of making merry and celebrating. That energy permeated the room.

He regarded the table alongside. Olivia

Dupree's expression never really changed. She looked down her nose at everyone. The Simmonds brothers, together with Walter and Scotty, shared a joke with Mandy and Enid. Alfie Stone and Didier chatted with some animation and appeared grateful to have met each other again.

The table beyond was occupied by four other Pals along with the Merryweathers and the Jacksons. The Pals had arrived from the North that morning. They'd set off early as all were slightly disabled and they'd wanted to ensure they arrived in plenty of time. Philip, as instructed, cast an occasional eye over to Miss Dupree's table in case anything suspicious might be happening. The waiters and waitresses scurried around them with bottles of wine, champagne and cocktails. Adam scanned the room for guests requiring service and delegated staff with a click of his fingers. Paul managed the desk and operations between the kitchen and the dining room. James let out a contented sigh — so far, so good.

The medley finished and Carlo lifted his baton and unleashed 'There's Frost on the Moon', a nifty number that prompted some to have a dance before the next course. Beth struck up a conversation with Juliet Brooks-Hunter by her side; opposite, Harry chatted with the couple celebrating their anniversary, so James arrowed in on the Carltons.

'So this is your first visit to Harrington's?'

The Major gave a curt nod and Cynthia, as if to compensate for her husband, exaggerated her enthusiasm. 'It is, Lord Harrington. I've heard many wonderful comments from people who have stayed here; well, I thought it was time to attend the famous Christmas dinner and dance. We'd probably still be sitting at home if I left it up to William to arrange; but when we heard John was performing, I thought it an opportune time to visit. I noticed the guests taking an interest in your photographic display.'

'The Pals, yes, our librarian Charlie Hawkins dug those up. I believe that he has a number stashed away in the reference library. Of course, his father and those of many of the villagers joined up.'

He raised his voice so that the Major could hear him. 'I say, Major, do you recognise the chaps here or in the photographs?'

The man visibly bristled and although it could have been the warmth, his face turned florid. James dismissed the heat notion: it looked more like anger, impatience or intolerance. Perhaps it was all of those things. The Major bellowed. 'Do you know how big that regiment was, Lord Harrington?'

James, who had served in the Royal Air Force during the previous conflict, had a pretty good idea of the size of regiments and battalions. He suggested around a thousand. The Major sneered and commented that this was probably a lucky guess.

'And did they fight together or was that simply a signing-on promise?'

The old man ignored the question. 'I don't recognise 'em and I didn't fight alongside 'em. My men were further along the trenches with the regulars; regular soldiers who knew how to fight; not that tinpot outfit, better at cricket than soldiering.'

His wife laid a hand on his arm. 'William, this isn't the place.'

At the next table, Eddie Simmonds had clearly heard the Major's comments. He leant back, balancing his chair on its back legs. His expression hardened.

'You watch what you're saying Major. Most of those cricketers fought a brave fight. Don't be telling me, or any of these men here, that we were a tinpot outfit or you'll get what's coming to you. If it weren't for our numbers, we would've lost the war. There's plenty of regulars who didn't have the stomach for it.' He mouthed an apology at James and returned his attention to the Major. 'And your wife is right. This isn't the place.' He righted his chair.

James, keen to change the subject, turned to John Carlton who was already dressed in his mumming outfit. This consisted of a *tatter* jacket, a thigh length coat made with strips of various coloured red rags and ribbons that were sewn on layer upon layer. Placed on the floor beside him was a top hat that, traditionally, the Morris men decorated to their own design. John's had a number of dog-eared beer mats slotted into the ribbon band at the base of the hat. Each Mummers' coat would be similar but sporting different coloured rags.

'What part do you play?'

'I'm Saint George this time around. I get to fight the Turkish Knight.'

'And come up triumphant, of course.'

'Of course; but not without a mishap on the way.'

Adam topped their glasses up and whispered to James.

'The Mummers are ready to perform, your Lordship.'

James acknowledged Adam and turned his attention to John. 'Looks like this is your moment. Do you want the staff to put some dinner by for you?'

'You've paid me to perform, Lord Harrington and I'm grateful for time with Mum and Dad. I'll pinch some Christmas pudding when we've finished if that's all right. We'll have a pint and some peanuts down the pub after. Thanks for letting me sit here in my rags.'

James indicated that Major Carlton

didn't seem to be enjoying himself. 'Is this not his thing?'

'Nothing's his thing, Lord Harrington. I'm surprised Mum got him here. He doesn't allow people in the house and he'll only come out if he can vet who he sees or sits with. Quite frankly, you're honoured that he's sitting here.' He got up. 'I think it all stems from the Great War. He's been like that ever since I can remember.'

John wandered through to reception where the rest of the Mummers were ready to march in.

Carlo brought the music to a halt and after settling the applause down stepped up to the microphone. '*Grazie, grazie*, you are too kind. Later, we will hear the wonderful Olivia Dupree but now, for your entertainment, something a little different.'

James stood, held up an empty glass and tapped his spoon against it. Their guests turned and gave him their full attention.

'Ladies and gentleman, I felt it was time to bring back the Christmas

Mummers' play. This is a centuries-old tradition dating back to pagan times but I believe this performance hails from the period of the Crusades. Please welcome the Christmas Mummers!'

A round of applause rang out as the men, dressed in their rag shirts and top hats, danced into the room, accompanied by a melodeon player and a fiddler. They quickly launched into the play and the first to speak was a splendid Father Christmas with a full grey beard dressed in green tatter rags.

'Then in comes I, old Father Christmas, welcome or welcome not,

I hope old Father Christmas will never be forgot.

All in this room there shall be shown, the hardest battle that ever was known.

So come in Sir Knight, with thy great heart, and in the battle quick do thy part.'

Each character stepped forward with a similar introduction. In came the Turkish Knight, the brave St George, Bold Slasher and the Quack Doctor. Bringing up the rear was the fiery dragon with a colourful papier-mâché head. Its lower jaw opened, snapping menacingly as its wearer paraded among the tables. A well-choreographed sword fight took place between St George and the Turkish Knight with each man goading the other in verse.

'I'll fight you St George, like a man of courage bold,

Let thy blood be ere so hot, I will quickly set it cold.'

'You may fight me Turkish Knight, like a man of courage bold, yes my blood be ere so hot, but you will not set it cold.'

All eyes were on the Mummers. James, along with the rest of the guests, chuckled along with the repartee and became engrossed in a convincing sword fight before St George collapsed to the ground and the call was put out for the Quack Doctor. The man, dressed in white ribbon rags with a modern stethoscope around his neck, knelt beside St George.

'I can cure the itch, the stitch, the palsy and the gout, whether your pain is in or out.' He examined John, who was doing his best to suppress a laugh. 'I have a bottle in the waistband of my belt, called the Golden Frosty Drop, drops of that will fetch this son to life again.'

He administered a few drops on the forehead and on the tongue. The Mummers stood back in preparation for St George to come to life. John twisted and convulsed. Someone on the next table commented on how good an actor he was. James frowned. He gripped Beth's hand. The character of Father Christmas kneeled down.

'John? John, are you all right?'

Cynthia rushed to her son and placed a palm on his forehead. Major Carlton sat transfixed.

James leapt up and whispered to Beth. 'Call George, he's at the pub.'

When he turned, Philip was already attending to the patient. The room hushed. James squatted down and muttered. 'I'm loath to ask, but are these the same symptoms as Olivia Dupree had?'

Philip wouldn't commit. 'Until tests are done, it's too early to say but they appear similar. Let's not alarm everyone. Keep your evening on an even keel.' He stood up and announced: 'A gastric bug, I believe, nothing to worry about.' He turned to the Mummers. 'Perhaps you can help get him through to Reception and we'll see about making him comfortable.' As the Mummers helped John from the dance floor, Philip pulled James to one side. 'You may want to get that bottle of Golden Frosty Drops off the Quack Doctor. John was fine until he had that.'

'Right you are.'

He cast a pleading glance to Carlo, who understood his predicament. Within a few seconds, his band had launched into Benny Goodman's 'Winter Weather'. The drama evaporated as the melody took hold. The Morris men traipsed out, disappointed not have finished their performance. Stephen and Anne, mindful of what had happened, stepped onto the dance floor and encouraged others to join them. Staff meanwhile busied themselves with clearing tables in preparation for the main course: roast beef, crispy roast potatoes, parsnips, sprouts, runner beans, Yorkshire pudding and gravy.

With the evening back on schedule, James joined Beth in Reception, where she was chatting with Paul. Didier scurried past to return to the kitchen.

'Where's our invalid?' James asked.

Beth explained that John and the man who had played Father Christmas were lodging with Mrs Keates in Charnley and that Dr Jackson had taken them there. Mrs Keates had fast become a part of the community ever since the investigation into the death of a local farmer the previous year. Paul leaned against the reception desk and confirmed that Dr Jackson would report back once John was comfortable.

'George is on his way,' Beth put in. 'I know something untoward has happened but we have to behave normally. As far as our guests are concerned, someone was taken ill and that's all. We wouldn't be standing here for someone who'd simply gone down with a bug.'

James instructed Paul to show George into the office when he arrived and to inform him of his arrival when it happened. Meanwhile, he steered Beth back to their table. Stephen threw a confused frown at him and he returned it with a reassuring smile. Olivia Dupree was singing 'Chestnuts Roasting on an Open Fire'. James dragged his chair in and caught the delicious aroma of roast beef. He picked up his cutlery and let Major and Mrs Carlton know that their son was fine and had returned to his bed and breakfast accommodation.

'I can take you there, if you'd prefer. It couldn't have been pleasant to see your son collapse like that.'

'No, not what I was expecting,' said Cynthia, hand on heart. 'It's not like John to be ill but I'm sure he'll be fine. He won't want us fussing around and he'd be annoyed if we gave up this evening because of a gastric problem. Perhaps it's something he ate.'

James hoped that her thoughts didn't reach Didier's ears. But this wasn't the food. No. John became ill as soon as that liquid was placed on his tongue. If it was strychnine, it looked to be a similar dose to that given to Olivia Dupree. Beth nudged his arm and gave a telling look at the Major. He'd brought his hand out of his pocket with a start and had turned as white as the tablecloth. He then scanned the room, in particular, the table alongside him. James followed his gaze. What was he looking for? Or perhaps he should ask *who* was he looking for?

'I say, Major, are you quite well?'

It took a while for the Major to register that he was being spoken to.

'Wh..what? Yes, yes, of course I'm well, why the hell shouldn't I be?'

James topped the Major's glass up. 'You looked a little peaky, that's all. Are you enjoying the meal?'

'What? Oh..yes..yes..quite satisfactory.'

Beth whispered, 'I think that's almost a compliment.'

They continued with their meal. The topics of conversation between guests varied from arrangements for Christmas to forthcoming holidays and general enquiries about one another's back-grounds. Harry, keen to get to grips with the running of the hotel, wandered from table to table chatting easily with the guests. James rested back in his seat and observed his son. He was certainly eager to help and had inherited the Harrington charm, engaging with guests from all walks of life and making them feel at home. There was no doubt about it: the future of Harrington's was safe for another generation.

'I-is our Morris man still h-here?' Stephen had squatted down between James and Beth.

'He's fine.' James said. 'Philip seems to think it was the same drug that Olivia Dupree ingested a few days ago.'

'H-have you told G-George?'

James checked his watch. 'I thought he'd be here by now. He was having a pint at the Half Moon. That's only a mile down the road. I wonder what's keeping him?'

Beth thanked Adam as he collected the dirty plates.

'Perhaps his car broke down.'

Adam leant in. 'DCI Lane is in the office, your Lordship. He arrived a while back but he asked us to wait for a natural break in proceedings. Dr Jackson is with him.'

Beth placed a hand on James' hand. 'You go. Harry and I will stay here and mingle.'

'I'll try not to be long. Stephen, could you and Anne find out a little more about the people on Olivia Dupree's table? Don't make it obvious but they are the only guests who were here a few days ago — except for our staff of course.'

He excused himself. Olivia Dupree commenced her set. The guests were oblivious to the seriousness of the situation and James was pleased to see the amount of dancing, chatting and laughter going on. On the surface, the evening was another roaring success. Privately, he was alarmed at the sinister nature of the attacks and wondered how on earth they were connected.

12

James escorted George and Philip through to the residents' lounge, a quiet room away from the main dining area, that housed a small bar, velvet wing-back chairs and a varied library. He snatched a bottle of brandy and three balloon glasses and the three of them made themselves comfortable. Harry poked his head around the door. 'Thought I'd find you here. Do you need an extra viewpoint?'

George felt his pocket for his pipe. 'Only if you've something to contribute.'

Harry took that as a cue to stay and ensconced himself, rather eagerly, beside James. James settled back in his chair, crossed his legs and afforded himself a silent chuckle. Harry had clearly got the sleuthing bug.

George went through his pre-investigative pipe-lighting ritual. A few puffs of fragrant tobacco drifted through the lounge. 'Right, we have two people, seemingly unrelated, who have been poisoned here at Harrington's. Philip, I've had it confirmed, by the way, that it was strychnine used on Olivia.'

A murmur went round the room. Philip confirmed that he thought that was the case. His dark curly hair flopped over his forehead. He looked like a romantic film star with his smouldering good looks and twinkling eyes. 'I belive that this attack tonight was also a tiny dose of strychnine. I've heard of athletes taking tiny portions of this stuff to enhance their speed. This is a heavier dose, but meant to debilitate, not kill. This is someone who knows what they are doing or has certainly researched the amounts that make the difference between discomfort and death.'

'Olivia, as you can see, is fully recovered,' added George. 'John Carlton is back at the bed and breakfast and being attended to by Mrs Keates.'

James swirled the brandy in his glass. 'And you can't establish any link between Dupree and Carlton?'

'Not had the time. I thought that Dupree might be targeted again; only because she seemed to rub people up the wrong way. But where John Carlton comes into it, I don't know.'

Harry reached across for an empty glass and poured himself a brandy. 'I had quite a chat with John before the dinner and this is the first time he's been to Harrington's. He seemed quite excited to see Olivia Dupree perform — said he was a big fan of hers but he didn't say anything about being involved with her or knowing her in any way. Do you think John was poisoned by mistake?'

Philip was quick to deny this. 'We have the bottle that the Quack Doctor used and I'm confident that George's people will find traces of strychnine in it. Whoever planned this knew who to poison and how to do it.'

'Crikey. Who had access to the bottle?'

George blew smoke up to the ceiling. 'Anyone and everyone. The Quack Doctor's bag was sitting in Reception while the men got changed. Doesn't take two seconds to add something to the contents.'

'It's taking a risk though. The place was

heaving with people,' said Harry.

James tapped his son's arm. 'Probably the best time to do it. People are milling around with overnight bags, handbags and purses. No one's going to take any notice if someone is fiddling with a piece of luggage, especially if they're pretending it's their luggage.'

A thoughtful silence descended. George eventually spoke.

'James, this is not something I particularly want to ask but I have to. If these incidents are not related, have you considered that someone is intent on hurting you?'

Harry baulked. 'Absolutely not.'

'Hold on, Harry,' said James. 'I would also say absolutely not but I may have upset someone and not know. I can't begin to understand the thought processes of my guests.'

'But we've not had any upsets here; the reviews are wonderful and most people keep coming back year on year.'

George shifted in his chair. 'I wasn't thinking so much about the reviews for Harrington's.'

Harry tilted his head at James who held a hand up.

'I think what George is suggesting is that someone from our previous investigations could be seeking to hit me where it hurts.'

'Over this last year,' George continued, 'you've helped with a number of enquiries and been the instigator of their resolution. Your business here is your living. If Harrington's gets a reputation for people falling ill and being poisoned, people will stop booking.'

Harry paled. 'But that means someone here knows a person who is in prison or has been hanged because of you and Dad.' He glared at James. 'Can you think who it could be?'

James pulled a face to indicate that he didn't.

'There are one or two vindictive enough to want revenge. George, perhaps you and I should go through your case files.'

His friend agreed. 'We're also going to need to check the background of every guest that's here.'

'Oh Lord, I don't like the sound of that.'

'Doesn't matter; the likelihood is that it's someone who also attended the first of December dinner but we can't ignore anyone else. We can't leave any stone unturned.'

James refilled his glass. There had been around seventy guests at Harington's that night.

Questioning them would lead to gossip and annoyance. Within a few months, the business could be ruined. 'I would far rather you look for a connection between Olivia and John before you start questioning everyone here.'

The door opened and Anne entered. She was quick to close the door behind her, before closing her eyes with a huge sigh.

'Sorry to barge in but something awful's happened.'

James felt his stomach sink.

'Mrs Carlton went upstairs to her room to have a rest. The Major's just gone up to check on her and found her dead.'

13

Urgently, James ordered Harry to return to the dance to update Beth and keep the evening ticking along. Meanwhile, Anne, George and Philip followed him upstairs to the Carltons' room. The Major and his wife had booked one of the more sizable suites with a large window overlooking the front of the property. During the summer, the vista provided a spectacular view of the hills as they rolled toward the sea. This evening, the snow provided a ghostly glow over the fields which mirrored the sombre mood in the room.

Major Carlton sat by the window, his jacket draped across his lap. His face wore an odd expression. James wasn't sure how to describe it. He'd expected to see a grieving husband but the Major was overcome by another emotion that he could only liken to fear. Of course, there was distress in the eyes but it was accompanied by a haunted air. Anne had gone straight across to join him, pulling up a matching chair as she did so. She held his hand and offered quiet words of sympathy, although he appeared to take little notice.

Philip examined the body of Cynthia Carlton while George scanned the room. James peered over Philip's shoulder and queasiness came over him. If Mrs Carlton had ingested strychnine, the person responsible for administering it had made sure it was a heavy dose. Her face was contorted and her body twisted unnaturally. Her terrifying strychnine grin forced him to look away.

George tugged his sleeve. 'Do you see anything untoward in this room? Anything placed where it shouldn't be? Anything missing?'

James gazed around. Everything appeared to be as it should be. George turned to the Major and, after a brief apology for having to ask, put the same question to him. The old man sat up straight and slowly studied the room. After a few seconds, he got up and opened drawers and wardrobes and checked his wife's vanity case. He shook his head.

'We brought clothes. The only jewels Cynthia had were for tonight and she's still wearing them.'

Not a robbery then, thought James. He watched as the Major slumped back in his chair. The reaction to his wife's death seemed unusual and he sensed that George felt the same. He quietly suggested to George that the Major might be more comfortable in the lounge. George opened the door.

'Major Carlton, I obviously have questions to ask but I don't want you distressed by staying here. Anne, perhaps you could escort Major Carlton to the lounge where we were sitting.'

Anne jumped up. 'Of course.'

She went to help Major Carlton but was rebuffed and advised that he was quite capable of walking unaided. Without glancing at his wife, he left the room. Anne followed behind and flagged up a helpless look at James who gave her a *what can you do?* shrug in return. He closed the door behind them.

'Is that a natural reaction to such an

awful death? I can see a mixed bag of emotions there but not much in the way of grief.'

George considered his question before answering.

'Shock affects everyone differently; but there was a resignation with him, don't you think?'

Philip got to his feet. 'I agree. It's as if he felt it was inevitable.'

James snapped his fingers. 'That's exactly what I was trying to convey. It really is as if he were expecting it.'

'Well,' mumbled George, 'I'll see what I can glean from him. Philip, your prognosis?'

'Professional opinion is that this was strychnine poisoning — a heavy dose in the jug of water.' He pointed to the glass lying on the floor next to the body. 'Make sure no one touches that or drinks from that jug.'

'Do we know who delivered the water?'

James undid his bow-tie and put his hands in his pockets. 'It's normally one of the regular staff. Everything comes from the kitchen and whoever has a free moment delivers the water.'

'Anything else to add, Philip?'

'Not that I can think of. I'll write up my report. Is the ambulance on its way?'

George confirmed that it was and that he would be sure to keep the glass and jug for evidence. 'The snow's not expected to last down in Lewes so I should have some help over the next few days. If anything changes, I'll let you know.' He slapped Philip on the back. 'Now I think that you need to get back down to that dinner. I want to keep things as normal as possible.' He winced as he spoke.

'You've done that a few times tonight,' Philip said. 'What's the problem?'

'I keep getting a stabbing pain here.'

Philip placed his hand on George's stomach. 'Any nausea?'

'A little, yes. Probably indigestion.'

'Not necessarily. Come to the surgery tomorrow and we'll take a proper look.' He turned to James. 'Sorry your evening's been spoiled.'

James groaned. 'Just make sure that everyone else is having a good time. Keep

Beth and Harry updated.'

'I will.'

After he'd left, there was a lengthy silence between the friends as he and George collected their thoughts. James went across to the window and closed the curtains. 'You did tell the ambulance men to come to a side entrance?'

George assured him that he was doing everything as discreetly as possible. There was a knock on the door and Paul entered. 'Sorry to bother you, but I wondered if there was anything you need us to do.'

'You could confirm who brought the jug of water up here.'

Paul caught his breath on seeing Mrs Carlton on the floor. He quickly met George's eyes. 'That would be Adam.'

'Did he prepare it?'

'No sir. We put a jug of water in all of the rooms. Didier would normally instruct the kitchen staff to prepare them and one of the waiters or waitresses would distribute them. As Mrs Carlton went up a little earlier than planned, that particular jug was brought up ahead of the others.'

'So anyone could have tampered with it.'

'Yes sir. The jugs are kept right by the door leading out of the kitchen.' He glanced at James. 'I'm attempting to accommodate Major Carlton in another room but we're fully booked.'

James ran a hand through his hair. 'Have a word with my wife. Miss Brookes-Hunter is a lady to whom we can offer accommodation at our place. She decided to spend a few nights here instead of GJ's cottage. Do that now before the evening comes to a close.'

Paul confirmed he would and left them to it. James stared at the body of Mrs Carlton and chewed his lip.

'What's the matter, James?' George asked.

'Mmm?'

'You look as if you've lost something.'

James was aware that he must have looked confused and he was. Something nagged at him and he couldn't think what it might be. He opened wardrobes and drawers, then stood motionless. He was aware that George was allowing him this time; that he realised something relevant might come out of his musings. What *was* it though? What little snippet of information had lodged itself in his subconscious? His gaze settled on the Major's jacket, still draped over the chair.

'Aha!' He dashed across and snatched it from the chair. 'Something alarmed the Major during dinner. He'd brought his hand out of his pocket and looked like he'd seen a ghost.'

George came closer as James delved into the Major's pocket and gently brought the item out. George sucked the air. 'You know the significance of that?'

'Yes, I do,' said James holding up a white feather. 'The sign of a coward or deserter during the Great War. 'Major Carlton was a notable war hero. Why would someone put this in his pocket?'

George frowned, contemplating Cynthia Carlton's body. 'And why kill Cynthia Carlton because of it?'

14

The dinner and dance continued without a hitch with no suspicions aroused over the missing Major and his wife. The couple had not mixed with any other guests so they were either not missed or it was assumed the pair had retired early. James and Beth spent the rest of the evening dancing and chatting and planting in their guests' minds the idea of a third dinner and dance for the following year. The suggestion went down well and, by the end of the evening, James had decided that an extra dinner and dance would indeed be on the cards the following Christmas.

The band packed their instruments away. The guests agreed, as they made their way upstairs, that the evening had been another roaring success. *If only they knew*, James thought.

At around midnight, in their own home, he prepared drinks for Beth, Harry and their guest, Juliet Brooks-Hunter. He and Beth were delighted to accommodate Juliet and she had jumped at the opportunity to stay with the people who had solved her sister's murder. Packing her belongings took little time as she always travelled light.

Harry stoked the fire into life and added a couple of logs for the flames to latch onto. Beth lit the candles and plugged in the fairy lights on the tree. She then placed cheese and crackers on the table and James distributed whisky and ginger for him and Harry and gin and tonics for Beth and Juliet.

'Well, Lord Harrington,' said Juliet in her matter-of-fact tone, 'you are a one for attracting a mystery. Tell me, do you intend to investigate this one? And there's no need to tell me that nothing happened tonight because your son's already spilled the beans.'

Some good humoured banter commenced between Juliet and Harry about James' investigations. He took it in his stride as he eased into his favourite armchair and stretched his legs out.

'The thing is, Juliet, something rather untoward happened on the first of December. Did Harry tell you about that?'

She glared at Harry. 'No he did not. I know that awful Dupree woman was taken ill but — .' She sat up with a start. 'Oh!'

James went through a brief outline of the events of that evening and how the police seemed to think that Dupree had been given a similar dose of strychnine to John Carlton. He added that she appeared to be disliked by anyone she came into contact with. 'I'm not sure that she actually has any friends, or acquaintances, even.'

Harry helped himself to a slab of cheddar. 'Mandy and Enid, her two assistants, say she's always opinionated and demanding.'

'Oh dear,' said Juliet. 'Unfortunate for her. I don't take kindly to egotistical behaviour; it's unbecoming of a woman.'

'I agree,' Beth put in. 'But what link does she have with John and Mrs Carlton?'

'Perhaps a distant relative,' suggested Juliet. 'That Major chappie is as standoffish as the diva — perhaps they're of the same blood.'

James held his palms open to indicate that it could be anything then picked up his whisky. Harry playfully kicked his shin. 'What are not telling us, Dad?'

He wondered whether to impart his news and decided there was no harm. Juliet had a good mind and he was interested to know her thoughts.

'I believe the nature of this crime relates to something historic, although how Olivia Dupree fits into it I don't know.'

Instinctively, his audience edged forward.

'During dinner, Beth noticed the Major go pale. He'd reached into his pocket and he looked like a rabbit in the headlights. When I asked if he was quite well, he dismissed my concern. Well, after Cynthia's death he left his jacket on the chair upstairs so I took a look. George was with me. I found a white feather.'

Juliet gasped.

'Does that mean what I think it

means?' asked Harry.

James confirmed that a white feather had become a symbol of cowardice during the Great War. 'They were given to conscientious objectors, deserters, that sort of thing.'

His son frowned. 'But why kill Cynthia Carlton? What had she done? And Major Carlton fought. He led men into battle. He received a DSO.'

'Someone thinks otherwise,' said Juliet. 'It wouldn't be the first time that a soldier made up stories of bravery.'

Beth questioned how someone in the Major's position would get away with cowardice. 'I mean, if he was leading men into battle, those men would know if he shied away.'

'There's something else too,' James said. He put his glass down, felt in his pocket and brought out a slip of paper. 'One of our staff found this. It's a record of a diary entry dated 1917. It hints at something untoward.'

Juliet took it from him. '*France April 12th 1917: His orders are vague.*' She studied the entry.

James motioned for her to turn the paper over. She did so and read on.

'France April 14 1917: This isn't war; it's slaughter. What's the point? These generals are miles away telling us where to fight. The plan is set up to fail. He's leading us to our deaths.'

'So, Dad, you're thinking that this plan being spoken of is something to do with Major Carlton?'

'I do.'

'Sweetie, have you shown this to George?' said Beth.

'No, I didn't think anything of it. I simply assumed someone had mislaid it. But I will do. My concern now is that the Pals may be involved. I checked the handwriting against the register but I can't see a match to this writing.'

'Mmm,' Julie pondered, 'handwriting may change slightly, but rarely very much. It's faded and difficult to read. The Pals must be connected. They're all jolly men who I've enjoyed spending time with tonight but this smacks of revenge. Something happened that's been bubbling under the surface all these years and now, someone

148

wants to cause harm.'

James looked to the ceiling. 'But why kill Cynthia Carlton? Why attack Olivia and John? If the Major is the cause of this anger, why not kill him?'

She sat up with a determined look. 'You need to investigate this, James, and I don't envy you. There is a hidden past that needs to be uncovered. You did it with my sister; you need to do it again.'

James groaned. 'Good Lord, I wouldn't know where to start?'

'With the Pals.'

Harry cleared his throat and winced. Beth frowned.

'What's the matter, dear?'

'If we're to do that, remember that Adam's and Paul's relatives fought in the Pals.'

'You're right,' said Beth. 'And our gardener has links too.'

James rubbed his chin. 'And Charlie. And don't forget that Didier played his part in the résistance.'

There was a thoughtful silence, eventually broken by James who began buttering a cracker. 'I don't even want to mention this but aside from the gardener, all would have had access to the water jug delivered to Mrs Carlton.'

Beth's eyes opened wide. 'You can't think our staff are capable of such an attack. They've been loyal and devoted; I can't imagine any of them wanting to spoil your good name. It's unthinkable.'

'My dear,' said Juliet, 'when revenge is this strong, common sense and duty become secondary. This was planned. The poisonings of Olivia Dupree and John Carlton were planned. Whoever killed Mrs Carlton arranged to do this tonight.' She turned her attention to James. 'Do you have people present at both evenings when the attacks took place?'

'The staff, of course, were the same. Then — '

'Did anyone push to volunteer?'

'Not that I'm aware of. We generally get the same people in because we know they do a good job. We had the four Pals, Carlo Pisani, Olivia Dupree and her two assistants, Mandy and Enid. The Merryweathers were here along with the Jacksons.'

'Strychnine is so dangerous. Who would know about its use and how to measure the dosage?'

James shrugged. 'Apart from Philip, I've no idea.'

'Appleton would,' Harry put in, explaining to Juliet that he was the gardener. 'Well, that's used for killing rats and moles, isn't it? And athletes, don't they sometimes use it?'

'I believe they did,' Beth said, adding that a relative used it once for a track event in around 1910. 'It was deemed to be a stimulant and supposedly used if you had an endurance event to help keep you going.'

James settled back in his chair. 'I don't know about any of that but Appleton wasn't at the dinners. He was at home.'

'Was he?'

James glared at Harry who returned it with a helpless shrug. 'Dad, you don't know for sure. We presume he was at home but he could have been up at the house.'

'But why?'

'My dear, that is your task,' said Juliet. 'You and your friend, George, must delve into the history of these people.'

Beth sighed. 'I, for one, would like to know why Olivia Dupree was poisoned. What links her to the Carltons?'

Juliet gave James a knowing look. 'Then why don't you start with her. She was the first target. Did you notice anything out of the ordinary on that evening?'

'An argument between Carlo and Olivia. Olivia becoming ill and accusing someone of trying to kill her. That's it.'

'She is your first line of inquiry, James. Why is someone trying to kill her? We must get to the bottom of this. Was this an attempt on her life or a warning of some kind? Once you clear that up, we can look at John and Cynthia Carlton. If Major Carlton is the target, why have *they* been attacked?'

James watched as Beth gathered the empty tumblers and plates. Juliet announced her retirement to bed; Harry escorted her up. James wandered around the room, switched the fairy lights off, blew out the candles and secured the fire guard. This wasn't going to be straightforward. People had been holding on to secrets, lies and revenge for forty years. How on earth could he unravel it? Beth slipped her hand into his.

'I think you should have a chat with Bert. He'll lead you in the right direction about Miss Dupree. If this is to do with the past, perhaps her parents will be of help.'

'Yes, you're right. I'll track him down tomorrow and see what I can find out.'

'He'll be here. It's St Nick's day tomorrow — we'll all be at church.'

15

Anne and the ladies of the Women's Institute had pushed the boat out for the St Nick's day celebrations. Fresh forest ferns, holly, hawthorn, mistletoe and tinsel were ornamenting the oak beams and the pulpit as well as the end of each pew. A beautiful wooden Nativity scene took centre stage.

The children had decorated a Christmas tree with baubles and tinsel and to the side of this was a huge wooden chair that Stephen had found at the back of the church. He and Anne had dusted it down, painted it gold and placed it by the tree like a royal throne. Under the tree was a pile of presents, each wrapped in brightly-coloured Christmas paper. The children gazed at them and chatted among themselves about what each present might contain.

Elsie Taylor distributed glasses of fruit-cup with cinnamon and the shelf normally reserved solely for hymn books had doubled up as a shelf for everyone's drink. James took a sip of the fruity cocktail. What a splendid idea: it certainly made this particular church service a social one. Bert slipped in beside them.

Stephen, as was his style, wandered up and down the aisles, promoting the season of goodwill and peace to all men. He chatted about St Nicholas, describing how he had originally been a Bishop in Turkey who was so poor he could not afford a dowry for his daughters. But, according to legend, he dropped a bag of gold down a chimney, which fell into a stocking that had been hung up to dry by one daughter. He then did the same for the others. As Stephen spoke, James found himself wondering where this gold had come from. Nicholas begged his daughters not to tell anyone what he'd done but word got out. Since then, when anyone received a secret gift, it was thought to be from Nicholas. Because of his great kindness, he was made a Saint: the saint of children.

Over time, St Nicholas had fallen out

of popularity but the Victorians, intrigued by the old stories, reinvented him. Although no one knew when he actually died, his bones were discovered on the sixth of December. So St Nicholas' day always fell on that date.

His congregation hung on Stephen's every word. He had a knack for story-telling, gesticulating and changing the tone of his voice as he strode up and down the aisle. He made his way to the front of the church and turned with a glint in his eye. 'A-and now, I believe that St Nick has arrived.'

The children shuffled.

'He p-particularly wanted to stop here, at St Nicholas' Church, to s-see the children.'

The vestry door opened and in walked St Nick.

James never failed to be amazed at the costume. It was the one they used every year but Dorothy Forbes looked after it as if it were gold dust. St Nick had a dark green hat that came to a point, with light fur around the brim. His matching robes, also furtrimmed, were tied by a large leather belt and an equally large metal buckle. His boots were made of sacking and his beard was bushy white. Anne had used stage make-up to give him a weathered complexion; his blue eyes sparkled. In one hand he carried a knobbly wooden staff and in the other an old sack tied by a length of frayed rope.

Underneath the costume and make-up was Mr Chrichton, who filled the outfit with the help of a small pillow. He certainly looked a jolly St Nick as he made himself comfortable in the golden chair.

Beth nudged him. 'Look at the children.'

He turned. Every child in the church had either made their way to the end of their pews or stood on the pews to see St Nick. Some were open-mouthed, some were pointing, but all were in awe. Stephen invited them to come to the front and they did so, en masse.

Anne scurried forward and instructed them to line up nicely. 'Don't worry, children, everyone will receive a gift.' Radley trotted up and sat by the throne in anticipation of a bone.

Over the next twenty minutes, James and Beth watched Chrichton distribute the gifts with a jovial laugh. He leant in as children whispered in his ear to ask for something specific at Christmas. Chrichton always responded with a diplomatic 'I'll see what I can do' and an instruction that the children must be sure to behave well.

As the boys and girls returned to their parents, St Nick rose from his chair and waved goodbye. Stephen settled proceedings down with a short prayer before opening the church doors wide. Bert dashed out, telling James he hadn't got all day.

James checked his watch. 'Did you want to come, Beth, or are you busy here?'

'I'll go over to Harrington's and mingle with the guests to make sure everything is in order.'

Harry straightened his tie. 'I'll come over too. George will probably be there by now asking questions. Shall I see if I can gatecrash?'

'He won't thank you for it,' said James. 'But if you can, see what you can glean. I shouldn't be long.' He put his gloves on. 'We don't have anyone checking out today, do we?'

Harry confirmed that all the guests would be staying until Monday with the exception of the Pals. 'They're going back to their own homes but, of course, they're local — well, the ones that attended both evenings anyway. Alfie Stone is leaving for Cambridge.'

'George will have it in hand, but he may want to have a good chat with Alfie Stone before he checks out. He's the one from Australia who recognised Didier. And don't forget that Eddie Simmonds put the Major in his place about the efforts of the Pals versus the regulars. No love lost there. It'll be interesting to know if Eddie knows more about the Major than he's letting on.' James pecked Beth on the cheek. 'I'll track you all down later. Are we having dinner at our place or up at Harrington's?'

'I thought ours, especially as Juliet is with us. We can discuss the day's events.

Graham left some pork chops for us yesterday. I'll do those with some mashed potatoes.'

'Splendid. See if you can get George along too.'

Because of the snow, traffic on the main roads was light and as Bert knew the way to Olivia Dupree's parents, they reached Shoreditch within the hour. What snow had fallen in London had quickly turned to a grey slush. That, coupled with the heavy clouds, cast a gloom on proceedings. The roads were lined with small, terraced houses, each of which had a door opening straight onto the road. Dotted here and there was the odd shop or café. They passed an opulent Victorian residence that James discovered was the grand and impressive Shoreditch College. After a few minutes Bert pointed him down one of the numerous roads that all looked the same. He parked outside Number 16, although the '6' had lost its top screw and had turned upside down. Two scruffy children ran up and stared at the sporty Austin Healey. Bert wagged a finger at them.

'Look after this car and they'll be a shilling for yer.'

'Each?'

'Cheeky buggers. Yeah, all right, each.'

James grinned at Bert as he knocked on the door.

A well-proportioned lady in her mid-fifties greeted them. She wore a floral apron which she hastily untied.

'You're earlier than I thought you'd be.' She looked at the sky. 'I thought you might get held up with the weather. I'm Mrs Brown.'

James introduced himself and Bert. Bert had managed to get a message through to the Browns via his contacts. He explained that the roads were not too bad, especially coming into London. 'It all melts rather quickly in the city, doesn't it?'

She held the door for them to go through to the front room. He and Bert made themselves comfortable on the sofa as Mrs Brown disappeared and returned with tea served on the 'best' crockery.

'Sorry about the mess. I've never had gentry 'ere before.'

161

James looked about at the spotless room. Like all front rooms, this was kept for special occasions and dusted to within an inch of its life. Mrs Brown appeared to be a homely individual and family was clearly important, judging by the numerous photographs around the room. He watched as she prepared the tea and distributed the cups and saucers. She opened the lid of a small wooden barrel.

'Biscuit?'

'Thank you.'

'Ta very much,' said Bert.

'It's kind of you to let us visit at such short notice, especially with Christmas coming,' said James.

'Well, we've not much to do at Christmas, except cook the dinner. My Joe's a grocer so 'e manages to get the food in and there's not many to cook for: just us two and our neighbours across the road.'

James cleared his throat. 'Does Olivia ever join you?'

Mrs Brown swallowed hard and blinked back her emotion. 'Diane? No. She sends a card and some money but that's about it.' She brought out a handkerchief. 'I

162

don't know why she don't come. It's like she's ashamed of us.'

'I can't imagine why. Perhaps her ambition to succeed has clouded her sense of what's important. Youngsters tend to forget these sorts of things. I'm sure she'll come around when she understands that.'

The door opened and a man of a similar age to Mrs Brown appeared. He took off his cap and extended an arm.

'Joe Brown.'

James and Bert stood up and introduced themselves. Joe nodded for them to sit down.

'You're wanting to talk about our Diane, is tha' right?'

Mrs Brown left, stating that she had potatoes to peel. James simply felt that she didn't want to break down in front of them. Joe sat down with a sigh.

'She 'asn't been back 'ere since she left to be a singer. The missus can't speak about her, Lord Harrington, she's that upset. She's our only daughter, see, and it's as if she's disowned us.' He reached across, opened a small cupboard and brought out a scrap book. He handed it to James. 'We've kept all the newspaper clippings and reviews. We're proud of her but she never mentions where she's from. We're a good community, look out for one another, but she always thought she was a bit above everyone 'ere.'

'Are you angry?'

'Not now. I was. When I see how upset the missus gets, that makes me angry. Nah, I'm more disappointed. We were good parents; never strict, always helped her with her school work and held birthday parties, you know, like you do.'

Bert helped himself to another biscuit. 'When did she scarper?'

'Just after her sixteenth birthday. She didn't even say goodbye. Packed a bag and left a note. We got letters to begin with but when she started getting famous she changed her name and the letters stopped coming. Now, we're lucky if we get a birthday card.'

James' heart went out to him. He couldn't imagine how it must feel to have your own children turn their backs on you. 'Does she keep in contact with anyone else? Any school friends?'

Joe chuckled. 'She don't keep in touch with anyone. Never really made friends — always had her head in the clouds dreaming o' stardom.' His eyes misted over. 'Well, she's got it now and I 'ope she's happy.' He picked up his tea cup. 'What're you interested in her for?'

'I won't beat around the bush, Mr Brown. We believe someone may have tried to harm her last week.'

Joe's jaw dropped as James went on to explain what had happened on the evening of the first of December. He gave an overview of who was at the table, the relationship between her and Carlo, and then waited.

'I know she's got a thing for that Carlo bloke. You can see it in those photographs from the papers. D'you think he's tried to kill 'er? These Italians can be a hot-headed bunch.'

James winced at the suggestion. 'No, I don't think that at all. I think this has to do with something from years ago, from the Great War.'

Joe frowned. 'But she weren't even

born then! What's that gotta do with anything?'

Bert pushed his cap back. 'It's too long a story mate, but she may have got involved in something without realising it. Do any of your family 'ave links with the Pals regiments fighting in the Artois region, you know, Arras and Albért, those places?'

A quick shake of the head answered that question. 'My dad was one of the first. He was with the Expeditionary Force up in Mons. Injured in the first few months.'

James enquired whether the name of Captain William Carlton rang any bells. A blank look confirmed that it meant nothing. Joe's worried gaze settled on him.

'Is my little girl safe?'

James felt disinclined to make any promises. So far, they had no idea what was going on; who was the target and why.

'No way to say,' said Bert. 'Whoever did it made sure it didn't do any damage. She's up and about with no 'arm done.'

'That's right,' James put in. 'Whoever did this has now moved on to the Carlton family. They appear to be the target. Are you sure you have no recollection of that name?'

'Absolutely not. Dad never mentioned much to do with the war, only the blokes he served alongside. He only saw the officers when they were ready to fight.'

'Did he keep a diary?'

'Nah. He weren't a writer, my dad.' He brought his chair closer. 'If you see my little girl, you tell her to come and visit. Tell her that her mum is distraught. I can't see that we've done anything wrong but if we upset 'er all those years ago, tell 'er we're sorry.'

James took that as their cue to go. He gave his assurance that he'd do his very best to speak with Olivia and encourage her to visit.

James watched as his friend tipped the kids for keeping an eye on the car. A young girl in her twenties strolled up and tapped Bert on the shoulder.

'Blimey, if it ain't little Gloria.' Bert turned to James. 'This is the girl that

167

went to school with Olivia. Me and her dad are mates.'

She gave Bert a hug. 'I 'eard you was coming up so I thought I'd wait outside like.'

Bert went through their reasons for visiting and James asked if Gloria was friendly with Olivia. She pulled a face. 'I was never friends with 'er. Right madam she was, always thought she was better than us.' She jutted her chin at the Browns' house. 'Mrs Brown was in a right state for years and she's ever so nice; a proper mum, that's what she is. Don't deserve a daugh'er like that.'

After a quick catch up with Bert, Gloria left, curtseying to James who was a little bemused by the gesture.

They got in the car and James slipped his gloves on. 'What do you think?'

'I dunno. There's nothin' that connects her to the Carltons or the war. Why don't you pop down to Mrs Keates and 'ave a chat with John Carlton? If we can't find a link soon, we're gonna 'ave to start thinking that you're the target.'

James felt his stomach flip. He'd put

that suggestion to the back of his mind but, here it was, shining like a beacon on Guy Fawkes night. Bert nudged him.

'Drop me at the East End Mission; I'm 'aving dinner with Gladys.'

James beamed. 'Are you really? Is this a blossoming romance or something?'

As Bert gave him directions, James ribbed him about a possible marriage, saying that he and Gladys had cut quite a dash on the dance floor during the wedding reception. Bert remained tight-lipped throughout and took it all on the chin. Outside the Mission, he took his cap off and smoothed his hair back. After a quick cheerio, he disappeared inside and James, with a mischievous grin, turned on to the main road, making a mental note to update Beth on a possible romance.

In the meantime, his next port of call was Mrs Keates.

16

He'd met Mrs Keates the previous year when trying to trace the estranged son of a dead farmer.

Although she lived in the neighbouring village of Charnley, her cooking skills were called upon for the many events and festivals celebrated in Cavendish.

She lived in a property similar to that of Mr and Mrs Brown: a two-up, two-down terraced house with a front door that opened straight on to the high street. The snow stopped and the sky cleared as he steered the car through the Sussex countryside. If it hadn't been so chilly, he would have put the roof down but he could imagine his ears dropping off with frost-bite if he did. He was glad to have wrapped up in a thick tweed jacket and cap as well as his scarf and gloves.

He pulled up outside Mrs Keates' house, leapt out of the car and knocked politely. Mrs Keates swung the door open and

James couldn't help but laugh. She stepped out onto the pavement and brushed flour from her apron.

'I've been making puddings and cakes and this flour gets everywhere.' She asked him in, catching sight of herself in the mirror as she followed him back indoors. 'Glory be, I've even got it in my hair. Come through, Lord Harrington, you know where to go.'

On the odd occasion that he'd visited, the conversation always took place in the small pantry at the back of the house where cooking appeared to be a continuous occupation. He took his cap and gloves off and unbuttoned his jacket.

'If we had cooking in the Olympics, Mrs K, I believe you'd win the gold every time. What are you making?'

'Some of your nan's mince pies. You remember you gave me the recipe last year.'

'Oh that's right; she used the old Georgian recipe.'

After a short discussion about Christmas and the preparations, Mrs Keates prepared a hot toddy for James, something he'd grown accustomed to having when he popped by in the winter months. She wiped her hands on a towel.

'You here to see John?'

'Yes. How's he faring?'

Her shoulders slumped. 'Inspector Lane was round earlier to see if he was up for the news of his mother.'

'And was he?'

'Well, it's never a good time, is it? Poor lad looks like his whole world's fallen apart. And at Christmas too. How's he going to have any good thoughts with such a memory hanging over him?'

James agreed that it would take a while to get over. 'No matter how old you are, the death of a parent is terribly sad.'

Mrs Keates agreed. She handed James a small tray with a second hot toddy and two gingerbread men on it. 'He's in the bedroom at the top of the stairs. Take that up to him and tell him I'll be up to see what he wants for dinner.'

Armed with refreshments and instructions, James made his way up the narrow staircase and knocked on the bedroom door.

'John, it's James Harrington. Are you

fine for me to come in?'

'Yes, come in.'

John was propped up in bed, staring out of the back window. He wore blue and white striped pyjamas and his thick, brown hair was dishevelled. He was a handsome man in a rugged way. James could imagine him hauling hay onto a wagon. But his red-rimmed eyes told their own story. He handed John the glass. 'A Mrs Keates special. Should hit the spot.'

'Thanks.'

James dragged a small wooden chair over to the bedside. 'I know it seems a silly question but how are you bearing up?'

In between the occasional sniff, James learned that John had recovered from the attack and had been all set to return to Harrington's to meet his parents when George came by with the news of his mother.

'I wasn't well enough for anything last night so he left it until this morning. I crawled back into bed and I've not moved since.'

'Quite understandable. You're in good hands with Mrs K; she's a godsend and won't allow you to leave until you're absolutely ready. Do you live on your own?'

The young man explained that he shared a flat with Simon, the man who played the Quack Doctor. He let out a half-hearted laugh. 'He's completely devastated; thinks it's his fault for leaving the bag out. But you don't expect someone to do something like this, do you?'

He stared into space. 'Inspector Lane said my mother was murdered; that it looked like the same poison that I was given.' He stared out of the window and then at James. 'Why would anyone want to kill Mum? In fact, why would anyone want to poison me? They must be quite insane.'

'That's what George is trying to find out and he's one of the best. Did anyone do or say anything untoward whilst you were at Harrington's?'

'Not that I can remember.' Without prompting, he went through his arrival with the rest of the Morris team; meeting his parents for a pre-dinner drink; the meal itself; the people he'd met at the dinner table and, finally, to the administration of the golden drop by the Quack Doctor. He blinked back the tears.

'I say, the man that plays the Quack Doctor, have you known him long?'

'Since primary school. We grew up together and started the Morris team.'

'Did anyone say anything to you last night that caused you to stop and think? It could have been something trivial but, thinking back, it seemed odd?'

Another shake of the head. 'Not that I can remember. Everyone was having a good time; I got chatting to the people on the next table, the Pals and the girls involved with Olivia Dupree but it was just general conversation.'

'And you don't recall meeting them before at all?'

John swigged his hot toddy. 'Oh yes, I've met Olivia Dupree and those two assistants of hers.'

James sat up.

'Yes, they were at the Grand Hotel in Brighton a few months ago for a dinner that I went to. I'm a bit of a fan of Olivia Dupree and I had one of her records so brought it along for her to sign.'

'Did she recognise you?'

'Last night? If she did, she didn't show it; neither did the assistants. I expect they get loads of people asking for autographs and things.'

'What about the Pals?'

John enthused about the stories they told and the camaraderie they shared. 'They didn't talk much about the war, more about the cricket team and how England played during the summer. They seemed like good company though.'

'Your father was in the Sussex Regiment, wasn't he? Did he not know them?'

'He may have done. I know he was pretty gruff with some of them but he's like that with most people.'

James hesitated before his next question. The lad had just lost his mother; but something bothered James about the father. 'When I mentioned the Pals to your father, he seemed to falter a little.'

John heaved a sigh and studied his hands. 'He's a hero, Lord Harrington, and he saw a lot of things in France that no one should see. I believe he feels bad for surviving. Anything to do with that time he tends to put the barriers up. We come from a military family and I did my National Service but I hated it. I thought Dad would hit the roof when I didn't stay on but actually he was pleased. He didn't want me joining up.' John reached across to check his watch. 'I really should get over to see Dad. I can't believe I'm lying here in my own misery when he's just down the road grieving.'

John stripped the bedclothes away. He placed his feet on the carpet and sat in thoughtful silence. 'Mum hadn't been the same for the last few months.'

'Oh?'

'I never discovered why. She became a little intolerant of Dad; impatient. She started going out more and socialising in the village. Perhaps she was just sick of stopping in all the time. Dad doesn't have anyone in the house that he doesn't know, or rather, trust. He has an underlying suspicion of everyone and according to Mum he'd been worse lately.' He wiped a tear away. 'I tried to get to the bottom of it because I felt Mum was holding something back but she never let on. Now I'll never know.'

'Did your mother involve herself in the Great War?'

John shrugged. 'Only did what other women did: knit scarves, pack up food parcels, that sort of thing. She helped out on one of the farms during harvest but that's about it.'

James got up. 'You get yourself straight. I'll wait downstairs and take you over to see your father.'

The young man thanked him and was quick to jump up and get organised. Spending too much time thinking would have brought him close to tears. Within ten minutes, he'd made himself presentable and had ambled down the stairs. After a grateful hug for Mrs Keates, John eased into the passenger seat of the Austin and James headed straight for Harrington's.

As they turned into the drive, James saw George directing two policemen and scanning the grounds. He parked at the entrance. His friend wore a concerned expression as he approached.

'Everything all right, George?'

George whispered. 'Major Carlton's disappeared.'

'Good Lord, when?'

'I'm presuming mid-morning. I had a brief chat with him first thing and then popped by to see John. Then I went and spoke with Alfie Stone and now I'm back here, one person short. Left most of his things and gone.'

John got out of the car and pulled his small bag of belongings from the back seat. 'I'm going in to see Dad.'

George cleared his throat. 'I'm sorry lad but that's not possible at the moment.'

James watched as George steered John toward Harrington's. This put a whole new perspective on things. Had Major Carlton run because of guilt? From what little he knew he didn't trust people and that was understandable with the things he'd witnessed. But was he a killer? They'd arrived late afternoon the previous day and, since that arrival, James had sensed his unease and, on more than one occasion, a look of anxiety on his face. Was he planning to kill his own wife? Did he see someone that frightened him? Did he know one of the guests?

Beth rushed to greet him. 'Have you heard the news?'

'Yes, it's all a little odd, isn't it?'

'I simply don't know what to make of it.'

James checked his watch. 'Is George coming to dinner later?'

Beth confirmed that he was. 'Didier's packed up some leftovers from the dinner yesterday so I'm doing my own version of the Boxing Day feast.'

In the villages of the district they still followed the medieval custom of distributing food to the poor on the day after Christmas Day. The traditional Boxing Day meal of cold meats and pickles was served with hot bubble and squeak which consisted of all the leftover vegetables and potatoes chopped and fried. Today, Beth was substituting pork chops for cold meats.

He took his gloves off. 'Jolly good. We

can have a good chat and establish where we are with all of this. I want to have a word with Charlie Hawkins about the Pals but I'll organise that for tomorrow. Has anyone spoken to Didier?'

Beth shook her head.

'And has anyone owned up to missing a part of a diary?'

'No, and that's important isn't it?'

'I think it's part of the jigsaw, yes.'

'Well, there was another piece found today. I think it fell out with that other part. It was in the same area but it'd fallen between the skirting board and the wall. Paul was about to throw it away and realised it was similar to the one he'd sent down a few days ago.' She handed it to him in a small envelope. 'As soon as I saw what it was I thought it may have fingerprints on it.'

'Good girl.' He opened it and noted the date — 1917. He slipped it into his pocket. 'I'll wait until I have the other piece before reading it. I'd like George to see it too, before he goes accusing me of withholding evidence.'

At the reception desk, James wanted

Paul's assurances that the guests were comfortable and happy. To his relief, the hotel was running like clockwork and any questions George had asked were asked with great diplomacy. Harry, he learned, had sat in on some of the interviews to ensure they remained informal. Satisfied that all was in order, he and Beth wandered back to the car.

A thought struck him that lifted his spirits.

Although he felt dreadful for being selfish at this time, the disappearance of Major Carlton indicated that this wasn't a vendetta against him personally. Something most odd was happening. A seemingly innocent woman had been murdered. There appeared to be no connection between Olivia and the Carlton's except for the autograph that John had asked for. Was there something more to that relationship?

And why was this happening now? Was Cynthia Carlton targeted in error? And why had her behaviour changed? Had Major Carlton left because he feared for his own life?

Whatever was happening, he hoped there would be some clarification during dinner that night. With George's update, the insightfulness of Juliet and Beth, together with Harry's inquiring mind, should, at least, lead them in some sort of direction.

17

George was the last to push his plate away. James watched as his friend took a deep breath and patted his stomach.

'I don't know why we only have bubble and squeak on Boxing Day. It makes a nice change to have it as part of a normal dinner.'

Beth tidied up the plates. 'Oh we have it now and again. It's a good way to use up leftovers.'

'Put in a chopped onion next time,' Juliet suggested. 'That adds a lovely bit of flavour.'

'How are you feeling, George?'

'Up and down, Beth, up and down. Philip wants me to have some tests.'

A collective groan went round the room and murmurs of how annoying it was when one became ill.

'Mother, shall I grab some cheese and biscuits?'

'Thank you, Harry.'

James ushered them into the lounge. While they waited for Beth and Harry, he stoked up the fire and poured everyone a glass of port. He drew the curtains and pulled up his favourite wing-back chair. George and Juliet sat on the sofa.

Harry placed a wooden board on the coffee table, with a selection of cheeses, pickles and crackers on it. He and Beth sat in armchairs on either side of the sofa. James tucked into the nibbles straight away.

'So, George, what did you glean this morning from your enquiries?'

'A great deal along with very little.' He perched on the edge of his seat and prepared some cheese and crackers for Juliet. 'A great deal in the fact that a lot of people had alibis — people able to vouch for one another — that sort of thing. Unless all of them were involved in a conspiracy, I'm able to whittle my investigations down to a handful of people.'

'How exciting,' said Juliet accepting the plate from him. 'Presumably those who have alibis are regular guests and people

185

who simply didn't mix with the victims.'

George confirmed that this was about the gist of it. James felt reassured when George explained that the regular guests had come to know one another over the last few years and they tended to gather at the same tables. Harry grabbed a copy of the seating plan. James brushed a crumb from his trousers. 'So we're concentrating our efforts on those that were at our table and where Olivia's group was.'

'That's right.'

Juliet asked James to remind her who was at his table.

'Me, Beth, Harry, Major and Mrs Carlton and their son, John.' He looked at Harry. 'What was the name of that other couple who were next to you?'

'Mr and Mrs Kitson. Both deaf as a post and not exactly young in years. They were celebrating their golden wedding anniversary. The weekend was a treat from their children. They live in Shropshire, have never been to Sussex before this dinner and have no links to anyone in the room.'

Everyone in the room was quick to

discount the Kitsons from their investigation.

'I say, what about the table the other side of Olivia's?' asked James.

Harry referred to the plan and winced. 'I wouldn't think so unless you want to accuse the Merryweathers, the Jacksons and two WI representatives. There were two Pals with them but both disabled.'

Two WI reps?' said George. 'What are they doing there?'

Beth shifted in her chair. 'We always give a couple of seats to the WI. They do such a lot throughout the year helping with the village festivities. They help decorate the house over Christmas and make fresh holly boughs and floral Christmas wreaths. We give away two seats and they raffle them off during the summer.'

George raised his eyebrows and expressed how generous that was. 'I'm taking it that these ladies are well-known in the village and open to questioning?'

Harry chuckled. 'They're getting on a bit and were founder members of the Cavendish WI. I can't imagine they'll risk missing out on a cake competition to murder someone.'

James smirked. He knew exactly what George would say and he wasn't wrong.

'Everyone is capable of murder, Harry. Your dad's found that out. Don't dismiss a little old dear with twinkly eyes. They can be the worst.'

'Of course they can, Inspector,' said Juliet. 'My sister killed a number of enemy agents when she was working for the government.' She chuckled at Harry. 'You can't imagine it, can you?'

'I have to say, Miss Brooks-Hunter, I can't. I stand corrected over the WI ladies but I still put them low down on the order of suspects.'

Juliet agreed. 'That leaves us with three families.'

James frowned. 'One family, Juliet — the Carltons.'

'No dear, three. The Carltons are a true family but I always put groups of people into families. Olivia Dupree, her two assistants and Carlo Pisani are a family and those Pals are a family.' She sat upright.

'Do you see?'

'Yes I do,' said James. 'They've spent as much time together as a normal family does.'

'And argue and disagree like family,' Beth put in.

George commended Juliet's way of thinking.

'Murder is generally committed by someone known to the victim and very often a family member.' He gave Juliet a considered nod. 'That's a good way of putting it — I like that analogy.'

'Thank you, Inspector. Could you pass me a slice of Wensleydale please?'

'Dad, how did you and Bert get on with Olivia's parents?'

'I felt quite sorry for them.' James went through their conversation and how the mother had never recovered from Olivia leaving and how disappointed the father was with his daughter. 'It sounds like she's dreamed of stardom since she could talk and to hell with anyone who gets in her way.'

'Is there no contact at all?'

'The occasional card when she can remember to send one. She wasn't liked and never made friends with anyone and hasn't been back home for several years.'

George cleared his throat. 'Did you establish any connection with what's gone on?'

'None at all. The mother is a hard-working housewife. She's kept a scrapbook of Olivia's career and there are photographs of her all over the place. The father is simply upset that he hasn't the relationship with her that most fathers have with their daughters. He's an optimist and hopes she'll come to her senses.'

'What a shame,' said Beth.

'Silly girl,' said Juliet. 'Chasing after stardom at the expense of a loving family. She'll rue the day she made that decision.'

George suggested this was a couple that were also down the list of potential suspects if not off the list all together. He turned to James. 'What did you make of John?'

'Nice chap, nothing out of the ordinary, devastated by what's happened. But he did let something slip.'

Everyone stopped eating and stared at him.

'Something untoward with Cynthia. Hasn't been herself for the last few months and wouldn't let on to John what it was. Also, he met Olivia and the two assistants a while back in Brighton. He's quite a fan, apparently, and wanted a record sleeve signed.'

'D'you think there's more to it than that?'

James pondered the question. 'I'm not sure. He didn't give any indication that there was more to it, but it may be worth asking. Did he say anything to you?'

George said that once he'd given news of his mother's death, he couldn't get much out of him at all. He sat back and felt for his pipe. 'It's interesting what you said about something untoward with Cynthia. You could say the same about the Major.'

'Gosh, yes,' said Harry. 'That Major Carlton was incredibly off-hand when George asked him why someone would want to kill his wife.'

'A reaction to grief?' James suggested.

George made a face to indicate that he didn't believe so. 'Ordered me to stop asking questions and get out there and find who did it. Seemed to skirt around the issue of why she was targeted. There's something more to it than he's letting on.'

'And now he's shut up shop and run. Has he gone home?'

'No. One of our men called in and the house is locked. We're checking to see if he's with friends. He has no other family.'

Juliet sipped her port. 'Scared.'

'Do you think so?' said Beth.

'People get angry if they feel scared or threatened by something or someone. It's human nature; fight or flight. He's too old to fight so he's taken off. He'll be with someone he trusts.'

James heaved a sigh. 'John said he never lets anyone into the house because he doesn't trust them. Sounds like he has to vet them first. Cynthia got fed up with the whole thing and began going out more.'

'He will have trusted someone,' said Juliet. 'From the past. You don't grow up not trusting anyone unless you've had a particularly bad childhood. He was happily married. Someone like Cynthia wouldn't marry a man frightened of his own shadow. He will have gone to someone he is comfortable with, from the days when he could trust.'

Harry clicked his fingers. 'Someone from his army days. He spent his whole life in the army.'

'Ye..s,' said James. 'There is camaraderie in the services that you don't get in civvy street.' He wagged a finger at George. 'If that's the case, you need to find out who he served with.'

'And,' said Beth, 'you'll have to put the Pals toward the top of the list. If he has gone to a military friend, then his mistrust of people came from his time in the army.'

'Crikey,' said Harry. 'He was in for twenty-odd years. That'll take a lifetime to find out.'

James held a finger up in inspiration. 'I don't believe it will. This goes back to the trenches of the First World War — 1917 to be precise.'

'Sweetie, how on earth do you know that?'

He reached in his pocket and brought out the diary extract. 'Because of this.' He leapt up and opened the bureau to take out the previous diary entry. He held it aloft. 'And this.'

George closed his eyes in frustration. 'Why do you always do this to me?'

'What?'

'I know nothing about these bits of paper. Why haven't you mentioned them?'

'I didn't think they were anything much until our conversation earlier. They're just diary entries that have come loose and Paul believed them to be lost property. But no one admits to owning them. If that's the case, they've now become relevant. This one was handed to me after the first dance. This second one was found in the same area, but not in plain view.'

'And you now have your fingerprints all over them.'

'I admit that the first entry will appear that way. But the second extract, well, Beth was quick to avoid contaminating it. You may find Paul's fingerprints but that's about it.'

'Come along, my dear,' said Juliet, 'read them aloud.'

James did so. At the end of the second entry, they all agreed that these spoke of something untoward. He picked up the most recent entry.

'I've not read this one myself yet.' Using a handkerchief, he unfolded it. *'France April 16 1917 : 9 shot today but it wasn't right. He did nothing wrong. He saw what I saw but opened his mouth and paid the price. I'll have to keep quiet or I'll go the same way. He won't get away with it — not as long as I'm alive. He'll get what's coming to him.'*

He puffed his cheeks and handed both entries to George. 'They look like originals. I checked the handwriting against the register but couldn't see anything conclusive.'

George scanned the text and sought out Juliet.

'What do you make of this?

'It confirms my suspicions,' she said. 'Major Carlton is running away. I believe whoever wrote this diary is referring to our Major. He did something during the war that he shouldn't have done.'

'Goodness,' said Beth, 'whoever it is sure holds a grudge.'

Harry scratched his head. 'So we need to investigate the Major and, presumably, he is linked to the Pals somehow.'

'You don't need to investigate anything. *I* need to investigate the Major,' said George. 'You get on with arranging your pantomime or whatever else you're doing this Christmas.' He started to rise, gripped his stomach and groaned. Harry leapt up and helped him back down. James insisted on calling Dr Jackson. George requested calm as the pain disappeared as quickly as it had come.

'I don't need a doctor. It's just a bit of indigestion, that's all. It's going off now.'

It took some convincing but James eventually gave his friend the benefit of the doubt. He requested the second diary entry back from George. 'I don't understand this. It says '9 shot today', which indicates nine people killed. But then it refers to 'he'. He did nothing wrong.' He held everyone's gaze. 'Who is 9?'

'And what,' said Harry, 'has this to do with Olivia Dupree?'

18

James looked on as Dorothy Forbes instructed the Cavendish Players to take their places for a run-through of that year's pantomime, *Cinderella*. She'd persuaded Beth to take the part of Prince Charming which she had reluctantly accepted after being persuaded by James, Anne and Stephen. Normally, Beth helped with the costumes and remained backstage but, after many assurances, she was convinced by all that she'd do well in the part. Although line-perfect, she wore an anxious expression as she stood on the small wooden stage.

He and the Merryweathers watched from the back of the room by the WI table. The Snoop sisters, Rose and Lilac Crumb, distributed teas and coffees and freshly baked mince pies. Elsie Taylor, who had come straight from closing her café, levered the lid off a cake tin and arranged some fresh gingerbread men on a plate alongside.

Dorothy ordered the men of the village, suitably dressed in overalls, to erect the scenery around her performers. She marched up the steps and onto the stage.

'Now, Lady Harrington,' she began.

James switched his attention to Didier who, this year, had opted to take part and play Baron Hardup. It was rare to see his chef out of his whites and he struck a fatherly figure in his dark trousers and cardigan. He was a short man with plump fingers who examined the gingerbread men with suspicion. Elsie thrust one into his hands and he took a bite. After a couple of seconds his eyes lit up.

'*Mais oui*, a perfectly made biscuit, Miss Taylor. You made these?'

'No need to look so surprised. I've been cooking since I was ten.'

Didier shrugged an apology and took another. James beckoned him over.

'I say, Didier, I'm interested to know what you did during the Great War. You must have been incredibly young; I mean, you're only in your early fifties now.'

Didier led him away from the main

crowd and they sat on two wooden chairs in the corner of the hall.

'I was fourteen, Lord 'arrington. I had to grow up fast. My father, he was a farmer in the Artois region and most of it was swallowed by the trenches. 'e grew many vegetables and we 'ad many fruit trees. I help him before and after school, all of my time. I was ready to follow in his footsteps but the war broke out.'

'Did the résistance come to you?'

'Non. We went to them. When my father saw his land disappear, 'e could not make a living; it was not safe for our family. At first, the war was a game. Those first few months in 1914, I would take food to the British soldiers. The sun shone bright and the meadows 'ad wild flowers with many colours. There was no fighting. I could not believe we were at war. But then it began.'

Didier went on to describe the increasing bombardment from both sides — the bombs, the gunfire and the mud. He spoke of his horror on seeing men and horses sucked into the dirt and left to rot; of rats and lice waging their own war on corpses that couldn't be retrieved. Tears welled in his eyes.

'Lord 'arrington, by the time I was fourteen, the war was raging. France was on its knees. My father could no longer provide for us. We moved from the farm and to my uncle. He lived in Albért. One night, I could not sleep and I over'eard a conversation between my uncle and a woman. The floorboards, they creak, they find me listening and pull me in. 'ow much did you hear?', the woman said.' Didier glared at James. 'I thought she would kill me but my uncle, he said I could be useful. 'e said no one would suspect a young boy.'

'So your uncle volunteered you?'

His chef nodded.

'Did you know what you were letting yourself in for?'

'At that age, it was an adventure, but I quickly realised how how important my actions were. I ran the lines, passing messages about enemy positions, where the guns were, troop movements. I took food supplies to points only the soldiers knew. Those boys, they 'ad nothing; they looked like rags on bones.'

'Did you ever get caught?'

'Once. That is when I became a man. A German foot soldier — he stopped me. I 'ad supplies of food and a message for the front line. He shouted at me to give him the food.' Didier shrugged. 'Well, I could not! If I had given him the basket, there would be no problem but — .'

'If you'd given him the food, he would have found the message.'

'*Oui, oui*. I told him it was for my grandmother, that she was sick. I offered him half the food and he struck me. He struck the side of my head and I fell. The food emptied from the basket. This soldier, he picked the food up and put it back in the basket and began walking away.' Anger contorted Didier's expression. 'I could not let my comrades down, Lord 'arrington. I had a knife in my jacket. My uncle gave it to me and said that I must not be afraid to use it.' He drew his shoulders back. 'I was not afraid to use it. I ran after that soldier and I stabbed him. He dropped to his knees. I stabbed him again. He died, there, on that spot. I grabbed the basket and I ran like I 'ave never run before. Through fields and country lanes until I found the drop-off point.'

'Good lord.'

'The English soldier waiting for me 'eard my story. 'e gave me water and ordered me to go and rest away from the rendezvous and take a different route home.'

Didier broke off a piece of gingerbread and put it in his mouth. James simply couldn't believe what he was hearing. He knew Didier as his chef and nothing more. A middle-aged genius in the kitchen who he could never visualise as a young man let alone a runner for the résistance.

'Can I ask, Didier, how did you become a chef after all of this?'

His expression brightened. 'This was my motivation. I always loved food, Lord 'arrington but I thought I would follow my father and be a farmer. But the farm was gone. My father opened a bakery in a village at the end of the war. He was happy but he missed the farm.'

Didier turned and faced James.

'I saw the pleasure my food gave those soldiers. I began to make special food. I baked fresh croissants and rolls and I cured ham. I made cheese and cider. The soldiers, they look forward to my parcels. They always ask for a delivery from me and I never let them down — not once.'

'So something marvellous came from that adversity.'

Didier pulled his shoulders back. 'That is why I was so angry with that woman — Olivia Dupree. She does not know this motivation for cooking. I fed those soldiers the best I could give. I am no different today. How dare she accuse me, Didier Le Noir, of poisoning her. Even if my worst enemy were to stay at 'arrington's, I would not poison him. I would not ruin my reputation for anyone.'

'It's pretty clear now, Didier, that something was put in her wine to make her ill.'

'Pah! She has the voice of angel and the manners of a camel.'

James couldn't help but laugh and, to his surprise, Didier laughed with him.

'I say, Didier, did you hear any rumours from the soldiers about coward-ice?'

His chef gave him a considered look. 'There were always rumours, Lord 'arrington.'

'What about officers?'

'Officers? I did not know the officers. I speak only to soldiers, the men on the front line and they speak of their comrades.'

'What about Captain William Carlton? Did anyone mention him?'

Didier held up a finger and narrowed his eyes. 'The man at your dinner, *oui*?'

'That's the one'.

'I cannot be sure, Lord 'arrington. I do not want to accuse a man without the facts. I 'eard rumour of a Captain who was not, 'ow you say, qualified to lead. There was a rumour that an officer made bad decisions. But,' Didier held his hands up, 'I do not know the name of that man.'

'Was he attached to the Cavendish Pals?'

'*Non, non.*'

James felt his shoulders fall. Didier

tapped the side of his nose.

'The Cavendish Pals were attached to his unit.'

Dorothy strode toward them. She clapped her hands.

'Mr Le Noir, I've been calling and calling! I need you on stage please.'

'*Je suis desolé.*' He got up and bowed to James. 'Je m'excuse.'

James's gaze followed Didier toward the stage.

What an extraordinary man. In all the years that Didier had cooked for their family — first his sister and now at Harrington's — none of them had had any idea of his bravery — and at such a young age too. And, although he was capable of it, he would not jeopardise his culinary reputation to kill.

Adam Franks, the waiter from Harrington's, caught his eye. He wore blue jeans and a navy blue turtle-neck sweater. James mused about how different people appeared when they were away from a uniform. He got up to join him at the WI table.

'What has Dorothy landed you with, Adam?'

The young man rolled his eyes. 'I'm props. I've been volunteered. I couldn't stand up in front of an audience and act. That'd be my worst nightmare. Are you taking part, your Lordship?'

James asked for a cup of tea and returned his attention to Adam. 'Not this year, no. I said I'd help out with programmes and getting people seated on the night. I'll do a taxi service for the folks at the old people's home. Christmas, this year, is a little busy, what with the wedding and two dances to organise.'

'Not to mention those people getting ill.'

'Yes, that was a rum do. Are you quite sure you didn't see anything on either of those evenings?'

Adam shook his head and reiterated his story. During the first dinner, he'd stood by the main door between reception and the dining room. During the one following, he'd more or less done the same but they had been a waiter down so he had filled in for him too.

'I didn't see anyone spike Miss Dupree's drink and I didn't see anyone go to that Quack Doctor's case. I know it was sitting in Reception for a while with the guests' bags but that's about it.'

'Tell me about your grandfather, Adam. He was in the Cavendish Pals, wasn't he?'

'Oh yes. He played football and cricket for Cavendish. Apparently, they were having one of those round-robin sports tournaments. It was during the summer of 1916. The football, tennis and cricket teams all took part from here, Charnley and Loxfield. I remember my nan saying there'd been some pretty awful fighting in France during that weekend and they wanted volunteers. I think it was decided in a drunken state outside the Half Moon and they all went and signed up. He was killed the following year.'

'Did you know much about him?'

Adam explained that his nan suffered terribly when he died. 'I don't remember her much; she seemed like an old woman to me but I don't think she was. Mum and Dad said she used to laugh a lot. I don't know if people can die from broken hearts but I think that's what happened to her.'

'I'm sorry, Adam, I didn't mean to stir up unhappy memories. Did he write home?'

'As much as he could have. Nan kept those letters in a box by her bed. They were always there, even years after the war.'

'Do you still have them?'

Adam looked away and shuffled his feet. 'I dunno. Mum prob'ly chucked them out. I'd better see if Mrs Forbes needs a hand. Excuse me, your Lordship.'

James sipped his tea and pondered the sudden furtive attitude of his waiter. Beth strode toward him.

'Did you hear me?'

'What?'

'Did you hear my voice when I was on the stage? I'm worried that no one will hear me. I hope I'm doing the right thing. What if I forget my lines?'

'Darling, you'll be perfect and Anne's helping you with your lines. You'll be wonderful and you're an adorable Prince Charming.'

She put her hands on her hips. 'What is this thing with pantomimes and women playing the men's role? It seems most odd to me.'

'It all harks back to those mad Victorians where ladies were forced to wear corsets and bustles. The only place they could rid themselves of such garments was on stage where they were permitted to wear costumes that showed a shapely leg. The only way they could get around it was for them to play the principal male role. No one objected because it also pleased the men in the audience.'

'That all sounds too bizarre,' said Beth.

'Speaking of bizarre,' he pulled her to one side.

'I've had a couple of enlightening conversations.'

Having grabbed her attention, he went through his chat with Didier and Adam, Beth interrupting with an occasional 'Oh' and 'Goodness!'.

'You don't seriously think they had anything to do with the poisoning, do you?' she asked.

'Good lord, I hope not. I seriously doubt that Didier has. His ego would forbid him to compromise his talents; but Adam became more than a little shifty when I probed him for information on those letters.'

'Do you think the family still has them?' She grabbed his arm. 'Do you think it's the same handwriting as the diary entries?' She squeezed tighter. 'Oh heavens, I hope he hasn't done anything stupid.'

James peeled her fingers off his arm and assured her that he thought it unlikely. 'I do need to get to the bottom of that story though.'

Before he could continue, Dorothy asked for all main players to go back to the stage. James selected a mince pie from the table and frowned. Was he wrong to dismiss Didier? His heroics were commendable but not only did this arm him with the ambition to cook and be one of the best chefs in Europe, it enabled him to be ruthless. He'd killed a man: it might have been in the context of war but he had shown no qualms about doing so.

And what was Adam being so shifty about? His demeanour had changed considerably when James had asked for more details.

If this was the background of two of his staff, what stories did the other descendants of the Pals have? He made a mental note to track down Paul and his gardener, Ernest Appleton.

19

The following day, James strolled around the gardens that surrounded their own property. There was crispness in the air and the little snow that had fallen crunched beneath his feet. He wore a pair of thick-soled hiking boots, dark brown corduroy trousers, a sheepskin jacket and a felt flat cap. He carried a shepherd's crook as he strode across the lawn toward the greenhouses and sheds at the far end. A fox dashed along the hedgerow ahead of him and he felt a rush of contentment. There was no denying it, being out in the countryside was his passion. He couldn't understand people who lived in the city with no fresh air and fields in which to wander.

Their gardener, Ernest Appleton, was busy in the greenhouse jotting notes down in a small book. He was a tall, wiry man with a weathered face and side-whiskers. James tapped the side of the greenhouse door.

'Ah, Appleton.'

Appleton tipped his battered trilby. 'Morning, your Lordship,' he said in a rural Sussex accent.

'Something the matter?'

James assured him that everything was splendid. 'I know I only come over when I want something done which is rather remiss of me. I thought I'd take a stroll and saw you hard at it. Much need doing this time of the year?'

The gardener scanned the garden. 'Just keeping on top of things really. Making sure plants don't get frost-bite, keep the birds happy and start preparing for the spring. That's what I'm doing now — logging the seeds I'm planting and where to put 'em. Make a note of what needs tending.'

James peered over his shoulder at the notebook full of dates, seasons and names of flowers and fruits.

'You're certainly industrious, Appleton. Anything new being planted for the spring?'

Ernest went through a list of flowers and shrubs that James wasn't all that familiar with. James loved the countryside and could happily tell you the different trees that dotted the area but where flowers were concerned, his knowledge extended only to the popular varieties. But, from what Appleton was telling him, they were to be prepared for an explosion of colour by May.

'It all sounds incredibly vibrant. I'm sure my wife will be overjoyed.'

James wondered how he was going to bring the subject of the Great War up when Appleton provided his opening.

'Looks like your Christmas dances were a success, your Lordship.'

'Yes, they're becoming a regular part of the guests' diaries now, so long may they continue. And you know we had a contingent of the Cavendish Pals here.'

'So I heard. Simmonds boys were there and Scotty Bull. Those three never left the village 'cept to go to war.'

'Your brother was in the Pals wasn't he?'

Appleton stopped working and gazed out of the window with a fond expression. 'Rider.'

'I beg your pardon?'

Ernest snapped out of his daydream

and faced James. 'We used to call him Rider. Always on your dad's horses at the stables, he was. Fancied himself as a stable-hand and said that once the war was over, he'd have a go and prove to your dad that he could run the stables.' He had a pained expression. 'Never got to live that dream though.' He heaved a sigh. 'Made it through the war but the gas got to his lungs. He was in that convalescent home on the coast for a while but then he got pneumonia and he didn't have the strength.' His eyes welled with tears as he held James' gaze. 'Only twenty three he was. Had his whole life ahead of him.'

'It was a sad time for many people. I'm sure he was glad to have such a supportive brother.'

'I did what I could.' He tapped his right leg. 'Of course, they wouldn't let me sign up.'

Ernest Appleton had a disfigured leg that caused him to limp. Running was impossible. The villagers had never questioned his non-eligibility for joining up. It was obvious the man had problems and they commended him for having tried to enlist.

James' father had known the young man was keen on the outdoors and had offered him a position working in the grounds. Gardening had been Ernest's saving grace. He learned his trade from the old estate gardeners up at Harrington's. The big house had become too much for him but, for James and Beth, there was no one else more qualified to manage the grounds of the house where they now lived.

'Did Rider write to you when he was in France?'

'He'd write when he could. Sounded horrific to me. I don't know how they put them men through it. I don't mean just the English; I mean all of 'em. The Germans had it as bad. I've got Rider's diaries if you want to have a read.'

His heart skipped a beat. 'That would certainly be of interest, thank you.'

Thinking the gardener would announce when he could deliver them, James turned to go. But to his astonishment, Appleton held up a hand and gestured for James to follow him next door to the shed. The shed was around the size of their garage and held quite a bit of machinery for jobs around the garden. At the back was an old oak sideboard that had seen better days. Appleton opened a drawer and brought out two small notebooks. He handed them to James.

'Be careful with 'em, won't you? I read 'em now and again when I stop for my flask of soup. Keeps me close to Rider, see.'

James held them up with a promise that he would keep them safe and return them in the next few days. 'I say, Jackson was speaking to me about poisons and he said that he hoped we kept ours under lock and key. Do we have poisons?'

'We've some strychnine to get rid of the moles and any rats. It's in the cupboard at the end there, locked up.'

'Where's the key?'

'Just behind you, hanging on the nail.'

He looked at it. So easy to steal; but people would have to know it was there. He thanked Appleton and strolled back to the house. Although he was feeling chilly, he perched on the edge of a cast iron chair on the terrace and read the first couple of pages.

1917! How extraordinary; everyone seemed to be writing about the same year.

The trenches are soft mud. The bread and jam has been stored in a sack covered in mud. My hands are covered in mud and everything tastes of mud. What I wouldn't give for bowl of Mum's chicken soup. We've been here five days and I've had three hours' sleep. I dozed off yesterday. Scotty woke me thank God. I've heard men are shot for that. I'm so tired, I can't think straight. The last tree standing got blown up today so I lost my bet. We'd bet a cube of chocolate each on which day it would disappear. I was a day out. Nice tree too. Ernest would have had it chopped up for the fireplaces at the manor.

He flicked through the pages, stopping every now and again to study the text. Then, he gently tapped the notebooks and put them in his inside pocket. The handwriting was not the same as in the papers discovered at the dances but he'd keep hold of them. Now convinced that his gardener was not a suspect, he wondered if the diaries might reveal something about

Captain William Carlton. It was a remote possibility but worth pursuing.

Beth's call from the living room snatched him out of his thoughts. He jumped up and went to join her. She announced that Stephen and Anne were helping the villagers decorate the tree on the village green and were then going to the Half Moon for a quick drink.

'They've dropped Luke, Mark and little Radley off at their grandparents for a couple of days, so they have some spare time. Can you come?'

'Of course. I'll change my shoes and I'm ready to go.'

As James parked alongside the green, Beth gazed through the windscreen. 'Oh James, it looks like a Christmas card.'

He got out of the car and opened the passenger door for her. 'It does look rather stunning doesn't it?'

The sun sparkled off the snow. Smoke swirled from the chimneys of the cottages surrounding the green and lights shone a welcoming glow through the Half Moon's windows.

On the green itself, Mr Chrichton

conducted his first year pupils in a chorus of 'Deck the Halls'. Children, were scampering around a large Christmas tree. Graham and Sarah Porter handed baubles to the children to hang on the lower branches. Helen Jackson directed where the decorations should sit. Charlie Hawkins was up and down one of the ladders, securing tinsel, while Philip fastened a silver star on the top. Anne held the base of another ladder while Stephen tied red ribbons to the ends of the taller branches.

'Be careful, Stephen!' James called. 'I don't want to have to collect you from the hospital again.'

On all of the cases James had helped solve, Stephen had been attacked in one way or another and James always seemed to be collecting him from the cottage hospital. Stephen gave him a knowing look, then focussed on the job in hand.

'What a shame your children are missing this,' said Beth.

Anne nodded but assured Beth that they would be helping with the tree where they were and no doubt Radley would be causing mischief too.

Over the next hour the villagers' efforts transformed a basic tree into a resplendent centre-piece for the green. Satisfied with the end result, the villagers dispersed in different directions; many of them to the Half Moon. James steered Beth toward the war memorial in the far corner of the green, where Stephen and Anne joined them. It was a fitting memorial with brass plaques screwed into the centre of each side. Two sides listed names from World War I and two from World War II.

'S-such an awful loss for a village of th-this size.'

Anne agreed. 'Especially in the Great War. It's a wonder the village itself didn't die out.'

'It's an ancient village,' said James. 'Many men didn't return.' He put his shoulders back. 'But we had many that did and a good number of boys who were far too young to fight. They were our future.'

Beth strolled around the memorial. The stonework was old and some of it was covered in moss and lichen. 'The Harringtons are represented in both wars.'

'Yes, we lost great uncle Edwin in the first and cousin Geoffrey in the second.' He examined all of the names while Stephen and Anne strolled toward the pub. A sense of pride ran through him. He knew the families of every name listed here and it pleased him that most had chosen to remain in Cavendish.

Paul skidded toward them on his bicycle and stopped alongside. 'Just going up to the house, Lord Harrington. Everything's in order up there and Didier has fresh rabbit on the menu.'

'Excellent.' James gave a nod to the memorial.

'Your father was a Pal, wasn't he? Is he still with us?'

'Yes he is. Fought in the first war and was in the Home Guard for the second. Lives with his brother in Eastbourne now. They lost their wives a few years ago and decided to share a home — more for company than anything. Loves it down there. All that sea air, he looks the picture of health.' He tipped his cap and went on his way.

James took Beth's hand and led her to

the pub. Inside, the atmosphere buzzed. The smell of hops permeated the bar. Tinsel and holly hung from every available beam and fairy lights were strung around the edge of the ceiling. Each table had a lit candle stuck into the neck of an old beer bottle giving a homely feel to an already cosy area.

Donovan and Kate filled the orders as if their lives depended on it and within a few minutes, James was holding a pint of Christmas ale with a thick head on the top of it. Beth opted for a warming whisky with ginger wine.

Graham Porter beckoned them across to the booth where Stephen, Anne, Bert, Charlie and Philip sat. James stood to one side for Beth to slide in ahead of him and, once seated, he raised his glass. 'An early greeting, I know, but Merry Christmas everyone.'

The group chorused the same in return. Graham slapped the table with the palm of his hand.

'So, what's going on up at the manor? Is it right that someone was poisoned?'

James was quick to play down the drama.

Philip said that it was an accidental over-dose of prescription medication. James spoke a silent thank you to the doctor. He didn't want rumours about murder and poisoning spreading around the village. It was inevitable that people would talk, especially as many of the villagers worked up at the house. Philip's suggestion would, undoubtedly, reach the ears of the gossips and, hopefully, things would quieten down.

Beth shifted in her seat. 'Graham, did your family fight in the war?'

'Absolutely. Not from here though. My dad joined the Derbyshire regiment. That's where he's from. Got through it too, which was a blessing. The Cavendish Pals are an interesting bunch though, aren't they? I was chatting to Charlie about 'em.'

'I've put a display up in the library,' Charlie added. 'I had so many photographs donated over the years that I thought I'd put an exhibition up to coincide with their reunion.'

'That's a wonderful idea,' said Beth. 'James, we should go and see that. I'm sure that'll interest the whole village.'

'Yes, you're right,' said James. 'Mr

Chrichton's bringing the school-children in tomorrow morning.'

Bert pushed his cap back from his forehead. 'That's who you wanna be showing that to. Keep the youngsters knowing what we did for 'em. There's plenty forgetting already.'

A collective nod went around the table. James thought back to the summer when he was investigating the smuggling ring. The moody teenagers and their attitudes had not impressed him at all. Bert was right: the children should be aware of what their grandfathers did.

Philip slipped out of the booth, announcing that he had appointments to meet. Graham checked his watch and decided he still had a few minutes. 'I went and saw Brighton play Derby on Saturday.'

Stephen looked deflated. 'Brighton lost. 2-nil.'

'Oi, whatcha doing supporting Brighton? You're from Oxford,' said Bert.

'I-I thought I'd switch allegiance to my l-local team.'

James supped his ale. 'I didn't know you were a Derby fan, Graham.'

'Oh yes, like to see a bit of football. I went down with Mr Bennett.' Mr Bennett was the elderly man who taught James how to fish as a boy. 'I used to play when I was a youngster; goalkeeper. Wasn't bad either.'

'I'm not surprised,' said Beth, 'I can imagine you in the goal with those enormous hands.'

Graham splayed his hands out. 'They've got bigger over the years hauling all that meat about and chopping it up.' He sat back and pondered. 'I wanted to be a centre forward, the one that scores the goals. Steve Bloomer, he was one of the best centre forwards in the country; he played for Derby. Best number nine ever.'

James' ears pricked up. 'Number nine?' He felt Beth grip his arm.

'Yeah, most centre forwards wear number nine. Not sure why but they do.'

Anne, bored with the subject of football, turned the conversation to the pantomime but James couldn't concentrate at all.

'Everything all right, James?' said Charlie. 'You look a little startled.'

'I say, Charlie, do you have archives in the library about the sports teams in the area?'

'Yes, we've a few. I don't know how extensive they are but there are some old newspapers with team sheets on.' He studied James. 'You want to look at them now, don't you?'

'Would it be too much of an imposition?'

Charlie made a face to imply it made no odds to him. He swigged the last of his beer down. James whispered to Beth that he was going to the library. Beth, keen to be a party to what was happening, made her excuses with a promise to Anne to meet for tea that afternoon.

Five minutes later and the three of them were ensconced in the reference library. Charlie scanned the shelves for box files marked in date order. He tapped each one and with a quiet 'Ha' he levered one out and put in on the table.

'Is this you putting your sleuthing hat on again?'

James gave him a wry smile. 'Your father was in the Pals, wasn't he?'

'He was but he got separated. All that talk about joining up and serving together didn't happen with Dad.'

'Oh?'

'My dad was a big bloke, muscular, so they volunteered him to dig tunnels.'

James recalled reading about the miners who dug tunnels. Their objective was to tunnel under No Man's Land and place mines beneath enemy positions. How perilous that work must have been.

'He was sent to Belgium with the Second Army. Managed to make it through the war but he suffered. Lots of lung problems, what with the fumes and the gas. We lost him when I was about ten. He spoke a lot about the camaraderie. Sounds like everyone dug in, excuse the pun. Officers and soldiers did their bit.' He patted the files. 'These are the local newspapers in Cavendish for between 1916 and 1918. I'll see if there's anything else to do with sports teams. Any sport in particular?'

James sat down and opened the box. 'Yes, football.'

Beth slid her chair as close as possible and peered over his shoulder. 'You know, in a way, I don't want to know.'

James stopped rummaging and felt his eyes glaze over. He didn't either. Whoever played number nine would be a name familiar to him and the Cavendish residents. He squeezed her hand. 'It doesn't prove anything, Beth. It's not evidence for murder.'

'But it may put suspicion on someone — an ancestor.'

'We'll just have to hope that whoever that person is has an alibi.' He picked up the flimsy newspapers, slid the box away and placed them on the table. Charlie left them to it, telling them to shout if they needed anything further.

James turned the whole pile of papers over. 'Sport is normally a few pages from the back.'

His first paper was listed for June 1914. He carefully leafed through until he came to the section he wanted. He scanned an article about the Cavendish cricket team having triumphed over Rottingdean, winning by 32 runs. He closed it.

'I need something between October and April.'

Beth gently lifted each document. 'This paper is so fragile. It feels like it'll disintegrate in your hand. Oh, here we are, this one's dated November 1915.'

James helped her open the paper up. He found an article for a match between Cavendish and Wivelsfield, a village near Brighton. The headline announced: 'Cavendish Win' and the article went on to describe a close-run football match where Cavendish won 2-0. Certain players had stood out, all of them from families that James was familiar with. He examined the article. 'I don't see a team sheet.'

Beth, meanwhile, had pulled out another paper.

'Here, try this one.'

It was dated January 1916. James leafed through the paper. 'A-ha. A team sheet.'

He examined the list of eleven players and groaned.

'What's the matter?'

'The number nine for Cavendish was Archibald Franks.'

Beth put her hands to her mouth. 'Oh no, that's Adam's grandfather.'

James folded the paper slowly and

placed the pile back in the box. Charlie appeared with a cloth.

'I thought I'd give this table a polish when you're gone. It's all a bit dusty, isn't it? Did you find what you were looking for?'

James got up and helped Beth to her feet. 'Yes, thanks, we'll see you at the next rehearsal if not before. Cheerio.'

Outside, he grabbed Beth's hand.

'Where are we going now?'

'The memorial.' When they arrived he pointed to the brass plaque listing the soldiers of the Great War. The names were in alphabetical order. He pointed. 'Archibald Franks is not on the plaque.'

He looked at Beth who'd paled. Tears formed in her eyes. 'Oh, James, I don't like where this is going.'

He wrapped an arm around her. 'Darling, Adam may have absolutely nothing to do with this.'

She opened her handbag searching for a handkerchief. 'But it points to him, doesn't it? Archibald Franks isn't on that memorial because he was number nine. Number nine was shot. He was a coward or a deserter.' Her eyes welled. 'Do you think Adam knew?'

He let out a sigh. 'There's only one way to find out and that's to ask him.'

As they reached the car, Beth pointed back to the library. 'Oh look. Isn't that Mandy Billings?'

James followed her gaze. 'Good Lord, yes. What's she doing here?'

They got in the car and watched as she skipped down the narrow path to Charlie's house and knocked. Charlie bounded out of the library and waved hello to her.

'Well,' said James, 'I knew that he was rather smitten with her last week. I didn't realise he was *that* smitten!'

He returned his attention to Charlie, who chatted with Mandy and checked his watch. After a brief discussion, he locked the library and they rushed to the bus-stop where the county service to Charnley had pulled up. James turned to Beth.

'Let's delay our chat with Adam. I believe Charlie may be escorting Mandy to Elsie's for tea. There's nowhere else of significance on that bus route. Do you fancy a cup? We may find out a little more about Olivia.'

Beth had a mischievous look in her eye. 'That is terribly devious, James. They won't want us intruding.'

'We'll take a timely stroll around Charnley so they have some time together first. Does that suit you?'

After some deliberation, Beth gave in. He put the car in gear and allowed the bus to go by before following.

20

James checked his watch. He and Beth had wandered around the green at Charnley and decided sufficient time had passed for them to drop by and visit Elsie's café. The doorbell jingled as they entered and a few customers glanced up to observe their arrival. Most tables were taken but one of the waitresses waved them across to a table for two in the far corner. At first, James couldn't see Charlie but then a hand sprang up. The librarian leant across the table to Mandy and then beckoned them over. They were sitting in one of James' favourite spots, a table for four by one of the bay windows. He motioned for Beth to lead them through. They stepped over handbags and shopping on the way and wished some familiar faces compliments of the season.

'Ah! Hello!,' said James, feigning surprise. 'I didn't expect to see you here — and Mandy Billings too. Do you live in the area?' he asked, 'I presumed you were in London with Olivia and Enid.'

They sat down. Mandy linked arms with Charlie before explaining. She spoke softly. 'Oh, Mr Hawkins invited me for tea, Lord Harrington. I'm still living at Mum's in Cowfold — when I'm not working that is. The rent's paid until the end of the month. Miss Dupree is taking a few days off so I'm sorting Mum's place out.'

'Yes,' Beth put in. 'I understand that your mother passed away recently. We're so sorry.'

Mandy sighed and explained how difficult it was to clear out the house. 'There's no end of things to do and the stuff she collected — it's taking an age to sort out.'

'I guess we all accumulate things through our lives.'

'I'm going to try to make sure I don't, Lady Harrington. I've never been one for ornaments or antiques so I've got a head start on Mum. She loved collecting. First of all, it was bird ornaments, then vases and the latest thing was bottles. All they did was catch the dust, as far as I could see.'

Charlie rested his elbows on the table. 'I said they could be worth a few bob, James. What d'you think?'

'I think you could be right. Someone's junk is another man's hoard.'

Mandy shrugged. 'I'm halfway through now. Done the upstairs. I've kept a couple of nice pieces as a memory but that's about it. Most of it looked like rubbish to me.'

Elsie approached their table, apologising for the wait. 'Christmas always brings my regulars out. What can I get for you?'

James and Beth examined the chalk-board which advertised home-made mince pies and Christmas cake. They looked at each other. Although it was lunch-time they knew exactly what they would order.

'Two teas and two slices of Christmas cake please, Elsie.'

'And we'll have a top up on the teas please,' added Charlie.

After a few minutes of small talk, the tea and cake arrived and James felt the time was right to steer the conversation his way. 'So, Mandy, how did you enjoy singing with Carlo Pisani?'

Mandy's face lit up as she described how excited she'd been, to be able to show what she could do. With a little prompting from Beth, she described her childhood in Cowfold; a standard education, a poor background and a love of music.

'My mum used to sing quite a bit. Just around the house when she cleaned or did the cooking.' Her expression hardened. 'That's before she got ill though. When she was ill, she never said a word — just curled up on the sofa staring at the floor.'

'Was this a long-term illness?'

'She'd get depressed. My dad left us and we didn't have any family to speak of. She used to go a bit odd and they'd take her into hospital. Well, it weren't a hospital, more like an institution but it didn't make much difference. Sometimes I think it made her worse. The doctors didn't treat her right,' she snapped.

'How awful for you,' Beth said. 'It's good that she had you to help her.'

'She's better off out of it. She's with family now — with Dad.' Her eyes lost their sparkle and, in an almost childlike voice, she said: 'Poor Daddy.' She blinked, coming out of her daydream. 'I'm not that religious but it makes you wonder when someone dies, don't it?'

James noticed that Charlie was quick to agree. He'd lost his wife at an early age, leaving him with Tommy and Susan to bring up and the feeling of loss was still raw with him, even though it was several years ago. 'Are you quite close to Olivia?'

Her brow knitted together. 'She's not someone you want to spend time with. She's picky and rude and treats me and Enid like dirt.' She brightened. 'But, we get to meet quite a few celebrities and travel a lot. I've been with her for three years now and I think I may move on soon. I've had a couple of offers but I might wait now and see what happens with the singing; or anything else. It'd be nice to be rich and famous.' She gave Charlie a coy smile.

'Even if the right man comes along, I don't think I could ditch it.'

'Was Olivia pleased that you stepped in for her at Harrington's?'

'You're joking, aren't you? She was evil that night. Accused me of trying to kill her. I couldn't believe it. After everything I do for her. I practically run her life so she don't have any stress. The one time I get to do something I love, she has a right go at me. It's not as if I'm gonna stop her from being famous. It was just one night at a country hotel — it weren't on the television.' She pursed her lips. 'And she left me in the lurch the other night. Didn't check to see if I had a lift or anything.'

Beth patted her hand down. 'She probably sees you as a threat. I heard your singing and I think the whole audience thought you were wonderful.'

Charlie grinned. 'I thought you were better than Olivia.'

Mandy tilted her head. 'Thank you, Charlie,' she said, her voice gentle once more, 'that means a great deal.'

'I say,' said James, 'are Olivia and Carlo an item?'

Her laugh was almost sarcastic. 'She'd

like them to be. She's besotted with him and who can blame her. He's handsome, rich, talented; she throws herself at him all the time.'

'And do you think someone was trying to kill her that night?'

She turned to face him. 'You're beginning to sound like a copper. You're friends with that detective bloke, aren't you?'

James held his hands up. 'Sorry, I find it intriguing and my chef was rather put out about the poisoning accusation.'

'Not surprised. His food was lovely and the old men on our table adored the pudding.'

'You got on well with them, I hear.'

She describe her grandfather, an old man who had passed away some time previously. 'He went into that convalescent home on the South Coast, The Royal Sussex I think it's called. I don't remember much about him. I was quite young when he left us.'

'What regiment was he in?'

'Sussex.'

James tried to remain calm. 'Really? Do

you know which battalion?'

Mandy pulled a face to indicate she had no idea.

'Mum didn't talk about it much and dad left us when I was about ten. Our family history is pretty non-existent.'

James bit into the last of his cake and checked his watch. Beth suggested to him that they should leave Charlie and Mandy alone. He stifled a grin. Was this his wife trying to match-make again? She and Anne had predicted the romance between GJ and Catherine. Was Charlie about to embark on a new romance? In a way, he hoped so. Charlie deserved it and James was sure he'd love his children to have a new mum. Whether it should be Mandy, he didn't know. Although she was obviously fond of Charlie, he couldn't see her being a mother. She didn't strike him as being maternal and her mood blew hot and cold. But Charlie enjoyed her company. After settling up with Elsie, James and Beth returned home where Harry was waiting on the top step by the front door. James opened the passenger door and called across.

'Everything all right?'

Harry closed the door and jogged down the steps toward them. 'You might want to get back in the car.'

'Oh dear,' said Beth. 'What's happened?'

'Adam's been taken in for questioning.'

21

The drive to Lewes was a frantic one. James focussed on the winding country roads and was mindful of the light snow and ice that had yet to clear. Beth, meanwhile, fired questions at Harry who insisted he had no answers for her. The only information he could impart was that it was George who had spoken to the staff at Harrington's and decided that he wanted more information from Adam. 'Adam didn't want his family to find out he'd been taken in. I think he felt a bit embarrassed about asking for you. You don't think he's guilty, do you?'

James came to a T-junction, pulled out and went past the sign that welcomed them to Lewes. 'I don't think he's guilty, no. I don't think he has that in him but there are questions that Adam needs to answer. I'm not entirely sure how much George knows.'

He drew up outside the police station

and the three of them leapt out of the car and up the steps to the main desk where James asked to see DCI George Lane. While they waited, they sat on wooden chairs in silence and stared at the posters on the walls. In a couple of minutes, George appeared, alongside Inspector Collins. James groaned to himself. Collins was that officious little Inspector he'd met in the autumn up at Cory House.

George's face was grey. Beth squeezed his arm.

'George, you look terrible.'

George explained that he *felt* terrible and that he was only staying on for this business with Adam and then going home. 'Inspector Collins is being briefed on everything. He's taking over while I have a couple of days off.'

Collins gave James a look of contempt. 'I've no business for amateurs so please don't keep coming in here asking questions.' Taking in Beth and Harry, he added, 'Adam Franks requested Lord Harrington, not the whole family. We can't have you all back here.'

James ignored Collins and held George's

gaze. 'Oh come on, George, we can fit around your desk easily.'

George held up a finger. 'No. Adam asked for you and that's all he's getting. He should be asking for a solicitor.'

Beth gasped. 'You haven't charged him, have you?'

'No, I haven't.'

'Mum, why don't you and I go and have a drink,' Harry asked.

'Good idea,' James replied. 'There's a café around the corner. Once I've finished here, I'll come and get you.'

Collins announced that he would continue reading the notes on the case and left. James couldn't hide his pleasure at this announcement. As far as he was concerned, the Inspector was an intolerant individual and one who would allow him no room to assist. Following George down the corridor, he enquired after Major Carlton. George shook his head as they reached his desk and took their seats.

'Nothing. No one's seen him. I'm trying to get hold of any army friends but they're proving elusive.'

'And how's John Carlton?'

'Much better. He doesn't have any idea where his father could be. But he's going down to his father's house tomorrow to see if he can get some contacts for us.' He reached across for his notepad and opened it. 'Right, Adam Franks.'

'Yes, why have you hauled him in?'

'I need him to be straight with us. He's being particularly cagey with his answers. He was at the scene for all of the attacks. He delivered the water to Cynthia Carlton. I tried to get some background on his family and he's uncomfortable answering anything to do with his grand-dad. Now he's clammed up and he won't speak with anyone but you and he's insisting I don't talk to his parents.' He studied James. 'Has he confided in you?'

James felt in his pockets for a cigarette and, after lighting it, said: 'No, he hasn't but he does have a story. What are your thoughts?'

'I think he's holding back. It's as if he wants to tell me something but he's frightened to. He could be covering up for someone.'

'If my own instinct is correct, I think

this may be more to do with shame for the family. Are you happy for me to lead the questioning? I know this goes against policy but I discovered a couple of things earlier. I was going to pass it on to you but I may as well do it here.' He leapt up. 'Lead on, DCI Lane, and let us speak to young Adam Franks.'

Adam Franks sat opposite them in a small windowless room that housed four wooden chairs and a table. A cold cup of tea had been pushed to one side. He was dressed in his work clothes; black trousers and a white shirt. He'd loosened his tie and James presumed he'd left his jacket at the house as it had been replaced by a baggy wool jumper. His hair, normally tidy with a side parting, didn't look as if it had seen a comb. His right leg trembled and his fingers drummed the table. He found it difficult to make eye contact with either one of them until James insisted he meet his gaze.

'Adam, I'm here as requested to try and help you but I believe you need to be open and honest with us here. I can't promise that our discussions will remain confidential but I'm sure DCI Lane will do his best to respect what you have to say. Understood?'

The young man confirmed his understanding.

'When we last spoke, you told me about your grandfather, Archibald Franks. You told me that he played centre forward for the football team and that he never returned home from the war.'

'That's right.' Adam looked at the ceiling and blinked back the tears.

'Why didn't he return?'

He swallowed hard and bit his bottom lip. 'He was killed. He was killed along with a couple of other blokes during the war.'

'You said your family never spoke about him. Why is that?'

'Bad memories I suppose. He was loved by everyone and no one wanted to get upset.'

'Adam, your grandfather's name doesn't appear on the memorial.' He saw George's reaction in his peripheral vision and noticed him jot this down in his notebook. Adam remained silent. James rested his arms on the table. 'One of the cleaners found a couple of diary entries on the floor.'

He'd expected a reaction but Adam simply looked confused.

'Diary entries?'

'Did your grandfather write a diary?'

'Not that I know of. He wrote letters to my nan but that was about it.'

George prepared his pipe. 'Does your nan still have those letters?'

Adam gave James an apologetic look. 'I said I didn't think they kept them but they did. Mum looks at 'em now and again. Do these diaries mention my grand-dad?'

'Not in as many words, no, but they speak of number nine being shot.'

Adam looked away, formed a fist and bit into it.

'Number nine was your grand-dad's football number. He was the man shot.'

It took some seconds for Adam to acknowledge this statement but eventually he gave a curt nod. George sat back in his chair.

'Desertion?'

Adam wiped a tear away. 'Nan said he

was suffering from shell-shock. She could see it in him when he was home on leave. Kept shaking and shivering all the time and if there was the slightest noise, he'd jump out of his skin. He went wandering off. That's what happened. He didn't desert, he just went wandering off in a world of his own and they shot him.' His eyes pleaded. 'They should have put him in hospital.' He buried his head in his hands.

James reached across and massaged his shoulder. George raised his eyebrows at this latest revelation. He heaved a sigh. 'The entries that James has spoken about refer to taking revenge. Whoever had written this diary spoke about putting things right. He'd served alongside your grand-dad. It suggested revenge. If you saw these diaries, Adam-.'

He stared at them. 'Revenge for what? I don't know anything about that. All I know is that he served with the Pals but I don't even know where they fought. Well, I do now because Mr Simmonds told me last week.' He stared at James. 'I didn't do anything. I didn't kill anyone. I don't know about any diary. I couldn't take another person's life; not for something I don't know anything about. Grand-dad lived in a different time, there were loads who were shot who should've been given help. I can't change things, I can't bring grand-dad back — what good would killing someone do?'

'What reason did your parents give for your grand-dad's name not being on the memorial?'

'Simply that he wouldn't have liked it and that they wanted to respect that wish.'

George sat up straight and made himself big.

'Adam, look at me.'

The young man did as he was told.

'Did you poison Olivia Dupree and John Carlton and did you kill Cynthia Carlton?'

Adam gritted his teeth. 'No. I did not. I swear on my mum and dad's lives. I never touched them.'

After some moments of silence, George announced that he'd send in some fresh tea. He signalled to James that it was time to leave.

'What about me?' said Adam. 'What

can I do to prove you've got the wrong man?'

George opened the door and called out for some refreshments. He turned to Adam. 'I'm going to call in and see your mum and dad. Just want to check up on a couple of things.'

This didn't appease the young waiter one iota; if anything he looked more anxious than before.

James asked George to hold on.

'Is everything all right, Adam?'

He explained that his parents were proud people: the thought of their son being hauled in for questioning over a murder would fill them with shame.

'George will speak to them with sensitivity, Adam. Try and keep your chin up. Is there anything you need?'

'If it's not too much of an imposition, have you got some biscuits? I missed breakfast and I'm starving.'

James smirked as George raised his eyebrows. 'It's not a ruddy hotel, Adam.' As they left the room, he turned. 'I'll get the constable to bring some.'

He closed the door. They wandered

through the corridors to the main entrance. 'What d'you think, James?'

'Unfortunately, I can't sway myself from thinking the best of people. Adam could easily have found out about his grand-dad from the Pals or even from his grandmother's letters. If William Carlton is the man who shot cowards, it could have triggered something in him. His family are good people, George, and I can imagine they'd want to put anything like this in the cupboard and lock the key. If it gets out that Adam is here in a cell, it will horrify them.'

'Well apart from me and Collins only you, Harry and Beth know.' He opened the main door to the entrance and pondered. 'To save their sanity, I'm going to suggest something that would enrage my superiors if they knew. And that upstart, Inspector Collins, is not my biggest fan because I let you stick your nose in; but in this case, I think it'll help.'

James raised his eyebrows.

'Why don't you pop round to his parents with Beth and Harry now? Make out you're doing some research on the

253

Pals and that Adam mentioned letters and would they mind if you see them — that sort of thing.'

'What if there aren't any letters?'

'Then ask some tactful questions.' He prodded him.

'You know what to do.'

James had a good idea. 'I'll toddle over there now and call you. If everything is tickety-boo will you release him?'

'I'm not promising anything. Go on; the sooner you report back, the sooner I can go home.'

James collected Beth and Harry and gave them a bite-sized version of events and their task ahead. Beth spoke about how to approach Adam's family and Harry looked at them in amazement.

'I can't believe that my parents are investigating a murder for the police!' James unlocked the car. As Harry got in, he continued, 'And I can't believe that I'm really enjoying this. Does all this come with the job of running Harrington's?'

They all laughed as James put the Jaguar in gear and sped toward Cavendish.

*   *   *

Mr Roy and Mrs Sue Franks were an unassuming couple. If you passed them in the street, it would be unlikely you'd remember them. Mr Franks wore grey trousers and a grey sweater and Mrs Franks wore a dull blue dress with a cardigan and a floral apron. James' arrival took them by surprise and no amount of reassurance from James, Beth and Harry settled them. Mr Franks dashed about and tidied newspapers off chairs and Mrs Franks reached far inside a cupboard for the best crockery. Once tea was served, Beth spearheaded the conversation. 'You really shouldn't have gone to so much trouble. We're here because we've taken a real interest in the Pals regiment.'

James observed the couple tense. He put his cup and saucer down.

'Charlie Hawkins gave us some photographs to hang up in Harrington's for some of the ex-soldiers who'd attended our dinner last weekend. They spoke about why they joined up and, although it was an awful time, we heard some wonderful stories of camaraderie and brave deeds.'

Harry agreed. 'I thought it might be a good project for my brother, Oli. You know he wants to be a teacher. It's good for the children to know what their ancestors went through. We know that Adam's grand-dad was in the Pals so we thought we'd pop in and find out what his story was.'

Mr Franks remained tight-lipped. His eyes darted here and there as if seeking help from an invisible angel. James felt for them. They knew. They knew Roy's father was shot for desertion. Mrs Franks twisted the hem of her apron.

'We don't talk about him, I'm afraid. We should do because he was a lovely man; but we have bad memories and he suffered terribly. He wouldn't want us to tell anyone. He was a brave and honourable man.'

'I've absolutely no doubt he played his part, Mrs Franks. We simply wanted to get an overall picture of what the Pals went through. Adam mentioned some letters his grand-dad had written.'

Mrs Franks softened. 'Oh yes, lovely letters.

They're in the cupboard here. They'd been married several years. He was a bit older than the rest of the Pals. They had a special love, Lord Harrington, like they were best friends. We were thinking about donating them to Professor Wilkins' museum but we think they're too personal really.'

Professor Wilkins ran the Cavendish museum from his cottage and had dedicated two of the rooms to displays.

'Does Adam know much about his grandfather?'

Mrs Franks sat back and let her husband take over. 'He knows the truth about his grandfather and we leave it at that. I'd be obliged Lord Harrington if your interest in the Pals didn't include Archibald. He was a proud man, didn't like any fuss.'

'Of course. We have no wish to upset you or the memory of Archibald. Thank you so much for your time.'

'Did you want the letters? I can get them for you,' said Susan.

'Would you mind if I had a quick peek?'

She got up and rummaged around in the back of a cupboard and bought out an old shoe box. The envelopes inside were small and the ink on the paper faded. She handed them to James. Beth and Harry steered the conversation toward Christmas and general conversation while James skimmed through half a dozen letters. After ten minutes he packaged everything back and thanked Mrs Franks.

'I think Wilkins would love to display these. He certainly appears to have been a devoted husband and father.'

Mr Franks agreed that he was.

Outside, James put his gloves on and motioned Beth and Harry toward the car. Harry got into the rear seat and rested his arms on the front seats.

'Well, that was a waste of time. And why didn't you take the letters? There could have been something there that you've missed.'

'On the contrary, Harry. If you're to sleuth with me, you need to read between the lines and I'm satisfied that Adam is innocent.'

'I agree,' Beth put in, adding that her decision was based on instinct alone.

James pulled across to the first phone box he found and called George. After going through his findings and answering a few questions, George said he'd release Adam on the understanding that he didn't disappear. James confirmed his waiter wouldn't be going anywhere and that he'd keep an eye on him.

On the drive back, Harry insisted on knowing what he'd missed.

'His father said that Adam knows the truth about Archibald and they left it at that. His body language, tone and the words he used suggests that the family have known for years. If William Carlton was the man who shot his grandfather, Adam could have killed him years ago. Carlton only lives the other side of Horsham.'

'And,' said Beth, 'Adam is too fond of us and Harrington's to carry out something so unsavoury at the house.'

James reminded Harry that Adam had a soft spot for Beth. 'He wouldn't do something like this because he knows it would upset your mother too much.'

Harry grinned. 'You'd better watch your step, Dad, you have a rival. He's a good-looking chap.'

Beth gave a knowing smile and asked James to continue.

'Mrs Franks also offered the letters up freely. She's more than happy to part with them so there is nothing incriminating. They are exactly what she says they are. Words of love and hope to a wife he adores. And the handwriting is not the same as in the diary extracts.'

He went on to explain the body language and how Mr Franks had flinched and appeared strained. 'He knows that we know. In his own way, he was requesting a plea for silence. They're a proud family who have not judged Archibald but are fearful that everyone else will.' He turned the car on to their drive. 'And I believe Archibald is a fighting man. One of those letters speaks of his impatience when sitting in the trenches, wanting to get out and fight. That doesn't strike me as someone who is cowardly.'

On stepping out of the car, Harry frowned. 'But how can the villagers not know about Archibald? If his name isn't on the memorial and he served alongside those Pals at the dinner, there must be a huge cover up going on.'

'It's probably the one piece of information that is awry. Adam mentioned that they didn't want his name up there. I think his grandfather would have been proud to have the Franks name listed so I believe they've created that lie. The Pals speak of their comrades as brave and professional soldiers. If there was a coward among them, I hope they would have said so. There is a cover-up, I'm sure, but who is behind it, I can't say.'

'Sweetie, this is getting so complicated. Could the group at the reunion be responsible?'

James opened the front door. 'It's improbable that the whole group is involved. They have a memory and a connection to a comrade; but would that lead to murder? And why so many years later? The Pals are all local. Why now?'

'What about Alfie Stone?' said Harry as

they wandered into the hall. 'This is the first time he's been back. He could have killed Mrs Carlton and now he's going after the Major.'

Beth frowned. 'But he wasn't in the country when Olivia Dupree was poisoned. And those other Pals who were at Stephen and Anne's table only arrived from the North that morning. And they weren't mobile enough to carry those crimes out.'

James heaved a sigh. 'I believe we are terribly close to an answer but it simply isn't showing itself.'

The phone rang and Harry picked it up. James watched with concern as his son's brow knitted together. He put the phone down. 'George has been rushed into hospital.'

'Oh goodness,' said Beth.

'Did they say which one?'

'Yes, Haywards Heath. Do you two want to pop down there?'

Beth was already shrugging her coat back on.

In half an hour they were at George's bedside to find him propped up reading a magazine. A doctor was completing notes on a chart.

Beth rushed to him. 'Oh, George, how are you? We were thinking the worst.'

James pulled up a chair for her. 'Did you see Jackson when you were supposed to?'

George shook his head and explained that he hadn't had time. 'They're taking me down to do some tests but they think it's an ulcer.'

The doctor explained that George would have to eat only light meals and spend a few days resting. 'His lifestyle and working hours are a contributory factor,' he said. 'If he's going home, he needs someone to play nurse. He's not to do anything for the next few days.'

Beth instantly confirmed that this wouldn't be a problem and that they would make room for him.

George wore a pained expression. 'Are you sure? I don't want to intrude. It's Christmas.'

'Nonsense,' said Beth. 'We have Juliet and Harry staying. One more won't make any difference. Besides, Christmas is still over a week away.'

'I was supposed to be taking John Carlton over to his dad's place tomorrow. I'll have to get a constable to do that.'

James felt the familiar surge of adrenalin. 'Have you discussed that with Inspector Collins?'

'No, I haven't. Why?'

'Well, why don't we do that for you? We were thinking of taking a spin out with the Merryweathers tomorrow. We haven't seen them much and they've freed up the morning. We could meet John and make it a little less formal.'

George's jaw dropped. 'This is police work. I can't have you and the Merryweathers trampling all over the Carltons' house. I should instruct Collins to sort this out.'

'But you can't stand the man.'

'That makes no odds, James. This is police work not a spy novel.'

James reminded George that he was to keep calm and assured him it would be low key. He reiterated the fact that John would be more comfortable with him rather than the police.

'Tch, everyone's uncomfortable with the police. That's not an excuse.'

'And the Merryweathers are a great comfort when there's been a death in the family.'

George glared.

'Now don't get yourself worked up, George. You know what the doc said; have your tests and take it easy. We'll report back to you and you can feed it back to Collins if you must. We'll come and pick you up when you're done here.'

His friend groaned. 'I can't stop you. I'll leave Collins to make his own decisions. If you are going, look for an address book and see if you can find something to show why Cynthia Carlton changed her behaviour. You report straight back to me when you're done.'

With arrangements in hand and an exciting morning ahead, James and Beth returned home. Harry lounged in the living room chatting with Juliet Brooks-Hunter. They were both quick to enquire after George. Satisfied that all was well, James prepared four glasses of whisky and ginger.

'Bert called while you were out,' said Harry.

'Oh?'

'He's found a few men who served around the area where the Pals were and he's having a word with them.'

James turned to Beth. 'Another one for dinner tomorrow?'

Beth always welcomed Bert but reminded him they'd have to cater for George. 'I'll get some smoked haddock; that's easy on the stomach.' She picked up her glass before opening the door to the hall. 'I'll call the Merryweathers to arrange a time for tomorrow morning. Where will I find Bert?'

Harry swigged his whisky. 'He's at the Sussex Arms in Brighton. The number's by the telephone.'

'What about John Carlton? Where do I find him?'

Juliet answered. 'He's back with Mrs Keates. I met him in the village earlier — he said he was stopping on one more day and going to his father's early tomorrow morning.'

Beth confirmed she would make the

266

necessary phone calls.

Juliet revealed she'd read through 'Rider' Appleton's diary and reported that there was no mention of Captain Carlton. 'I returned them to Mr Appleton. He is not your man.'

22

James steered the Jaguar to a parking place in the main street in Hazeldon-upon-the-Mole.

It was a quaint village about twenty miles from Cavendish. The Mole was a small stream that meandered through the village green. Small, ornate, stone bridges crossed from one side of the stream to the other although, in fairness, one could easily jump across. As in Cavendish, the green was surrounded by a pub, a church and shops, including the butcher, greengrocer and newsagent. Surrounding the green and in roads branching off were whitewashed cottages with tiny windows, and strands of smoke trailing from the chimneys.

The pale sun struggled to throw out any warmth so the pavements remained icy. A Christmas tree stood by the vicarage at the far end of the green and a number of people were making their way toward it.

Getting out of the car, James, along

with Beth and the Merryweathers, buttoned up their coats and put their scarves and gloves on. James checked his watch.

'Looks like we're in time. Shall we get a hot toddy before it begins?'

During Beth's telephone conversation with him the previous evening, John had mentioned a carol service due to take place around the Christmas tree. It was a tradition in the village and was scheduled to begin at eleven o'clock. Keen to make the most of their morning out, James suggested they join in with the carols before going on to meet John at Major Carlton's house.

Collecting a hot toddy each from the pub, they wandered across to the tree to be greeted by the villagers. An elderly vicar was distributing song sheets and appeared a little doddery on his feet. James noticed he had a rather florid expression. Perhaps an over-indulgence in hot toddies, he surmised. The vicar examined Stephen and did a double-take. 'Merryweather — am I right?' he slurred.

James caught Anne's smirk. The vicar was clearly tipsy. He swayed a little as he observed Stephen who recognised him immediately.

'W-we met at the ecumenical m-meeting a few months ago.'

'Of course.' He steadied himself. 'How are you getting on? You're in Cavendish, aren't you?'

'That's r-right.' Stephen quickly introduced everyone to the Reverend Joseph Lee.

The vicar's eyes opened wide. 'Lord and Lady Harrington! Welcome to our little service. I'm surprised you've come all the way here for this. Don't you have your own little thing going on down there?'

James explained that their main reason was to visit John Carlton. The vicar sighed.

'Oh yes. A sad business. Cynthia was very well liked in the village, you know. She belonged to a number of clubs; was on the committee for our charity work. I heard that someone did her in — that's not right is it?'

James gave him a quick shake of the head. 'We're not entirely sure what happened.'

The vicar raised an eyebrow then took

a step forward to keep his balance. Anne wrapped her hands around the warm glass. 'Do you know Major Carlton well?'

The vicar made a face. 'Been here twenty years. I can count on one hand the number of times I've spoken to him. He's a total opposite to Cynthia; and their son John.'

'H-he's a war hero, isn't h-he?'

'John?'

'N-no, the Major.'

'Ah yes, the Major. Saw some bad things I gather. Maybe that's why he doesn't come to church. I would imagine your faith would be tested.' He frowned. 'I thought if anyone would get killed, it'd be him.'

James gave a start of surprise. 'Why would you think that?'

'We-ell, you hear rumours you know, small village and all that.' He lowered his voice. 'He took exception to people asking where his medals were. They wanted to display them but he was having none of it. Got quite rude.' He handed them a song sheet. 'He's generally an unpleasant man. I know I shouldn't be

271

scathing of my parishioners but if it were up to me to decide who ended up dead in that family, I would have gone for the Major.' He looked up to the sky. 'Forgive me, Lord, but I can't help what I think.' With some hesitancy he stated: 'I can imagine he's made a number of enemies.'

Before James could put another question to him, the vicar swung round and ordered everyone to come closer. As they did so, they heard the distinctive sound of an organ. Beth's jaw dropped.

'Where's that coming from?'

A villager nearby pointed to a young woman who was seated with an antique pump organ.

'Good Lord,' said James.

He watched as the woman pumped the bellows with her feet while playing the introduction to 'We Three Kings'. With the vicar conducting, they launched into the carol with great gusto. It was certainly a jolly way to spend an hour and they managed to get through six carols before the children did a solo turn with 'Away in a Manger'. At the end, a charity box was passed around to collect funds for a new door to the village hall.

The Reverend Lee staggered across. 'Thank you so much for coming. You're off to see John now, are you? One of the villagers has just told me the Major's missing. Is that right?'

James explained that they were simply paying John a visit to see how he was. He was reluctant to divulge anything more. The vicar was knocking back the drink like it was going out of fashion and he could imagine him having a loose tongue.

'You don't think he killed his wife, do you?'

'I think that's unlikely, don't you?'

Anne handed her song sheet back to him. 'You don't know where he might be staying do you?'

The vicar uttered a drawn-out 'No', collected the sheets and wished them well. 'Tell John that my door is always open.'

Back in the car, Beth and Anne burst out laughing.

'W-what are you l-laughing about?'

'The vicar,' Beth replied. 'That was the best piece of free entertainment I've seen in a long time.'

'Did you see him swaying as he conducted? I thought he was going to fall flat on his face.'

The ladies continued giggling as Stephen explained that he remembered him having had a tipple the last time he met him. James grinned at the hilarity, fired up the engine and drove out of the village toward Major Carlton's house.

The property was surrounded by iron fencing with ornamental spikes on top. The gates opened onto a long gravel drive that led to a huge red-brick house; in some ways, very similar to James and Beth's residence but with far more acreage. James' father had insisted that their land remained as part of Harrington's country hotel and, although they still had a substantial plot, it didn't compare to the sprawling estate he saw here.

James parked by the front steps and, as they emerged from the car, John opened the front door to greet them. He looked pale but managed a greeting as he thanked everyone for coming.

'Did you enjoy the carols?'

Beth and Anne were quick to share their delight and enquired after the vicar's health. John grinned. 'I've never known him not be sloshed. He gives quite an amusing sermon, especially if he helps himself to the wine.' He pushed the door open further. 'Please come through.'

They were shown into a large lounge with windows along one side and French doors that opened on to a small paved area. Beyond this were extensive lawns with shrubbery to the rear and behind that the spiked iron railings that bordered the property.

James surmised that the Carltons were not gardeners. Although they had an immense amount of land, there were few trees and relatively little in the way of flowers or shrubs; unlike James and Beth who specifically employed Ernest Appleton to bring their landscape to life.

John brought a tray of tea and biscuits in and placed it on a large table in the middle of the lounge. There were half a dozen comfortable wing-back chairs surrounding the table and a long sofa to one side. They each opted for a chair and sat in a circle while John poured the teas. James accepted his with a thank you. 'How are you bearing up, John? It must still be raw for you.'

John appeared reluctant to speak. Emotion hovered beneath the surface and one show of sympathy appeared likely to set him off.

'I'm bearing up. I'm still in limbo; I can't quite take in what's happened. I mean, we were plodding along as a normal family and then suddenly things take a turn. I can't quite get to grips with what's happened to Mum. And where the hell has Dad got to?'

Stephen accepted his tea and shifted to the edge of his chair. 'I-I'm aware that you may not have a faith, John, and if you do it is likely to be tested; b-but please be assured I am here should you wish to talk. As is A-Anne. I can p-promise to steer clear of religion if it suits.'

'You're very kind. I suppose I do have a faith. I used to go to Sunday school when I was little and Mum is . . . was always involved with the church. I tend to go when you're obliged to — Easter,

Christmas, you know.' He sipped his tea. 'I may take you up on that, though. You're more my age group than that old codger we have in the village. And you're not part of the village. The vicar here is less than confidential when he's had one too many.'

Stephen and Anne immediately suggested popping in later in the week. James crossed his legs and looked out of the window. 'Your parents have quite a place here.'

'Yes, it was a culmination of inheritance. My parents were not rich people, Lord Harrington. They were among the upper classes but not to this extent. A number of family deaths allowed them to purchase this house. We're a small family and there were very few people to leave an estate to so everything came their way. Mum and Dad moved here when I was around four years old.'

'Where were you before?' asked Beth.

'In a house near Wisborough Green.'

James knew the village well. He'd always thought it pretty and well laid out with two pubs; he'd frequented one of them with the cricket team — it was aptly named The Cricketers. The church stood on a small hill overlooking the village green. He and Beth remembered taking Oliver and Harry there as children to feed the ducks that had taken up residence on the pond. Stephen gave him a subtle wink. They'd agreed earlier that they didn't want everyone involved in the investigation so Stephen steered the conversation toward the many books lining the shelves. He and Anne got up to peruse the titles. Anne was quick to spot a number of children's books. John joined them.

'Mum loved children's books and collected a number of first editions. Why don't I show you next door? She kept a small library.'

As he ushered them out, Anne turned and gave James and Beth a thumbs up. James rolled his eyes. Anne loved a mystery and made no bones about it. When John returned, James settled back in his chair.

'John, we'd all love to help you make sense of what's happened. Perhaps talking it through may help. You said, when you were staying with Mrs Keates, that your mother had been acting strangely.'

John stared at his tea. 'That's right. It started about eighteen months ago, two years at the most. I visit quite a bit — I only live a few miles away but she was agitated for a while and hinted that Dad was getting paranoid about things.'

'What sort of things?'

'Claimed he was being followed — that someone was spying on him. It sounded a bit too far-fetched for my liking. I mean, Dad's always been a bit off with people. He doesn't trust anyone. You only have to look at him odd and he'll read something into it.'

'But what would make him feel that way?' asked Beth.

'Can you remember a time when he wasn't like that?'

'Not really, but the last couple of years has been more intense. And it's only recently that Mum acted strangely too. She started going out more; attending more social gatherings and getting involved in the community. It's as if she was annoyed with

279

Dad and had finally lost all patience with him.'

'And this all started a couple of years ago?'

'I believe so.'

'And what do you know about his exploits during the war — the Great War. You hinted that it might be something to do with that.'

'He received a commendation for bravery but he threw his medals in the drawer. Mum's always wanted to display them but he won't have it. He's never discussed the reasons why. Whenever I asked him about what he did, he'd get angry. Mum said that it was because of what he'd seen; that a lot of the men who served choose not to talk.'

'Did he keep a diary?'

'If he did, he never told me.'

'Have you gone through any of his belongings? There may be something there that would shed some light on this.'

John confirmed that he hadn't and felt apprehensive about doing so. 'I fear that there's something dirty at the bottom of all of this. And if Dad found out I'd been looking through his things, I'm not sure how he'd react.'

Beth empathised with him. 'And you have no idea where he could be?'

'We have no relations and I can't remember the last time he actually had a friend.' He gazed out of the window. 'I hope he's not lying dead in a ditch somewhere.'

'Oh, dear,' said Beth, 'you mustn't think like that. Your dad is probably suffering from shock. He certainly appeared shaken when this happened. Grief affects us in different ways. He may have checked into a hotel to be on his own.'

'Perhaps.'

'I say, does he have an address book or anything? If we take a look through that, there may be a contact that you don't know about. Perhaps an old army colleague or something.'

John led them through to his father's study. This was opposite the lounge and was a much smaller oak-panelled room with a solid oak desk and another set of doors leading to gardens at the side of the house. John opened the drawer and pulled out an address book. Beth squeezed John's arm.

'We'll do our best to find him.'

John expressed how grateful he was and suggested more tea. Beth was quick to offer help in the kitchen.

As the door closed behind them, James sat on a worn leather chair and reached down to open four drawers that hung on either side of the desk. None of them gave up any secrets. He focussed his attention on the address book. At first, the contacts appeared to relate solely to Cynthia: Women's Institute, knitting circle, the local choral society and the ladies' bridge club. Then, as he flicked a few pages on, one name leapt out. General Niven Short. The address was a Sussex one: Hove, just along the coast from Brighton.

James snatched a piece of paper and jotted down the details and the telephone number. He continued flicking through the book and raised an inquisitive eyebrow as he read a familiar name. The Royal Sussex Convalescent Home. How many times had that name cropped up in conversations recently?

Underneath this was an entry for the Sussex Regiment Museum. He added the details of these to his list and sat back. The walls were bare except for a couple of landscape paintings. He felt a twinge of disappointment. There was nothing here to highlight a problem. Beth peered around the door and announced that fresh tea was available. He thanked her and wondered if he could find an excuse to see the bedrooms.

He was about to join her when Stephen and Anne scurried in. The door slammed behind them. Stephen grinned.

'You've found something, haven't you?'

'Oh James, I think we have,' said Anne rushing to him with a book in her hand. 'This was on the table. I sent it flying when I tripped over the rug.' She opened it up to show the pages had been cut out to form a secret box. In it were a handful of letters.

'We-we've read one and i-it's rather disconcerting. I'm not sure that showing them to J-John would be a good thing.'

'Showing me what?'

They looked up. John stood in the entrance.

'I heard the door slam and wondered if

you were all right. Have you found something?'

James waved a piece of paper in the air. 'I have a couple of contacts of your father's that I'll pursue — see if we can't track him down for you.'

'I'd like him here for Mum's funeral.'

They made to go through to the lounge but John stopped them. 'What else did you find? I'm going to have to know and, if it's bad, there's never going to be a good time.'

James hastily suggested that they return to the lounge where Beth had poured fresh tea. As they entered, he could see from the look on her face that she sensed the anxiety etched on their faces. Anne pressed the book into James' hands. Stephen sat down and rested a hand on John's arm.

'A-are you quite sure you w-want to know.'

John swallowed hard and nodded. James opened the book, took out six envelopes and checked the dates on the postmarks. Satisfied he was opening the first letter, he took out a single sheet of paper and unfolded it. On it were two sentences made up of letters cut out from a newspaper.

'You're the guilty one. You're no more a hero than I am.'

James scanned the group and his gaze settled on John. 'Does that mean anything to you?'

John shook his head and motioned for him to continue. James pulled out the second message:

'You murdered him to save your own skin. You played a hand in every death.'

James felt the bottom of the envelope and peered in. His heart sank as he pulled out a white feather. John's shoulders slumped. He stared at the ceiling but then motioned to James to continue. Anne pulled her chair closer to John and held his hand. James pulled out the third piece of paper.

'I'm watching you. You'll get what's coming to you.' Again, a white feather accompanied the communication. James chewed his lip. 'I think we get the picture with these. I'm sure the rest are more of the same.'

'Please,' said John, 'read them.'

The fourth was a little more detailed. '*You sent men to their deaths. You claimed the glory but you never fought. You are a fraud and shouldn't be here.*' The fifth reiterated the last message. The sixth stated '*I know what you did*'. Each was accompanied by the now familiar white feather. James stacked the envelopes together. 'Has there been any more post since your parents left for Harrington's?'

John looked at him as if he didn't understand but James could see that the young man was trying desperately to hold his emotions in check. John ran his hands through his hair.

'Yes, yes, there has been post. I didn't think to look at it.' He made his way out of the room.

Beth nudged James and mouthed the word 'fingerprints'. James called out to John and told him to handle everything with a handkerchief. As he returned with the post, James put his gloves on and explained that he would need to take these particular letters to George. John handed him three envelopes and returned to his chair. Two were bills; the third had a similar type on the envelope to the others. He examined the type and couldn't identify anything particularly unusual. He supposed the police could make a match if they found the typewriter. He took out the letter and groaned.

'*I'll see you at Harrington's.*'

'Oh God,' said John. He gripped Anne's hand.

'That arrived the day they left. He never opened it.'

'D-did your father n-not report all this to the police.'

John was quick to confirm that he wouldn't. 'I know what these letters mean; I know what the white feather means. No matter how much I want to deny that my father was a coward, the way Mum was over the last few months, she must have discovered something. She must have done — why else would she have changed?' He closed his eyes. 'He'd built up a lie. If Mum found out, and I've no doubt she did, this would have had a domino effect.'

Beth frowned. 'How?'

John let go of Anne's hand. 'Don't you see? A coward who's deceived his friends and neighbours, it would be disastrous. His name would be dragged through the mud. If she had lived, my mother would have been ostracised by the villagers. They'd have had to move. If this comes out Dad will have no choice but to move.'

'B-but this person who has t-targeted your father — how would th-they know? They may have their f-facts wrong.'

James was loath to pour water on Stephen's small ounce of hope but he had to be realistic. 'John's right. Cynthia Carlton was clearly, from the small amount of time we spent with her, an astute woman. She knew something was awry with her husband. And this person who's sent the letters — they've done their homework. They've been stalking William Carlton — they've overheard a conversation — they knew he was visiting Harrington's.' He addressed John. 'Did your mother speak of any new friends she made?'

The young man stared blankly and shrugged.

Beth sighed. 'You know what that means, don't you?'

James met her gaze. 'It means that whoever poisoned our guests and murdered John's mother, was a guest at Harrington's.'

Anne shifted in her chair. 'I still don't understand why Olivia Dupree was targeted.'

He asked John to confirm that he didn't know Olivia. John reiterated that the only time he'd met her was to ask for an autograph.

'Well, that link will remain a mystery for the time being. But whoever is responsible for these attacks was, I'm sure, at both dinners.'

'A-and had the t-time to visit the village and e-eavesdrop on the Carltons.'

Beth checked her watch. 'I'm so sorry to break this up, but we have guests for dinner tonight, James. We really must make a move.'

James and Beth said their goodbyes and left John to have a moment with Stephen and Anne. They were the ideal couple to bring comfort and solace to a lost soul and, when they emerged from the lounge, they had already made arrangements to meet for afternoon tea the following day.

'I-I will telephone you tonight. I-is the telephone still connected here?'

'Yes.'

James swung round. 'Will you permit me a short call to DCI Lane?'

'Of course. The telephone is on the desk in the study. You will have seen it earlier.'

James dashed into the study and, after a couple of minutes, was connected through to George. After enquiring after his health, he confirmed that they were returning home and that he'd plenty to impart.

'I have a concern, George.'

'What's that?'

'These anonymous letters; I'm concerned about John's safety. Someone targeted him before; his mother is already dead. Does this person intend to murder John? He's on his own here.'

'It'll be a brave man to attempt another murder when such an investigation is going on but, yes, I'll get in touch with the local constabulary. I'll see if they can place someone in the vicinity to keep a look out.'

Feeling more settled about leaving John in such an enormous house in the middle of the country, he tucked the vicious letters away in pocket and they made their way home. He was keen to know what George would make of them and whether Bert had discovered any news from his 'Tommies'?

23

Beth was relieved to be home in time to prepare the meal but, to both her and James' surprise, Juliet and Harry had already dealt with the cooking.

'My dear,' said Juliet, 'if you are being Watson to James' Holmes, you won't have time to prepare dinner too. The haddock is in the oven, I've just put the potatoes on and I've opened a tin of peas. That should suit your Inspector nicely.'

Beth hugged her. 'I think I'm more like Mrs Hudson than Watson, Juliet.'

'Can I be Watson?' said Harry with a grin.

Twenty minutes later they were digging into a plain but tasty dinner. Juliet had poached the fish in milk and sprinkled it with pepper and drizzled it with a small knob of butter. James and Beth recounted their visit to Major Carlton's house and the contents of the letters, along with John's shock over the discovery of his father's past. George held a finger up.

'Was that shock genuine? Do you think he suspected anything?'

'Absolutely not,' replied James. 'He suspected something was wrong because of his mother's behaviour but he'd no idea about what it could be. I think this was the last thing he expected. He looked completely bamboozled.'

Bert scooped up a forkful of mash. 'What about Olivia Dupree? I don't get why she was poisoned.'

George sipped his water and looked at it in disgust. 'Yes, that's stumped me. I can't get a connection.'

'My dear,' Juliet put in, 'have you considered that Olivia could have been a trial run?'

George sat back and stared at her.

'I say,' said James, 'that's a thought. Perhaps it was to confuse things.'

'Blimey, if that's what 'appened, this bloke's sparing no one's feelings.'

George used his fork to flake the fish from its skin. 'I had another word with Olivia Dupree.' He took a mouthful before continuing. 'But you know what she's like; claims someone tried to kill her but nothing's happened since and nothing's happened before. Either she's linked in some way to the Carltons or, as you say Juliet, the killer was testing out the dose.'

'Oh, that sounds too horrid,' said Beth.

Harry topped his wine glass up. 'That sounds feasible. Poison is only poison if the dose isn't right. I mean, we've already said that athletes have used strychnine to improve their performance but then our man Appleton uses it to kill moles.'

Juliet dabbed her lips with her napkin. 'You should leave Olivia Dupree out. There are no leads for you there, Inspector. You do have clues for your other victims and they may give up a connection to Olivia later in your investigation.'

James was impressed at his guest's forthright observation. 'She's right, George. Unless another attempt is made against Olivia, I think you need to focus on the Carltons. The entire family's been hit; John is given a similar dose to Olivia, Cynthia was given an overdose and the Major's up and run.'

Beth waved her knife at George. 'Ran in fear, I shouldn't wonder.'

'And where's 'e scarpered to?' asked Bert. 'I reckon he's latched 'imself onto a mate somewhere.'

James confirmed that was his suspicion too, explaining the entries in the address book. 'I tried to call this Major Niven Short but he wasn't answering.' He sipped his wine. 'What about your chat with the Tommies, Bert? Harry said you might have some news.'

Bert scraped his plate clean before pushing it away. 'Yeah, interesting blokes. I popped into the British Legion in Brighton — I thought that'd be the best place to ask.'

The British Legion helped servicemen and raised money for functions and Remembrance Day. Many clubs held dinner and dances for ex-service personnel and James, Bert and George all supported their branch of the Legion in Lewes.

'There's a lo' of talk about shooting cowards and it turned a bit nasty for a while,' said Bert. 'Nothing vicious or anything but tempers went up depending on what you thought.'

James asked him to elaborate.

'Well, there's two sides. There's those that were cowards and those that weren't. Those that weren't are the ones who weren't capable of fighting. You know, the shell-shock. There's blokes that went off their nut and just wandered away. They didn't know where they were or what they was doing. Then there's the proper cowards, the ones who slipped away. Nothing wrong with 'em physically, just didn't wanna fight.'

A murmur of understanding went around the table.

'There's a couple of Tommies who saw one of their own slide off. He didn't wanna die; he'd just got married and 'ad a kid on the way. He wanted to go 'ome.'

'How old was he?' asked Beth.

'Twenty.'

'Oh, how sad.'

'It's right though. The army's built on trusting the man you're fighting with. You trust the bloke next to you with yer life. We all 'ad loved ones at 'ome. We all had families waiting for us. You can't go wandering off.'

James agreed. 'That's why they were shot. If you simply fined them or put them in prison, more people would have deserted. They had to set an example.'

George pushed his plate away. 'What about the officers? Did the Tommies hear about any officers being cowards?'

'Yeah, they did. They don't 'ave names but they 'eard rumour of an officer in the Sussex Regiment who was dodgy. Didn't lead the men into battle — let the men down.'

'But how?' said Harry. 'How could they get away with that? Surely someone would say something.'

'Ah, but remember those diary entries,' said James. 'If the Major is the coward — and we think he is — he's shot whoever witnessed this and terrified another into keeping quiet.'

'Beastly,' Juliet said. 'He sounds like a coward. Running off when his wife's been killed and his son attacked. And now the son has to arrange the funeral with the worry of where his father is hiding his pathetic carcass.'

James raised his eyebrows and she held a hand up.

'I'm sorry, James, but he came across

as a pompous ass at that dinner last week whereas, in reality, he's a timid mouse frightened of his own shadow.'

Beth agreed and pushed Bert for any more information.

'Not much more except that one bloke said you should get down to the Sussex Regiment museum. They've got quite a few bits and pieces down there about the battalions and who's been commended and what battles they fought in. You might find something there.'

James nodded. 'I'd be interested to see the museum, especially if our Pals are featured.'

Beth announced that she'd dish dessert up in the kitchen. Harry accompanied her. George meanwhile expressed his thoughts about specific names in respect of who committed the crime.

He went on to announce that his questioning of all the guests had proved useful, if only to eliminate them from his enquiries. Many had been able to verify one another's stories; a good number were regular visitors and, on cross-checking their statements, George confirmed their alibis were sound.

'The table next to you, James, and the one that the Merryweathers were sitting at. Again, they're regulars who attend every year. Their alibis check out with the girls waiting on the tables. The Pals that were with the Merryweathers are disabled and they gave no hint of knowing the Carltons. I'm confident they wouldn't have been able to carry out a crime like this.'

'So we're left with the table where the Pals, and Enid and Mandy were sitting,' James summed up.

'You're forgetting your staff, James.'

James announced that he felt he had good reason to discount them. He noted George's expression, one that questioned his sanity. He held a finger up.

'One: Didier. He is rather demonstrative in his opinion of cowards. He's capable of killing and has it in him to do so. Although he had nothing to do with the Sussex Regiment he ran the lines where they were fighting. He could have witnessed something that, as a result, affected him and the résistance. However, his handwriting does not match the diaries. His ego and reputation would not allow him to commit such a crime at Harrington's. Any cowardice shown between an officer and his men is nothing to do with Didier or his family.'

He held up a second finger. 'Two: Adam. His family history in respect of the regiment is known to myself and George. However, there are no diaries, only letters, and again, the handwriting doesn't match. Those letters also speak of getting impatient and wanting to fight. His words didn't strike me as those of a coward.'

He raised a third finger. 'Three: Ernest Appleton. His brother wrote diaries but, again, the handwriting doesn't match. I can't see any motive or what Ernest would gain from such an act.' He met Juliet's eyes. 'And four: Paul. Juliet, I believe you spoke with him earlier and got the same story as me.'

'Yes, a pleasant man. His father served in the trenches. He did what he was told, never caused trouble, didn't win any bravery awards but never shied from his duty. Claims he knows nothing about cowards. His father came out unscathed and lives with his brother in Eastbourne.'

Bert knocked the table. 'So a couple may 'ave a motive but it's not likely.'

'I do not believe them to be guilty.'

George let out an impatient sigh and James held his hands up.

'I know you think I'm wrong to dismiss them so easily but I have good reason. These men have been in my employ for years. They have given me no reason to challenge them on anything, inside or outside of work. Carlton lives just a few miles from here and I cannot imagine any one of these men wishing to sour the good name of Harrington's and, indeed, mine or Beth's name by committing an offence at such an event. They've all had every opportunity to target Carlton away from their workplace. Why carry out such an act and make yourself a suspect?'

Bert said that this was fair enough and that George's instinct must agree with that.

'I must admit I do,' said George, 'but I've still got to check these people out to tidy things up.'

'But,' said Juliet with a twinkle in her eye, 'these people are not at the top of your list. Excuse me for asking, Inspector, but have you checked Enid and Mandy for any links?'

'I have, Miss Brooks-Hunter, and I'm struggling to find anything. Enid's family are in Devon but her grand-dad was in the regular Sussex regiment. He was fighting near where our Pals were. Collins is trying to find out a little more. Mandy isn't sure. She knows her grand-dad was in the Sussex regiment but that's about it. She doesn't recollect any diaries and hinted that both her dad and grand-dad were very childlike with their writing skills. Her grand-dad died when she was young and she doesn't remember anything. He was her father's father and she said the dad left them when she was young.'

'Yes, I remember her talking about that. The mum's just died. She's been clearing the house out. I say, you know that Charlie is rather smitten with her, don't you?'

Bert snorted. 'What, Mandy Billings?'

'I think he was rather taken by her voice and looks. He's walking around like a love-struck puppy.'

Harry and Beth came in with bowls of treacle sponge pudding and custard. Harry gave George a small portion of custard, explaining that treacle sponge wouldn't help his ulcer.

'Oh, James,' said Beth, 'you're talking about Charlie and Mandy. We met them in Elsie's yesterday. He is quite enamoured with her although we didn't think she was terribly maternal.'

James added that he felt she could be a bit moody. 'She struck me as blowing hot and cold during our conversation at Elsie's.' He turned to George. 'What about the Pals?'

George rubbed his chin. 'Alfie Stone definitely wasn't here for the first attack and I can't trace any motive. Scotty Bull and Walter Anderson have no motive and seem genuine enough. The night that John was taken ill, Didier said they were chatting with him. They were on the dance floor when we think the water jug was taken up to Cynthia. And both Scotty and Walter are big men with chunky fingers. It would have been quite a feat to do this without being noticed, especially preparing the bottle of drops. Billy and Eddie Simmonds, again, are playing down any involvement but Eddie seems a little nervous. I've made enquiries but I can't find anything dodgy about him.'

Beth sat down. 'So, do we have any plans?'

'Yes. If George will allow me, I'll pop down to the museum. It sounds pretty interesting and I can ask to look at any paperwork they have about the heroic Major.'

'Pah,' Juliet responded. 'Heroic, my foot.'

Harry piped up. 'I've promised to help Mum and Mrs Merryweather with the rehearsal for the carol service. The Reverend Merryweather is over at Loxfield and finding it difficult to fit everything in.'

Beth gave James a playful shrug. 'Sorry, you're on your own.'

'This is police business,' George put in. 'Inspector Collins will have to go down.'

'Piffle,' said Juliet. 'He sounds intolerant of constructive help. I'll accompany you, James, and we'll report back to you, George. You can pass it on to that odious little man.'

George glowered.

'You've no need to be boorish, Inspector. I'm far more qualified than either of you to trace documents and dissect useful information. And anyway, the museum is open to the public so you cannot stop us having a morning out.'

James grinned. Juliet, of course, had been an agent for the government many years previously and assisted in ways he could never imagine. George heaved a sigh of resignation.

24

The following day, James and Juliet rose early and enjoyed tea and toast together. She had dressed in a gold tweed skirt and a rust-coloured wool coat with a matching felt hat. Although elderly, she cut an elegant figure and took pride in her appearance. James had opted for navy wool trousers, an Aran sweater and his trusty sheepskin jacket. After calling ahead to ensure the museum was open, Juliet put her hands together and beamed at him. 'Can we take the Austin?'

Like her sister before her, Juliet was a spritely lady who loved adventure and living life to the full. In ten minutes, they were speeding through the Sussex countryside.

The regiment's museum was a large, white structure with a colonnaded front-age. It stood at the end of the main road on the outskirts of Hove and was an imposing building among the surround-ing smaller offices and shops. When they entered the building, a woman approached them. She was a buxom lady in her mid-seventies and dressed in a tweed two-piece costume. Even indoors, she wore a navy blue felt hat. Strands of grey hair curled under the rim. She strode toward them, blustering in a mannish way.

'Ah, Lord Harrington, I presume. Is this your mother?'

'No dear, I'm Juliet Brooks-Hunter, no relation.'

James bit back a chuckle. The woman stretched out her hand.

'Mildred Clatterthorpe, OBE.'

She offered a firm hand shake and invited them to follow her. She took them on a route march across the main hall, shouting information as she went.

'Museum's been here for five years. We're moving to a more permanent site next year. Medals on the right; photographs on the left; history on the far right; current status of the regiment on the far left. You can't get lost, signs everywhere and a map here at the bottom of the stairs.' She turned. 'Ground floor is public, first floor reference. Your enquiry this morning suggests you'll need the reference.'

She began marching up the stairs but stopped when Juliet asked, 'May we view downstairs first? Lord Harrington is keen to see the exhibit about the Pals.'

She marched back down and led them to the history room. She stood to attention and pointed to the far end. 'Pals are in the corner. When you're ready for the reference section, you'll find me in the curator's office.'

'Most kind. Are you a volunteer?'

'No, Lord Harrington, it's a paid role. Never get rich on it. My family are Sussex Regiment. Trace them back to when the regiment was formed.'

'You had siblings in the Great War?'

'Of course. Army. Fought at Ypres.'

'Did they manage to get home?'

'Two brothers did, one cousin dead.' She clicked her heels. 'I'll leave you to it.'

As she retreated to the main reception, Juliet turned to him. 'Should have sent her out to fight on the Somme; she'd have terrified the enemy into submission.'

They chuckled and wandered over to the Pals exhibition. It took up quite a large area and included the history of how and why they were formed, where they fought and the villages they signed up from. Alongside were photographs donated by family members as well as official army portraits depicting young men with hope in their eyes. Against the walls were glass cabinets containing handwritten letters, diary entries and medals.

They made for what attracted them. For James it was the photographs. Juliet, meanwhile, studied the letters, personal items and diary entries.

James scanned the walls and soon found a selection of photographs relating to the Cavendish Pals. There were several sepia portraits with name tags pinned to the bottom of each photograph. He recognised many of the names local to Cavendish. A splendid picture of Paul's dad gazing beyond the camera mesmerised him: a handsome man with deep-set eyes and a pencil-thin moustache. Next to this was a similar picture of his gardener's brother, Rider. James imagined them lining up as if waiting for their school photograph, each instructed to sit still and gaze beyond the camera. At the end of the line was a picture of Adam's grand-dad, Archibald, in that same pose. He was a good ten years older than the rest of the Pals. He also featured in a group photograph with the football team and, further along, in a rather grim pose in the trenches. James leaned in to study his expression. Archibald looked a determined man as he polished his gun; a cigarette between his lips and an assuredness about him. James was reluctant to judge a man by a photograph but this didn't look like someone scared of fighting. A true soldier kept his equipment in working order. He appeared to be a strapping man, concentrating on the job ahead, which linked in with the letters he'd read. Juliet interrupted him.

'My dear, this is interesting.'

She had now moved on to the photographs further along from James. He joined her to look at a rectangular black and white image. He moved closer. Six men were in the photograph. He recognised Adam's grand-father straight away. Three other privates stood alongside who weren't familiar. The other two were officers, one of whom was William Carlton.

'Good Lord.' He stared at Juliet. 'He *did* know the Pals.'

'Never mind that; look at the caption.'

He returned his attention to the photograph and read the names out loud. 'Private Archibald Franks, Private Arthur Strong, Private Andrew Brown, Private Peter Shotover, Captain William Carlton, Major . . . ' His jaw dropped. 'Major Niven Short.'

Juliet sighed and nudged him. 'You really are infuriating, James. Did you interrupt your teachers when you were a boy? Read to the end.'

He grinned and returned his attention to the typed label. 'Special unit formed to take out a strategic enemy position.' He stepped back and frowned.

'D'you think there's something about that mission here?'

'We'll have to ask Matron. She'll be in her quarters.'

'Before we do, did you see anything in these diaries of any interest?'

Juliet confirmed that she hadn't. 'Mainly love letters, requests for chocolate and tobacco and complaints about how muddy the terrain is.' She screwed up her nose. 'Lots of rats and trench foot.'

They discussed how awful it must have been as they made their way to Miss Clatterthorpe's office which was, effectively, a converted cupboard underneath the stairs. James repressed a chuckle. Miss C was a corpulent individual and seemed to fill the available space. He wondered why she didn't situate herself somewhere a little more comfortable. She edged her way out of the area and smoothed her skirt down.

'Ah; ready for the reference section?' The wooden steps echoed as they followed her up.

'I say, Miss Clatterthorpe, do you have any information up here about a special assignment? It was led by a Captain William Carlton and Major Niven Short.'

'If they're Sussex, they should be here.'

They reached the landing and she strode straight ahead into a large room with a huge varnished table at its centre. Surrounding this were floor to ceiling shelves full of books and box files.

'Do you know what the special assignment was?'

'Taking out a strategic enemy post.'

'That doesn't narrow it down, Lord Harrington. Captain's name?'

'Carlton. William Carlton.'

Juliet answered. 'He received a DSO. I wonder if he received it for this?'

Miss Clatterthorpe positively beamed. 'Much more helpful.'

She headed straight to the far end of the room and scanned the box files. James and Juliet strolled over. He could see that the files covered years and letters of the alphabet. Miss Clatterthorpe heaved out one marked 'C'. She summoned them over to the table and slid the box toward them.

'These are documents relating to soldiers whose names began with the initial C who received medals and commendations. Whatever your chap did to earn that will be in here.' A telephone rang downstairs. 'I'll leave you to it.' She turned on her heels and marched out.

James held a chair out for Juliet and sat down next to her. He lifted the papers out of the file and placed them on the table. Many of the documents were so thin he could almost see through them. Juliet pulled her chair closer.

'Let's halve it. You look at one pile; I'll look at the other.'

They began examining the papers. James handled each document with great care; partly out of respect and partly because some of them looked as if they might fall apart. Some ten minutes went by before Juliet announced that she'd found something. She placed a document between them, showing a regimental emblem at the top. James read it through.

This was a letter of commendation to a higher authority, recommending that Captain William Carlton be awarded the DSO for his part in the taking of an enemy post. He'd led a small band of men across No Man's Land and took out the stronghold, with only one casualty from his unit. He looked at Juliet. 'DSO is one down from the Victoria Cross.'

'Normally only awarded to Majors but they make exceptions.'

'But how could he have received such

an honour and be a coward? Perhaps our killer is mistaken.' He returned his attention to the document. It continued to detail how the stronghold was taken and what Carlton's involvement had been. The more he read, the more he felt that the handwriting was familiar. He couldn't place it but the sweeping loops of specific letters were distinct and he felt sure he'd seen this recently. He caught his breath when he saw who had signed it.

'Major N. Short.' James examined the document.

'This handwriting is annoying me. I've seen it somewhere.'

'Diaries?'

'No. The diaries I've read are from the Pals; farmhands and labourers. This is the writing of an educated man. Look at the way his writing flows: it's almost an art form.'

Juliet pushed him to delve deeper and suggested places where he might have seen it. 'Something in the library perhaps.'

He shook his head and read through the document again. Realisation dawned on him. He slid round in his seat to face Juliet. 'The registration book at Harrington's. That's where I've seen it. I'm sure that's Carlton's handwriting.' He held the document up. 'There's only one way he could have received this award and that's by being in cahoots with his senior officer.'

'Why don't you telephone Paul and see if he can describe Carlton's handwriting to you.'

A few moments later, James was in the foyer dialling Harrington's while clutching the commendation. To his relief, Paul answered immediately.

'Harrington's, how may I be of assistance?'

'Paul, Lord Harrington here.'

'Yes, your Lordship.'

'Do you have the registration book to hand?'

'It's here on the desk.'

'Can you go to the page where Major Carlton signed in? I'd like you to describe the handwriting to me.'

'Certainly.'

James visualised his maître d' wearing a

bemused expression. He no doubt knew that his employer was sleuthing so would take it all in his stride. He could hear Paul flicking through the pages.

'Right. I have the page here. Major William Carlton.'

'I'm loath to prompt so please simply describe the writing to me as best you can.'

Paul did so. He provided a clear image of the writing: how specific letters sloped to the left; the loops at the base of the 'F' and the artistic, swirling 'A'. He emphasised where more pressure had been placed on the paper and where the writing tailed off. James felt elated with each piece of information and by the end was convinced that the letter of commendation was written specifically by Major William Carlton. He thanked Paul and asked if there was any news on the Major's whereabouts.

'None sir. The Reverend Merryweather telephoned just two minutes ago to see if you were here. I believe he has something he wishes to share with you.'

'Right-ho. I'll speak to him later.'

He rang off as Juliet descended the stairs. She grinned.

'You have a glint in your eye, James. I presume your telephone call was a success.'

'You presume correctly, Juliet.' He turned to thank Miss Clatterthorpe for her help. 'I say, how far is the convalescent home from here?'

'Turn right at the end of the drive — continue for four miles. It's on the right-hand side. Can't miss it.'

He took Juliet's arm and escorted her to the car.

'This convalescent home keeps cropping up. Why don't we take a visit and see what we can find out.'

'Don't you want to call in to see this Niven Short? Pound to a penny our missing Major is cooped up there hiding. Snivelling individual.'

James smirked. Compared to the heroics that Juliet and Delphine Brooks-Hunter had performed during hostilities, he supposed that Major Carlton would strike her as she had described. Instinct told him to visit the home first and, as it was nearby, they might as well call in.

'You never know,' he said as he turned onto the main road, 'we may glean a little more information. At the moment, all we have are ideas and assumptions — nothing tangible.'

Juliet settled back and teased her hair. 'Then don't spare the horses, James. Let's see what this pretty little car will do on the straight.'

25

The Royal Sussex convalescent home stood in its own grounds. The brickwork was painted a brilliant white which gave it the appearance of having risen up from the snow. It was a huge, two-storey rectangular building with large windows giving a pleasant outlook to the sea. The lawn ran down to the main road, on the other side of which was a shingle beach.

As they emerged from the car, the bitter breeze reminded them that it was mid-December. They dashed to the main entrance to be greeted by the warmth of a log fire and a welcoming hello from a nurse dressed in a blue uniform with a white pinafore apron. She was in her mid-twenties with a short bobbed hair-style and a white cap on her head. She smiled brightly.

'Are you visiting?'

After introducing themselves, James explained that they were trying to find out about any Pals who had stayed there during and after the Great War.

'Well, we have a small room through there with bits and pieces that may be of interest. I'll need to sign you in if that's all right. We like to know who's coming and going.'

They followed her to the main desk which had been decorated with tinsel and holly. In the corner of the room was a Christmas tree with many colourful wooden ornaments hanging from its branches. James guessed they were hand-made, no doubt, by those convalescing there. A record player was on the table next to it which, as they added their names to the visitor's book, played 'O Come All Ye Faithful'. The nurse studied the names and did a double-take.

'Oh. Lord Harrington.' She curtseyed.

James held his hands up to stop her. 'No need for any of that,' he peered at her name badge, 'Molly. I say, that's a rather charming name.'

Blushing, she showed them through to a room adjacent to Reception. 'This is where all of our history is kept. I'm not sure that it's in any particular order but you're welcome to have a look. I'm afraid medical details aren't here; they're confidential.'

'My dear,' said Juliet, 'are there any ex-servicemen still here who fought in France during the Great War?'

'We've a handful, yes.' She tilted her head in a sympathetic way. 'Poor things. They haven't got any family and never really got over the shell-shock. It did terrible things to those men. They're not too bad but they wouldn't be able to cope on their own so they're here for the duration.' She stood in the doorway. 'Did you want to speak with them?'

'I think that would be rather splendid. Perhaps we can seek you out a little later for an introduction.'

Molly's eager grin confirmed she'd be happy to do that. Five minutes later, she returned with two cups of tea. 'Sounds like you're going to be here a while so you may as well be comfortable.'

James wandered around the room. It wasn't a terribly big area; more like a back office with odd armchairs dotted about. The carpet was slightly worn and the room had a musty smell to it. Juliet clapped her hands together. 'Right, what are we looking for?'

He reached into his pocket and brought out a slip of paper. 'Anything to do with Privates Brown, Strong and Shotover. Archibald Franks was shot for desertion. One of the others, presumably, was the casualty on the mission. Oh and, of course, Niven Short and William Carlton.'

'I'm sure we won't find anything on those two. Major Short probably sat behind a desk for the whole time and if Carlton was the coward we think he is, he would have no more shell-shock than Mickey Mouse.'

James grinned to himself. He dreaded to think how Juliet would react if she met Major Carlton again. They rummaged through photographs, flicked through books and manila files full of papers and documents. As interesting as some of the material was, it wasn't shedding any light on the individuals in question.

'Molly was right, nothing's in any

order. I'm beginning to think this was a fruitless exercise.'

Juliet knelt on the floor and heaved at a large volume. James crossed to help her. Once it was free, he studied the title, discovering it was a list of patients between the dates of 1900 and 1920.

'Good show, Juliet.'

'Not sure this should be here. Isn't this confidential?'

He shrugged and helped her to her feet. They pulled two armchairs together and opened the volume up. James thumbed through the pages for any dates from 1917 onwards. On finding it, he spread the pages wide. Juliet examined the left-hand column showing the surnames of soldiers. After turning the pages several times, she sat back.

'Shotover.' Her index finger moved to the right. 'Peter. Private. Cavendish Pals. Address in Loxfield.' She frowned. 'Is that right?'

James explained that the Cavendish Pals came from three villages, Cavendish, Charnley and Loxfield. 'Cavendish was the biggest village at the time and the decision to form a Pals unit was made at a sporting tournament on our village green.'

'How quaint.' She continued along the column. 'Admitted for shell-shock. Discharged in 1925.'

'Good Lord. He was here for eight years.'

Juliet continued studying the book until she reached the year 1920. She slammed it shut.

'Nothing else here.'

'Shall we track Molly down and see if we can chat to some of these veterans?'

They wandered out to the reception area where the record player was now playing Leroy Anderson's 'Sleigh Ride'. As they waited, Juliet swayed to the beat of the bouncing melody and James tapped a rhythm with his fingers on the desk. Molly appeared from another room.

'Oh hello again. Did you find what you were looking for?'

'Not as much as we'd hoped but we'd like to find out a little more about Peter Shotover. He was here between 1917 and 1925 with shell-shock.'

Molly reminded him that detailed medical reports were confidential. James held a hand up in apology and requested that they could, perhaps, chat with some of the veterans. 'Do you know if any served under Captain Carlton?' he asked.

'You sit there. Let me go ask. That'll make things a lot quicker for you.'

James put his hands in his pockets and wandered around the reception area. He studied the wooden ornaments on the tree and took in the various landscapes that lined the walls. The small plaque by each one stated which patient had painted them. On hearing Juliet gasp, he turned.

'Everything all right?'

'My dear, look.'

He wandered across and looked up to where she was pointing. Above the reception desk was an oil painting of a distinguished-looking officer in full uniform, wearing a pompous expression. Underneath, it read: Major Niven Short, Patron.

'Good Lord!'

Molly reappeared. 'I've found someone who knew of your Captain Carlton.'

'Splendid. I say, before we go through,

I notice that Major Short is a patron of the hospital. Does he live nearby?'

'I think so. My friend Sally'll know. She's been here a few years and knows everything. Follow me.'

Juliet went ahead. A flutter of excitement rushed through him as he sensed a possible breakthrough.

Molly led them through to a huge, airy room that looked out toward the English Channel. It was easily the size of a tennis court and had a number of plush armchairs scattered about. There were various large tables where a number of men were playing cards, chess and draughts. A large Christmas tree stood in the corner and paper lanterns hung from the ceiling. Paintings of the countryside and spring meadows provided a relaxed and pleasant environment.

About twenty men were in the room and those who were not playing games sat reading or smoking pipes or cigarettes. Some appeared oblivious to anything or anyone and simply stared into space. Those who were aware of their surroundings and themselves waved a greeting; a couple of men stood up when they saw Juliet. She insisted they sit down. Molly chuckled. 'Real gents, aren't they? Always standing up when a lady comes in.'

In the middle of the room, she turned to face them. 'I'm going to introduce you to Corporal Fluff Irwin.'

James was aware that he must have looked a little bemused. Molly explained that Fluff was a nickname.

'He tried to grow a moustache when he enlisted but it ended up like a piece of cottonwool, so he was nicknamed Fluff and it's stuck ever since. Anyway, Fluff suffered terribly with shell-shock at the end of the war and he came straight here in 1918. He's come on leaps and bounds but he's one of those who wouldn't last five minutes in the real world.'

'Are there any subjects we should avoid?'

'Oh no, he's doesn't get troubled or lash out or anything; he's just a bit simple.' She led them across to a chair by a large window. 'Fluff, you've got some visitors.'

James helped Molly manoeuvre two

armchairs across. Fluff gazed at them, his eyes bright with anticipation.

'They've come to see me, Molly?'

'That's right. Not just anybody neither. This is Lord James Harrington and his friend Juliet Brooks-Hunter.'

James and Juliet shook hands with him and declared how delighted they were to meet him. He wore grey trousers and a chunky cricket jumper. He no longer sported a moustache but he still retained a mop of greying hair. His eyes had innocence about them, as if he'd never seen anything bad in his life. James hoped that he hadn't deleted the memory of the war completely. Molly announced that she'd leave them to it and would be back with fresh tea. Fluff held his hand up.

'Can I have some cake, Molly?'

She squeezed his hand. 'I can do you a slice of walnut or lemon sponge.'

His eyes opened wide. 'Cor, lemon sponge.'

James and Juliet placed the same order.

'I've never had a Lord visit before. Are you related to the Queen?'

'I'm afraid not, Fluff. I have met her

though; just the once.'

'She's pretty.'

Aware that he needed to gain Fluff's trust as you would a child, they spent some time chatting about his life and hobbies. Juliet, like Beth, had the knack of making people feel comfortable. The tea and cake arrived and over the next twenty minutes James learned that Fluff was originally from Balcombe, a tiny village outside Haywards Heath, and that his family were farmers. Before the war, Fluff helped get the horses ready to plough the fields and in the evenings, he'd shoot rabbits for the weekend stew. He had a sister but she died and his parents succumbed to the flu pandemic shortly after the conflict. He was now on his own. James' heart went out to him. The story was told as if by a ten year-old — in a very matter-of-fact way as if Fluff didn't really understand how serious it all was. Fluff shifted in his chair and brought out a bald teddy bear with one eye missing.

'This is Pinky.'

Juliet stroked the bear. 'My dear, how sweet. Where did you get him?'

'I've had him since I was tiny. I call him Pinky 'cos he's pink.' He chuckled.

James chuckled along with him. 'Did he join the army with you?'

Fluff nodded and then whispered. 'He didn't sign his papers. I smuggled him in my kit bag.'

'I say, he's been on a lot of adventures with you.'

The man rocked in his seat and gave Pinky a cuddle. 'He came to France with me. I kept him warm in the quarters. I put a note on him to say where he lived just in case I died.' He met James' gaze. 'Some of my friends didn't come back. But that's all right, they're in heaven now.'

'And you knew Captain William Carlton, is that right?'

'That's right. We were all together.'

'Can you remember what year that was?'

'I was 15.' He chuckled and whispered again. 'I was under-age. Shouldn't have joined up. I'd just celebrated my birthday. 5th of January 1917.'

Juliet smiled fondly. 'You must have

been one of the brave men asked to go on a special mission. How exciting for you.'

'No, that weren't me. They never asked me.' He grinned. 'I knew about it though. They should've asked me. I would've done a good job. They thought I was too young. But I wasn't. I shot rabbits when I was five. I'm not an idiot.'

James assured him that they couldn't imagine anyone thinking he was an idiot and encouraged him to tell his story, in particular, anything to do with the mission.

'It was a secret. No one was supposed to know but I was friends with a couple of 'em. We used to smoke cigarettes together and share chocolate. I like chocolate. Molly brings me chocolate. She likes me.'

Juliet held Fluff's hand. 'And who did you know on the mission?'

'Pete and Arthur.'

James pulled out the paper he'd been writing on and checked the names. 'Peter Shotover and Arthur Strong.'

Fluff looked at him in amazement. 'D'you know 'em?'

'I'm afraid I don't but I'm interested to hear about them. Pete was here for a

332

while, wasn't he?'

'I liked Pete. He was a Pal. Arthur never came back. He went to shoot a German and never came back.'

'This was during the mission?'

Fluff shifted in his chair. 'Something bad happened.'

James' his heart skipped a beat. 'Can you tell me what?'

The man scanned the room and chuckled again.

'I'll only tell you if you promise not to tell. If that Captain Carlton finds out, he'll tell me off. I like it here. I don't want to be taken away.'

'My dear, they'll have to get past us first. You will remain here for as long as you please.'

He positively beamed at her. After one more cursory look around the room Fluff leant forward. 'Captain Carlton wanted to blow up a trench opposite us with Germans in. He didn't choose any soldiers from his section — he went over to get Pete and Arthur and there were two others too. I didn't know them but they was all together. The regulars had a name for

Captain Carlton.'

James tilted his head. 'Oh?'

'Custard Carlton.' He chuckled again and nudged James. 'You know what that means, don't you?'

'Do you?'

'I didn't used to. I thought it was because he liked custard.' He whispered. 'It means coward. Cowardy custard.' He chuckled to himself.

'Extraordinary,' said Juliet, 'why would they call a distinguished officer such a thing?'

Fluff nibbled his lip. 'They say he never went with 'em.'

'Never went with who?'

'The men. The men went to the trench but one didn't come back. Captain Carlton went half way. He said he was injured but he didn't look injured. Pete said he let the men take the post while he hid. I'm good at hiding. We used to play hide and seek on the farm.'

'The man who didn't come back, do you know what happened to him?'

'He got killed. Do you want the rest of your cake?'

James handed him the remainder of his sponge. 'So one was killed on the mission and three came back to their unit. Peter Shotover, Arthur Strong and Archibald Franks.'

'Archie got shot.' He looked down. 'That's not a nice thing to do.'

'And Arthur Strong? What happened to him?'

Fluff held Pinky tight and his eyes shifted from side to side. James squeezed his forearm. 'It's all right, Fluff, I'm not going to tell anyone.'

'Cross your heart?'

'Cross my heart.'

Fluff answered in a quiet whisper, 'Custard Carlton killed 'im.'

James stared at Juliet and then at Fluff. 'Are you quite sure?'

The man appeared strained. 'Arthur threatened 'im. I don't why but I 'eard that Carlton killed him; made out that he'd run away. But he 'adn't run away.'

Molly appeared behind them. 'Do you want more tea?'

James and Juliet declined but Fluff requested another slice of lemon sponge announcing to all that it was his favourite. Once he'd settled back with his cake, James continued. 'So Peter Shotover was the only one left.'

'He came here. He was my friend but he couldn't stop shaking. We played tiddly-winks. He liked that but he couldn't keep his hands still. I had to help him flip the counters.'

'But he got better, didn't he?'

Fluff stared at the floor. 'He went home to his family.' He stuck out his bottom lip. 'My family are in heaven.'

James felt Juliet grip his arm. 'My dear, he had family?'

'He had a son. His son was married and they had a little girl.'

'Are you still in touch with him?'

'He's in heaven. He shot himself.' Fluff bit into his sponge and began to chat to Pinky. 'Shame you got no appetite, Pinky, this is right lovely sponge.' He looked at James. 'I'm a bit tired now.'

'Of course, we're sorry to have taken up so much time.'

As they stood, Fluff grabbed James' hand. 'Will you visit again? I don't get many visitors and I like you. And you,' he added to Juliet.

'We'll be sure to stop by.'

Back in Reception, Molly handed him a slip of paper with Niven Short's address on it. James thanked her. 'Molly, is Fluff allowed out?'

'As long as he's with someone responsible. Why?'

'I wonder if he'd like to be a guest at our pantomime in Cavendish. I could arrange to pick him up and drop him back here.'

Molly put her hands together. 'Oh, he'd love that. Let us know when and what time and we'll make sure he's ready for you.'

Satisfied with their visit, James and Juliet made their way to the car. He opened the passenger door for her.

'James, I'm beginning to dislike Carlton more and more. Are we now paying a visit to Niven Short?'

'I think so. I believe Carlton is there, don't you? Be interesting to see what they both have to say for themselves.'

26

Major Niven Short lived in a detached house about two miles along the coast from the convalescent home. The house was a 1930s style residence with bay windows and a small garden. Clearly, this man didn't have the wealth in his family that William Carlton had. James took his gloves off and rapped on the door using the lion's head door knocker.

When the door opened, he couldn't hide his surprise. The painting above the reception in the Royal Sussex depicted Niven Short as a pompous oaf but the man standing in front of him was anything but. He stood around the same height as James and wore clothes more in keeping for a country walk. He looked welcoming and swung the door wide.

'Hello? Come to see me or are you lost?'

'Major Short?'

'Guilty as charged. Do I know you?'

James began the introductions and asked whether they could perhaps speak with him about his army days. Suspicion darkened his face. 'May I ask why?'

Juliet stood straight. 'We'd like to know about your service career with Major William Carlton or, as he was back then, Captain Carlton.'

'Ah, now, just a minute. He's not here if that's what you're thinking.'

'Which means he *was* here,' Juliet put in.

'What? Well, no, well, I mean to say —'

James suggested he invite them in for a chat. 'I don't want to involve the police, Major Short. You do know they're looking for him, don't you?'

'He's done nothing wrong! Poor chap's just lost his wife, you're aware of that, are you?'

'She was murdered at Harrington's, I'm hardly likely to forget it.'

A silent bell seemed to ring in the Major's head.

'Ah, yes, Lord Harrington! Of course, you're the owner, aren't you?' He suddenly looked resigned. 'You'd better come in.'

As they followed him through to the front room, Juliet nudged James and winked at him. Clearly she was as excited about this as he felt himself. The room was a cosy one with a fire roaring in the grate and a small Christmas tree in the corner with presents lying underneath. On the mantelpiece were family photographs. Copies of magazines and books lay on the sofa and small coffee table. The Major gestured for them to take a seat.

'The wife's out at the moment; shopping. I'd rather we have this conversation before she gets back.'

'Of course.'

He made for a bureau where he grabbed a bottle of whisky and three glasses. 'Oban single malt. Will you partake?'

James and Juliet both nodded. He poured the drinks and placed the bottle on the table between them.

'Help yourself if you want more.'

He flopped down in his armchair and heaved a sigh. 'How did you find me?'

'It's been a wild goose chase but a few clues led us this way.'

James went on to outline the whole series of events to date — the attack on John Carlton, the murder of Cynthia Carlton, the discovery of the white feathers and poison pen letters. Juliet added little bits of information here and there; the constant mention of the convalescent home, the suspicions that Cynthia Carlton had about her husband. James highlighted the diary entries that had been found and the discussions he'd had with the Pals during the dinner and dances. Finally, they detailed their visit to the regimental museum and the commendation that appeared to have been falsified, along with their discovery that William Carlton had acquired the nickname 'Custard'.

James cradled the whisky in his hand. 'I realise that Major Carlton is a friend and comrade but there are too many things here to discount. I believe that his past has caught up with him. He's being targeted for something he did in 1917.'

Niven Short studied the amber spirit as he swirled it in his glass. Juliet sat upright and took on the expression of a pompous headmistress. 'Major Short, covering for your friend is commendable but not wise. His son is mourning the loss of his mother and having to arrange her funeral without him. He's discovered the truth about his father and is trying to come to terms with this. Your friend is continuing his cowardly behaviour by running away from his responsibilities even now. I wonder if the man ever had a backbone.'

Short swallowed hard and poured himself another whisky. A few seconds ticked by before he spoke.

'You're right. This charade has gone on long enough. In a way I'm glad that it's coming out. I owe it to the men who lost their lives.'

'Tch,' said Juliet. 'It's too late for them. You should have thought of that at the time. You're just as guilty as he is.'

James reached across and patted Juliet's hand. He didn't want Major Short to put up his defences and he didn't know the Major well enough to start wading in with opinions. Juliet took her cue and sat back.

Short sighed. 'It's probably best that I

start at the beginning.'

'We're all ears,' said James.

'He went to my school. I was a junior master back then, fresh from university. When William enrolled, I looked out for him. He reminded me of my own younger brother, who died when he was only ten. William was a sickly child, not terribly sporting and not that academic, if truth be told. He was an average student, never really got into any trouble. Steered clear of it. But boarding schools are renowned for bullying and Will got his fair share of it. Nothing serious but it made Will into what he was — a man lacking confidence. His father was the complete opposite: a strict tyrant who expected Will to be a man's man, leading from the front.'

He smoothed his hair back.

'The war came and because our pupils were privately educated there was some stuff and nonsense that they would make good officers. Well, by that time, I'd joined up. I'm from a military family so it was a natural step for me. I did my time at the military academy and was promoted several times.' He put his shoulders back. 'I was a damn good soldier.'

'So, William Carlton was trained as an officer, even though he was young and had no experience of life?'

'Compared to the men he was to lead, no. Officers were being shot down like tin cans on a shooting range. He wasn't cut out to be a soldier — not a field soldier, but his father insisted he fight the good fight and make him and the family proud.'

'And he was put in charge of this special mission.'

'That's right. Take out an enemy post that would gain us a few hundred yards. It was all pretty hush hush but the hierarchy thought it would prove to be a turning point where that particular area was concerned. William was ordered to select four men and take the unit out.'

'And why,' said Juliet, 'did he select Pals?'

Niven closed his eyes for a while, before meeting Juliet's gaze. 'He wanted to have people with him who didn't know him. He didn't want to fight. On the night of the operation, he went forward with the men but for every yard they covered, he fell back one. He realised, of course, that he'd backed himself into a corner. One of the group challenged him; told him to fight with the rest of them but he didn't. He scrambled under cover.'

James asked for permission to smoke and lit up. 'One man died.'

'That's right.'

'And Private Franks?'

Major Short struggled to make eye contact with James. 'Franks was already showing signs of shell-shock and..'

'He threatened to expose William Carlton for what he was.'

The Major nodded. 'How he found the strength to shoot him, I don't know.'

Juliet baulked. 'My dear, Carlton wouldn't have done. He would have ordered a firing squad to carry out his dirty work.'

'Yes, of course.' The Major's shoulders dropped. James pushed again. 'And Arthur Strong?' Niven explained that he'd heard he'd been shot. 'Found dead the day after the operation.'

'Our understanding is that Arthur

Strong made the same threat as Archibald Franks.'

'That's correct.'

'And that left the last of the four Pals, Peter Shotover.'

James realised that the Major was saying less and less. Reliving this episode was becoming uncomfortable and difficult for the man, so he decided to outline his thoughts. Major Short was bound to put him right if his version of events was wrong. 'Peter Shotover was suffering from shell-shock. No one believed anything he said. He was deemed to be unfit and, at the time, of unsound mind. But he remembers what happened. He wrote a diary and documented what had happened during that mission. He was tormented by it. So much so that he committed suicide.'

The Major fidgeted.

'Major Carlton,' James continued, 'has received anonymous letters that accuse him of cowardice. Someone, recently, has read those diaries and is taking revenge.'

Major Short's swirled the whisky in the tumbler. Juliet slammed the table with the palm of her hand. Short flinched.

'And still you do nothing!' she cried. 'Why on earth did you sign a commendation? A commendation written by Carlton himself?'

'He was just a boy. He shouldn't have been there. I felt sorry for him.'

James sighed. 'But why not let the whole thing slide into history instead of making him out to be something he's not?'

'I thought it would give him confidence. It would make his father proud.'

Juliet huffed. 'Oh, for goodness sake!'

The Major's face turned red. 'He turned into a bloody good officer. Once he was off the field, he came into his own.'

'Because it's easy to be an officer when you're sitting at a desk, detached from the real world. So he went all the way to the top and didn't lift a rifle again. He lived on a lie and began to believe it himself, pompous oaf.'

'I did what I thought was right at the time and there isn't a day goes by where I don't regret it.' His eyes blazed at Juliet.

'It's not easy fighting a war.'

James put an arm across to stop Juliet from leaping up. 'Major Short, you're speaking to a lady who has worked undercover in Germany during the two wars, right under the noses of high-ranking officers. I would be careful with your allegations.'

Major Short flopped back in his seat. 'I'm sorry. I'm more angry with myself than with anyone else.'

'Presumably Major Carlton came here to hide from his attacker.'

Niven explained that he'd pitched up on the doorstep a few days previously. 'He told me about the letters he'd received.' He frowned. 'I don't understand it, though. Will is adamant no one but Shotover knew what happened. When the man killed himself, Will relaxed — thought it wouldn't haunt him. It was years ago. But then those accusations came, along with those ghastly feathers.'

'Shotover may have died, Major Short, but the diaries remained. There is a family member out there wanting revenge.'

He shook his head in disbelief. 'I heard the son committed suicide too.'

'Peter Shotover's son? When?'

'I don't know. A few years ago. He left a wife and daughter.'

Good grief, James thought, *a woman is responsible for this.* Juliet slapped the table to attract the Major's attention.

'Do you know Olivia Dupree?'

'The singer?' He considered. 'Well, not personally, no. I've heard her sing, of course, but that's about it.' He stared at James. 'Why are you asking about her?'

'Because the week before all this happened to the Carltons, Olivia Dupree was poisoned in the same manner as John Carlton.'

'A mistake?'

'Impossible, old chap. The Carltons weren't there that evening. We're trying to establish a link.'

'I can't help you there, I'm afraid. Will's never mentioned the woman except to say she was singing that evening at your place.'

'Why did he leave here? Has he gone home?'

'I'm not sure. He received a letter and he said he had to leave.'

'A letter? Did you read it?'

Niven explained that Will wouldn't let him read it. It had been posted through the letter box by hand.

'He paled a little and said he needed to help John arrange the funeral. It all sounded above board so he went. He hadn't brought much with him.'

'No, he left most of his clothes at Harrington's.' James pushed himself up from his chair and helped Juliet to her feet. 'I think you've told us everything we need to know. Thank you for your time.'

As Major Short opened the front door, he appeared like a man defeated. 'I'm pleased to have told someone. I understand if you have to report me to the authorities.'

'I think you can see now how signing that document and covering for your friend has escalated. Lives have been lost. I would suggest you contact the authorities yourself.' He provided him with George's details and left the decision to him.

On the drive back to Cavendish, James asked Juliet if she thought Niven Short would telephone George. She gazed through the windshield at the snow-covered branches.

'I believe he will telephone George and the Regiment. He's from a military family. Hopefully, he'll do the right thing now.'

'But who the hell is Shotover? That name hasn't cropped up until today.'

'Then we need to find out. Shotover left a son with a wife and daughter. The son is dead. We're looking for a woman and that narrows it down to three: Mandy, Enid and Olivia. Perhaps Olivia poisoned herself to avoid suspicion.'

James manoeuvred the car through the country lanes and arrived home around an hour later. Stephen's little Austin was parked by the front steps. Beth rushed out to meet them.

'At last! We've been trying to reach you for hours!'

As they took their coats off, James apologised and explained that they'd much to tell. Harry came out and helped Juliet with her coat.

'Come in and tell us. I think you'll also

351

want to hear what Stephen and Anne have to say.'

They stepped into the lounge. George made to stand but James insisted he stay comfortable. His friend had more colour in his cheeks than on the previous day. Stephen opened his mouth to speak but Anne was so animated she couldn't help but go ahead of him.

'We went to visit John today and had a wander through the village. Stephen happened to pop into the post office to buy some stamps and got chatting with the postmistress. She's a bit of a gossip and asked what we were doing here and Stephen explained who we were visiting and mentioned that the house was big and a little out of the way.' She paused for breath. 'Well, she didn't have anything nice to say about William Carlton; thought he was stuck up and full of himself. Never mixed with anyone.'

Juliet clicked her tongue. 'I told you, James: pompous oaf.'

James grinned and sat down opposite his friends. 'Anne, you're clearly excited about something but how about scooting ahead and letting us know what that is?'

'Oh. Sorry. Yes. Stephen, you tell him. It's your news — I'm hogging the limelight.'

Stephen rolled his eyes. 'I-I kept her speaking about the M-Major and she commented that I-I was taking an unusual interest. Then she said someone else had b-been asking about him over the previous months.'

James frowned.

'You'll never guess,' said Anne. She put her hand to her mouth. 'Sorry!

'E-Enid Carmichael.'

James stared at Stephen. 'The wet weekend? Enid Carmichael?'

'Dad, you don't have to be a weightlifter to poison someone.'

'And,' Beth put in, 'they say that poison is a woman's *modus operandi*.'

He turned his attention to George. 'What do you make of this?'

His friend added that he had called the postmistress and had quite a chat with her. 'She'd apparently seen Enid now and again over the last year or eighteen months. Popping in to the village for a cup of tea. She said that she and her chap were thinking of moving there so were getting familiar with the area.'

'It's no wonder she knew Carlton's every move. She must have stalked him; sat next to his wife at coffee mornings; probably chatted with her in the newsagents. Quite disturbing.'

'Well, I've let Inspector Collins know so he's sending a constable down to get a statement.'

The telephone rang. Harry stepped into the hall to answer it. Two minutes later he returned. 'That was Collins.'

'H-has he arrested E-Enid?'

'Unfortunately not. She appears to have done a runner.'

27

'But none of this makes sense,' said James. 'Enid's family are in Devon; didn't you check that, George? Isn't her father still alive?'

He nodded but reminded James that the grand-dad fought for the Sussex Regiment. 'We'll have to find her. It's too suspicious that she's stalking Carlton and now she's gone missing. People lie and she's deceived all of us.' He checked his watch. 'It's getting late. Don't you have a rehearsal to get to?'

James scratched his head. He'd been certain he was getting better at judging characters and Enid Carmichael didn't come across as a cold-blooded killer. But then neither did Mandy or Olivia. Oh, they had their annoying quirks but that was about it. Did Enid lie about the chap she was walking out with? He was Devonshire too. All of this was easy to check. Surely she wouldn't have left herself so open by lying about all of this. Yes, she'd had an opportunity to poison Olivia Dupree and the Carltons but he simply couldn't envisage it. But perhaps that's what had made her slip his mind. The quiet ones attract little attention. He snapped out of his thoughts. 'George, I think you need to hear what we've discovered.'

'Tell me on the way to the village hall.'

Juliet travelled with the Merryweathers and updated them on the day's events. James did the same for Beth, Harry and George. At the hall, both he and Juliet were met with concern and disbelief. James insisted that he had no more to tell them and it would be impossible to answer questions without making assumptions. He held the door to the village hall open. As Anne passed him, she tried to query something but James held a finger to his lips to indicate no.

George jotted down a few notes and said he'd follow them in as he wanted to update Collins on James' news. James gave him a reassuring squeeze on the shoulder.

'Good luck with that, George. You'll probably have strict orders to arrest me for poking my nose in. But he really needs to be finding out about this name, Shotover. If he can link Enid to that name, he has his proof.'

Inside, the Snoop Sisters busied themselves making teas and coffees. Elsie Taylor opened a huge tin of scones and fairy cakes and arranged them on a china platter. Harry delivered a selection of mince pies that Beth had baked earlier to Grandma Harrington's traditional recipe.

Dorothy Forbes led from the front and instructed her players to take their positions. Little groups of villagers huddled in various parts of the hall, going through their scenes. Graham Porter, Charlie Hawkins and Philip Jackson hammered scenery into place while their wives rehearsed in front of them. Children raced around the hall playing tag.

Beth joined Dorothy; Anne skipped across to sit with the ladies making last-minute adjustments to the costumes and Juliet and Stephen discussed the Yule Log and Christmas services.

Bert slapped James on the back. 'Oi, oi.'

He swung round. 'Bert, where the devil have you been? You've been conspicuous by your absence.'

'Christmas innit? I told you I wouldn't be about much. I've 'ad a few orders for stuff.'

Harry laughed. 'I'll bet you have. What's on everyone's list this year?'

'What I can get me 'ands on and I've a few things left. Wagon Train annuals, Pelham puppets, Corgi cars, Space Patrol walkie-talkies, skipping ropes; er..Enid Blyton books and some Ponds beauty kits and portable record players. That's about it.'

'Don't let DCI Lane hear you.'

Bert scanned the room. 'He's not 'ere, is he?'

James smiled. 'He's just through those doors, making a phone call. And what's that under your arm?'

Bert relieved himself of the box and placed it under the WI table. 'I know you don't like dealing with me in this way but I got my hands on the Meccano set you wanted to get Luke and Mark.'

James picked the box up and gave it to Harry along with his car keys and instructions to put the box in the boot of the Jaguar. He fished out his wallet and paid Bert.

'I'm grateful, Bert, but I feel terribly guilty for purchasing goods like this.'

'Don't worry about it. Selfridges and 'arrods ain't gonna go out of business because I'm selling a few knocked off toys. Listen, I've got someone you may wanna chat to about Major Carlton.'

James picked up his cup and saucer. 'Oh?'

'Eddie Simmonds.'

'Our Pals Eddie Simmonds?'

'That's right. Put yer tea down, he's just outside.'

'Well bring him in here, it's ruddy freezing outside.'

Bert pursed his lips and marched through the wooden double doors at the back and dragged Eddie in. In his fifties, Eddie was the younger and quieter of the two Simmonds brothers. He'd enjoyed the dinner and had danced with several ladies during the evening, leaving with his fellow Pals around eleven o'clock. James remembered Eddie's attitude to Major Carlton on the evening of Cynthia's death. He certainly had no time for the officer; that much was obvious. Eddie held out his hand.

'Evening, Lord Harrington. Thanks for seeing me.' He surveyed the hall and waved a quick hello to several villagers. 'I've booked tickets for this. Bringing my little grandson. He's five.'

'Good show. Just the right age for a pantomime — is the whole family coming?'

'Just me and the grandson. He's latched onto me at the moment and he didn't want anyone to come except me.' He tutted. 'Hope he doesn't change his mind at the last minute.'

James assured him they'd be able to squeeze his son and daughter-in-law in should the need arise. He steered Eddie to a quieter area. Bert nipped over to deliver a couple of annuals to Helen Jackson.

'So, Eddie, you have some information for me.'

'We weren't straight with you when we saw you, Lord Harrington.'

'We?'

'Me and Billy. The others don't know anything but Billy said we can't not say anything, 'specially with what's been happening.'

James put his hands in his pockets and waited. It was no use pushing him. Eddie was struggling with his conscience and wanted to do this in his own time. After a few seconds he pulled his shoulders back and looked James in the eye.

'We knew Adam's grandfather, Archibald Franks. He was one of us and he wasn't a coward. He was ill. The shelling, the gunfire, the gas, it got to him. He'd been fighting with the rest of us but there was some heavy bombing close to him over a few weeks and he changed. He went from being someone we looked up to, to a jabbering wreck.'

'You've no need to explain,' said James. 'I discovered what happened. He should have received medical help.'

Eddie blinked back the tears. 'But there's something you don't know.' Eddie motioned for him to move further from the crowds. He scanned the room before lowering his voice. 'Billy and me were in the firing squad.'

James's jaw dropped. Words failed him. Eddie stared at his feet to compose himself and slowly returned his attention to him.

'There was ten of us. Five rifles had bullets, five had blanks so we don't know who actually killed 'im. It's supposed to make us feel better about it but how can you? How can you feel better about something like that? Archie was one of us. He played in our football team; he was our bowler in the cricket team.'

'Were you aware who ordered the firing squad?'

He shifted on his feet. 'No. We had an inkling. It happened straight after a mission he'd been sent on. Then another one of 'em got shot. Arthur Strong. He played cricket for Loxfield. I didn't know him well but he was one of us; one of the Pals.'

'Firing squad?'

'No. They found him face down in a

ditch. They called it accidental but it was straight after that mission.'

'Do you know what the mission was?'

'No idea. The boys were hand-picked. But we know who picked 'em.' Eddie stared at James. 'Captain William Carlton.'

'Did you hear any rumours about Captain Carlton?'

'Not at the time, no. When we got home we wanted to forget it. We didn't speak about it for years. Me and Billy didn't even discuss it on our own. We couldn't face the Franks family. To this day, they don't know me and Billy were in the squad. I couldn't live with myself if they knew.' He grabbed James' arm. 'You won't tell 'em will you?'

'Certainly not. You have my word.' He offered him a cigarette and after lighting it asked him what he'd discovered later. Eddie tilted his head in question. 'You said you didn't hear any rumours at the time.'

'Oh. Yes. I got chatting with someone a few years later at a Remembrance Day service; someone in the regular army who served under the Captain. Kept referring to him as 'custard'. I thought it was just a nickname.'

'But you discovered something different.'

Eddie let out a sarcastic laugh. 'Cowardy custard. I've no proof. I don't know what happened on that mission but every one of those Pals ended up dead. One on the battle-field, one suspicious, one murdered by firing squad and one shot himself.' He puffed his cigarette. 'That ain't right.' He checked his watch. 'I'd best get back. I don't know if that's been any help. I've no proof about what happened to our comrades but I do know this. Something happened on that mission that destroyed my mates and their families.'

'Do you know where Shotover's family are?'

Eddie shrugged and explained he never met them. 'They weren't Cavendish; they were Loxfield and I think they were pretty new to the area when war broke out. Moved away years ago.'

James watched him go. This placed new emphasis on William Carlton's reputation as a coward. And Eddie's last words ran through his head. *Something happened on that mission that destroyed my mates and their families.* That something was enough to kill. Was Enid Carmichael the grand-daughter of Private Shotover? Did she discover her grandfather's diaries?

Bert's return brought him out of his thoughts.

'Helpful?'

'Very.' He felt his pockets for some loose change.

'I'm going to make a quick call.'

As he opened the door, he noticed George sitting at the back of the hall. 'Did you get through to Collins?'

'He went home at five o'clock and won't be back in until tomorrow afternoon. He won't get promotion doing that. I left a message with my sergeant but he thinks Collins is too fixated on finding Enid to take any notice, especially when I mentioned that you'd provided the information. That's a sure sign he'll put it at the bottom of the list.'

'Perhaps you shouldn't have let that slip.'

'Perhaps.' He nodded at the stage. 'Has

Beth been on yet?'

'Yes, she's still up there. Why don't you go and sit down? You're supposed to be taking it easy, not pursuing a murder enquiry.'

George didn't argue and went through to the main hall. James stood by the phone and leafed through a tiny address book. He studied the name selected and dialled the number. On hearing the pips, he fed coins into the slot.

'Ah, is that Gerald Crabtree? Good show, Lord Harrington here.'

Gerald had attended GJ's wedding but James didn't realise he'd be calling on him again so soon in his official capacity. His place of work was Somerset House where all the births, deaths and marriages were registered.

With the pleasantries out the way, James got down to business. 'I wonder if you could shed some light on Enid Carmichael and her family.' He went through the information he had about her; her roots in Sussex and Devon and the military career of her ancestors. The pips went and he fed more coppers into the slot.

Gerald cleared his throat. 'So you need to establish that she's on the level.'

'Exactly right. She's being hunted down for murder but I'm not sure that she is our suspect.'

'Do you know who is?'

'I've a suspicion but absolutely no proof. Having confirmation about this from you would solve that. The name Shotover has cropped up in the last couple of days and I can't establish who that belongs to.'

'Well, give me the names and I'll see what I can find out.'

James imparted two further names: Olivia Dupree (née Diane Brown) and Mandy Billings. 'I don't have much to tell you. Olivia Dupree's people are from Shoreditch and Mandy's are from Sussex.'

Gerald double-checked that he was talking about *the* Olivia Dupree and James confirmed that he was.

'Well, that would cause a scandal, wouldn't it? Leave it with me and I'll see what I can rustle up for you.'

Happy that he was moving in the right direction, he returned to the village hall, delighted to see that he hadn't missed

Beth's entire rehearsal. With actors line-perfect and with costumes being adjusted as they were worn, the dress rehearsal rolled by without a hitch. Satisfied that they were as now good as they could be, the whole ensemble transferred to the Half Moon to celebrate a job well done.

★　★　★

At 10:30 the following morning, Gerald rang James with the news that Enid Carmichael was telling the truth. He'd traced the family back to the mid-19th century in Sussex and a later move to Devon. The family had men listed in the Sussex regiment in Italy. The grand-dad was discharged and is still alive. The Shotover name did not appear to be linked.

'James, I've not had an opportunity to check the other names. I've quite a bit on at present so I'll have to do this when I have time. If your Inspector chap put in a formal police enquiry, I could probably get something done quicker.'

After the call, James replaced the

handset. The chances of getting that ghastly man, Collins, to expedite anything would be like betting on a rocking horse to win the Derby. But at least one name had been taken out of the equation.

28

Philip Jackson had picked George up to take him to the hospital for a check-up. With Beth and Anne in discussions with the Salvation Army over a carol concert and Harry running things at the hotel, James invited Juliet along to speak with Mandy Billings. Charlie had given him the address of her mum's place in Cowfold where she was doing the last of the clearing out.

Cowfold was a small village on the road between Horsham and Shoreham, dating back to the 13th century. It hosted a regular ceilidh in the village hall which he and Beth had often attended. They were also customers of a local farmer in the area whose wife made delicious rabbit pies.

The house was in a row of terraced cottages a five minute walk from the main square. They were narrow houses, each with a tiny garden at the front. On finding the correct property, he peered through the dusty window but detected no signs of life. *Perhaps she's in the back room*, he thought. Juliet searched for a doorbell or knocker and, on finding none, rapped on the door itself. They waited a few minutes. He stamped his feet on the pavement. 'My word it's cold!' he said, mist emerging from his mouth as he spoke.

'Seems we may have had a wasted journey,' said Juliet.

'Can I 'elp you?'

James turned to his left to see a neighbour leaning on the fence. She wore a wrap-around apron and a headscarf.

'Ah, hello! We were hoping to see Mandy. Is she about?'

'I ain't seen 'er today.'

Juliet approached the fence. 'We have some news regarding her late mother's estate. It's vital we see her. Do you know if she managed to complete our paper-work?'

The woman made a face to indicate she had no idea. 'Why don't you take a look? I keep a spare key. Always 'ave done.

You're from the solicitors, are you?'

James took the key. 'That's right. We won't be long. I'll get this back to you in a few moments.'

She waved and carried on brushing the front step. James huddled by the front door and grinned at Juliet. 'That was extremely devious of you,' he said, as he opened the door.

The house was as cold inside as out and their footsteps echoed as they crossed the linoleum floor into the front room. Juliet went on through to the kitchen.

'Cupboards are bare,' she informed him. James scanned the room. 'Not much in here either.'

All the furniture had gone except for a compact sideboard. He opened the various drawers and squatted down to see inside the lower cupboards, which all proved to be empty. He stood up and examined the shelves to the side. These must be some of the bottles that Mandy had spoken about. Six shelves full of blue and green bottles; all shapes and sizes and of varying ages. Some were recent designs and some were clearly Victorian or earlier.

He squatted down and checked under the cupboard. Something caught his eye and he reached underneath to scoop up debris by the skirting board. Among the dust were some scraps of newspaper letters.

He leapt up and held the clippings high. 'We have her. Look, odd letters from newspapers. A pound to a penny these will be a match with those letters sent to Carlton.'

'If she's been that careless, there may be more evidence.'

James pointed to the back. 'The dustbin, let's try that.'

In the small garden at the back, they lifted the dustbin lid. Keeping his gloves on, James pulled out a selection of newspapers; old copies of the Daily Express and the Evening News that dated back several years. He leafed through them and Juliet was quick to spot something.

'Look there,' said Juliet.

James retrieved a chemist's script. Juliet peered at the prescription.

'This is for Mandy Billings. If my

memory is correct, this is for severe depression. And she's not presented it. It's over a month old.'

James slipped it in his pocket and took out the layer of newspapers. 'Well, well, what have we here?'

At the bottom of the dustbin was a wooden rack with half a dozen tiny bottles. Unlike the bottles on the shelves, these had elaborate labels on them. They were faded but their origin was what had taken his interest. 'Juliet. Look at these,' he said, picking a couple up.

Juliet took the rack from him. 'These are bottles from a pharmacy. They're dated 1880. Look at this one. Strychnine.'

'Does strychnine go off?'

'No, it doesn't. Her mother probably bought these at a market or something.' She leant in close. 'This bottle's been used. Look. There's no dust on this one but the others haven't been dusted at all. Put everything back. The police will need to fingerprint these.'

They returned to the main room where Juliet stopped in her tracks. 'Look, a typewriter.'

'This is our murderer, Juliet.'

There was a knock on the door and the neighbour entered. 'Found what you were looking for?'

'Ah, no, I think she must have those papers with her. Looks like Miss Billings has done a good job of clearing everything.'

The neighbour frowned. 'Miss Billings?'

Her expression put a seed of doubt in his head.

'Yes. Mandy Billings? Her mother died. Mandy's the one who's been sorting everything out.'

She laughed. 'Gawd, I 'aven't heard that name for a while. Billings. I knew Ethel when she was a Billings.'

James frowned. 'Ethel?'

'Ethel Shotover.'

James forced himself to remain calm. 'Ethel Shotover?'

'Yes, Mandy's mum. Billings was Ethel's maiden name. I've known Ethel since school. We lived in the same road back then and now we're neighbours. Poor thing. She had a rotten life.'

'In what way?'

The woman folded and unfolded her cleaning rag as she relayed the story of Ethel Billings. She spoke of a timid girl whose wish was to have a husband and a family and nothing more.

'She got 'em too,' said the neighbour, 'but, oh dear, what a life she had. Her father-in-law came out of that awful war with shell-shock. They kept 'im in a home for years but because he had family, they let him out. Came to live here, with them, he did.'

She described days and nights where they'd find him cowering in the garden and shouting at demons.

'He weren't old; probably mid-forties when he put a gun to his head.' She pointed towards the back garden. 'Down there it was, behind the shed. Ethel wanted to throw that gun away but her husband was having none of it. He locked it in that cupboard there.'

James opened the cupboard door. He brought out a leather pistol holder and opened it. Empty. Juliet's face mirrored his concern.

'I say, was Mandy born then?'

'She must've been around six I think.' She twisted her apron-string round her fingers. 'Then the dad did the same.'

'What? I thought he'd left.'

'He did. But he didn't go far. Went down to Beachy Head and threw himself off.'

Beachy Head was a beauty spot on the South Coast with incredibly high cliff tops. Many a time he and Beth had walked along the coastline there and stopped for a picnic. How tragic that Mandy's dad should make such a decision. He rubbed his forehead.

'Why did Mandy's dad take his own life? He had a wife and daughter who presumably loved him.'

'Affected by his dad. When his dad came from the convalescent place, he weren't right in the head. It put a shadow on this house. Ethel withdrew and got ill — suffered with depression. She was in and out of mental homes till the day she died. And when he jumped off Beachy Head, well, she got worse. I'm not surprised she poisoned herself. She had enough of the stuff.'

James and Juliet exchanged alarmed looks. The neighbour began speaking about the bottles. 'She used to go to markets and second-hand shops buying tat. I remember her showing me things she'd bought. Look at the pretty labels, she'd say. She loved the writing on the bottles from the chemists. I know she had quite a few. I hope Mandy's chucking 'em all away.'

Juliet pulled her scarf tighter and shivered. 'James, I think we've probably learned all we need to here. Don't you think we should try to track Mandy down?'

James agreed. Time was of the essence. Mandy had drawn her net around Major Carlton and now they needed to establish where on earth she'd taken him. They thanked the neighbour for her time and returned the key to her. When they'd entered the house, there had been a chill in the air. Now snow-laden clouds gathered in the distance. James started the car and put the heater on full blast. He turned to Juliet.

'Where d'you think she's taken him?'

'I don't know. We can't go dashing around the countryside on a wild goose chase.'

He put the vehicle into gear. 'Let's go home. Perhaps she's left a ransom or something.'

'I doubt it. Mandy Billings is not driven by money. She has one thing in mind for Major Carlton and I don't believe it entails him living much longer.'

The roads were damp. Although snow threatened, only a few flurries of sleet swirled down and disappeared before touching the ground. James pressed his foot on the accelerator and, for a brief moment, relived his racing and rallying days from the 1930s. He took the racing line around bends and went up through the gears on long stretches of tarmac. He revved the engine and slowed as he turned into the drive, coming to a halt at the steps leading to the front door. Juliet let out a satisfied sigh.

'My dear that really was the most invigorating run. We must do it again.' Without waiting for James, she got out of the car and breathed in the fresh, still air. 'I wonder, while we're discussing our next move, whether I could have a glass of water? I'm quite parched.'

James quickly opened the front door. 'Of course. It was remiss of me to drag you away all morning without a break.'

As if on cue, Beth peered around the kitchen door.

'Good timing; tea's just made.'

In the lounge, James and Juliet updated George, Beth and Harry with their news. George frowned as he listened to Juliet's thoughts about Mandy's intentions.

'She's going to kill him, George, mark my words.'

Harry paced the floor. 'But where would she go? She lived with her mum — she didn't rent anywhere else, did she?'

James looked at his son. 'Should we telephone John?'

'No need,' said Harry, 'he called earlier to ask if we'd heard anything. We were having a chat but someone was at the door so he had to go.'

They sat in silence. James spoke his thoughts aloud. 'There must be some-where significant to her. She wouldn't take him to a random place.'

George agreed but suggested that it would be more significant to Peter Shotover. 'This is all about what happened in 1917 so she must be planning something in line with what happened to her grand-dad.'

'Don't forget that her whole family was affected,' said Juliet. 'She didn't know her grand-dad that well. She's only been planning this for a couple of years so I would assume that that's when she found the diaries.'

James felt a jolt of panic. 'Harry, you said someone was at the door for John.'

His son's eyes widened with alarm. 'Crikey, do you think that was Mandy?'

James jumped up. 'I'll telephone him.' He dashed out to the hall and dialled John's number. It rang and rang. 'Come on, John,' he muttered, watching the seconds tick by on the clock. Beth and the others gathered, willing John to answer. James shook his head and replaced the receiver. He picked it up again and dialled.

'Ah, hello, Charlie, it's James here. I say, have you heard from Mandy at all?'

There was a small period of silence before his friend replied. 'No, James. I probably won't be seeing her again.'

'Oh? Why's that?'

'She's a bit of a Jekyll and Hyde. When you get to know her she seems a bit . . . I don't know how to describe it.'

'Unhinged?'

'Well . . . yes, that would cover it. What's going on?'

'I'll update you later — got to dash.'

'I take it,' said Juliet, 'that the librarian has seen another side to Mandy.'

'He has indeed,' James replied, relating what Charlie had said.

Nonplussed, James stared at his feet. Was there something in Ethel Shotover's house that could have given them a clue? Was there something the neighbour said or something they'd seen?

George placed a call to his office and requested a police presence at the house of Major William Carlton, adding that they were to break in if there was no response. After a couple of minutes he finished the conversation and turned. 'It may be that she's got them there.'

Beth held Harry's hand. 'Oh, I feel so helpless.'

James churned over his earlier conversation in his mind. The thought he wanted was there. As if it were at the heart of a maze, it stood tantalisingly close, yet so far away.

And then it appeared. He slapped his forehead with the palm of his hand. 'Of course! The poisoning, the shooting, it all makes sense!' He clicked his fingers and pointed to Juliet'

'Beachy Head.'

Juliet's face lit up. 'Oh, James, how inspiring. That's it?'

Harry looked confused.

'I'll explain on the way. Come along. We've wasted too much time as it is.' He turned to George.

'Are you well enough to travel?'

George's indignant glare answered his question.

They shrugged their jackets on, grabbed their scarves and gloves and raced down the steps.

Beth, Harry and Juliet squashed themselves into the back of the Jaguar and George sat up front with James. As he turned onto the main road, sleet began to fall. Harry sat forward.

'Come on, Dad, why Beachy Head?'

'I think she's recreating what happened. She has her grandfather's gun so she will have the upper hand on getting John out of the house. I think she's driving them both to Beachy Head. Her grandfather, Peter Shotover, shot himself. Her father threw himself off the cliff. Her mother poisoned herself. She wants Major Carlton to go through the same emotions, feel the same way she does; have that same sense of loss and go through the same death.'

'So she's poisoned Cynthia and now she's going to kill John.'

'I think she will shoot John and shove William off Beachy Head.'

Harry groaned and sat back. James gritted his teeth and put his foot down.

'Careful,' said George, gripping onto the seat with every corner.

James ignored him.

'Mmm,' said Juliet as she peered through the window.

'You have a thought?'

'Quite inappropriate really but I wonder if you could switch your radio on. Your aerial's up and they're presenting a carol concert on the Light programme.'

James checked his rear view mirror to catch Beth smirking. Juliet didn't care for William Carlton and, he believed, didn't care one jot whether he lived or died. But, John, on the other hand didn't deserve the fate Mandy had in store for him. He reached over and turned the radio on. Greeting them was the Winchester College boys' choir singing the Sussex Carol. He focussed on the road ahead. Christmas was almost upon them. The first night for the pantomime would be in two days' time and the pub dinner and Yule Log ceremony would be the next night. Peace and goodwill to all men! *Let's hope my instinct is right*, thought James. *Let's pray we're heading in the right direction. If not, both the Major and John will be dead.* He notched the speed up.

29

Beachy Head was home to England's highest chalk cliffs and, when viewed from the ocean, appeared as a curtain of dazzling white against a blue sea. Over the centuries, it had been the site of many a shipwreck and during World War II, the Royal Air Force had set up a forward relay station there, where they listened to signals coming from France.

Today, the iron grey sky had cast a blanket of gloom across the landscape. James drove along the main road, looking for a convenient place to pull over. He slowed the car down and peered through the side window. To his right were the grasslands that led to the cliff top.

'Look,' Harry pointed. 'Tyre tracks.'

James pulled over and followed the tread. Thank you for damp slush, he thought, as he drove the car across the undulating cliff-top. He hoped he didn't hit a pothole or get stuck in a hidden ditch. The windscreen wipers cleared the screen of sleet and it was becoming difficult to distinguish between the colour of the sky and the snowy ground. George pointed to the front.

'There.'

James saw a small red car stop in the distance. The Major stumbled out of the passenger seat, his hands tied. Mandy opened the boot to allow John to climb out at gunpoint.

'Pull up here. We don't want to distract her,' George ordered.

James did as George suggested and switched the engine off. He turned, rested his arm on the back of his seat and addressed the ladies.

'I'd really rather you stay here. If she has a pistol, she could shoot the lot of us. The woman is psychotic so there's no telling what she'll do.'

'Fiddlesticks with that,' said Juliet. 'Harry, let me out. I didn't come all this way to watch you play the hero. If you go, we all go.'

'Absolutely not,' said George. 'This is a police matter, the woman is armed and

I'm not taking responsibility for people getting hurt. You stay in the car.'

Juliet reached over Harry to open the door. 'I don't need you to take responsibility for me. I'm quite capable of making the decision for myself.' She nudged Harry, who gave James a helpless stare and got out.

James pointed at Beth. 'Don't you dare think of following! I almost lost you to some idiots last year and I can't go through that again. Harry, I insist that you stay here with your mother.'

James and George got out of the car and gently closed the doors. They pulled their scarves close, crouched low and made their way toward the red car. They ducked down and judged their timing for scampering on. Juliet, although elderly, was sprightly and kept step with them all the way. George signalled for them to go to the side of the car where they would remain out of sight. James nodded. He kept his eye on Mandy. She only needed to turn and she'd see them. He frowned. She wore no coat and appeared oblivious to the sleet and chill coming in off the ocean. When they got to the car, they scurried around to the side, and peered over the top of the bonnet.

Mandy and the Carltons were around fifteen feet away. She waved an old army pistol and shouted for them to walk to the cliff-edge. John's response was taken by the wind but he held his father back. Mandy screamed at him.

'Don't play games with me! If you don't do as I say I'll shoot where you stand. It makes no odds whether it's here or over there. You will be shot today, John Carlton.'

Major Carlton relied on John's strength to keep him up. He reached a hand out.

'Please, spare my son. I'll do whatever you want me to do but please, not John, he's done nothing wrong.'

James' blood chilled. Mandy's laugh was manic; hysterical. She stabbed a finger at herself.

'I did nothing wrong. My dad did nothing wrong. But because of what you did, Major bloody Carlton, our whole family suffered. You drove my grand-dad mad.' She brought a small book out of her pocket. 'It's all in here, he wrote it all down but no one believed him, 'cos they said he was mad. Do you know what he did? I'll tell you. He shot himself.' She held the gun in the air. 'With this pistol. He couldn't live with himself. My dad found him. Poor dad was raised by a madman and it sent him crazy too. D'you know what my dad did?'

William cowered as John struggled to keep him steady. The old man struggled to stay on his feet. Mandy waved at the ocean.

'He jumped off this cliff. Left me and Mum. And now Mum's gone. Poisoned herself.' She waved the gun. 'Do you understand now? Do you understand what's going on? You caused my grand-dad to shoot himself so I'm going to shoot John. You caused my mum to poison herself, so I poisoned your missus.' She moved closer. 'My dad jumped off the edge here and you're going to do the same Major William bloody Carlton.'

William shook his head and cried. 'No.'

Mandy sneered. 'What's the matter? Too cowardly?'

John held his father tight. 'Surely, we can talk this through. I didn't realise what you'd gone through. Dad would never have wanted so many people to suffer.'

Mandy repeated his words in a sarcastic tone.

''Dad would never have wanted so many people to suffer.'' She spat on the ground. 'He knew what he was doing.'

'He was ordered to lead. He had no choice. If you'd come to us and spoken to us we could have helped your parents.'

'Not my dad, you couldn't. He'd already jumped.'

'Well, your mum then. She didn't need to suffer like that.'

Mandy's expression suddenly changed. In a flick of a switch, she stood like a small child lost in the wilderness. 'My mummy's a nice lady. She makes my favourite tea on a Saturday.'

James caught his breath. John asked her what her favourite tea was.

'Smoked haddock and a slice of bread and butter. She always makes that for me.

Every single Saturday. She's got some in.'

James nudged George. 'Do you have a plan?'

'Not while she's waving that gun around, no.' He looked at James. 'Do you?'

'Yes, I do but it's completely insane and may not work.'

Juliet's eyes lit up. 'I saw it too. Now is the time.'

George glared at her and grabbed James' arm.

'Don't be bloody stupid. What could you possibly do to stop her?'

'Charlie said Mandy was a Jekyll and Hyde character. Did you not notice a complete change in her character? Trust me.'

His heart beat like a tympanum and the saliva in his mouth disappeared as he stood up. He strode toward her and tried to keep his hands from shaking.

'Ah Mandy, thank Goodness I've found you!'

Mandy turned, glassy-eyed.

'The hospital's been trying to contact you about your mother. She's feeling a lot better and is asking for you. She said she may be a little late serving dinner.' Mandy continued staring as if trying to make out what he was saying. James put his hands in his pockets and strolled toward her as if nothing was wrong. 'She has a Christmas present for you. I have my car just along here so I can take you to see her.'

Her arms dropped to her side. 'Mummy. You've seen my mummy?'

'I have and she's asking for you. She wants to put up the Christmas tree and she said it's not the same if you're not with her to do it. Would you like me to take you to her? She's worried you'll catch cold.'

'Yes please.'

'Come along then.' Behind her, John and William remained rooted to the spot in terror. He hoped they'd remain like that. Any sudden movement could push her back to the present. Mandy stepped toward him.

'Is Mummy all right?'

'She's absolutely fine, Mandy. Come along, we don't want to keep her waiting.'

She walked toward him in a daze and gave him a blank stare. James reached down and gently took the gun and diary from her hands. He put the diary in his pocket and held the gun out of reach as he wrapped an arm around her. He waved for Harry and Beth to join them. George and Juliet got to their feet as James insisted that John and William to stay out of sight.

'Mandy, we'll take your car. My friend George will take you to your mother and my son will drive.'

They helped her into the back of the car. George sat beside her and put the handcuffs on. When the cuffs locked she came out of her trance and screamed.

John brushed past him, opened the car door and punched her hard across the cheek. She fell back, unconscious. George glared at him. The young man held his hands up.

'Arrest me if you want.'

'I'll turn a blind eye.'

'Dad,' Harry shouted, 'you're a bloody idiot, you could have got yourself killed! Promise me you'll never do anything like that again. If you do, I'll take it that you're as mad as her.' He got into the driver's seat. 'John's probably done you a favour, George. At least she won't be screaming all the way to Lewes.' He started the engine and looked up at James. 'I'm proud of you Dad but *please* don't do that again.'

James assured him he wouldn't and once the car was on its way he sought out Beth who, along with Juliet, was helping William.

'Sweetie, could you bring the car to us. I don't think he'll manage to walk.'

'Of course.' He ran across the clifftops to fetch the Jaguar.

* * *

As James drove home, the car heater began to warm Major Carlton who sat in the back between Juliet and Beth. He peered over his shoulder to see Juliet rubbing his hands. He was pleased to see that she'd succumbed to her soft side even when dealing with a man she clearly loathed. But Carlton's pomposity had given way, revealing a vulnerable old man. Beth spoke quietly with him about normal things; getting home and having tea and crumpets. He appeared to respond to this well. A signpost for Cavendish came into view. James stole a glimpse at John, who hadn't spoken a word since they'd left Beachy Head. He had a haunted look about him.

'Things will be all right, John.'

The young man looked defeated. 'I can't face going home tonight. Could we see if Mrs Keates has her rooms available?'

'We can do a little better than that. Come and stay with us. Dr Jackson can give your father the once over and give you a sedative to help you sleep.'

'I'd like that. I'd like that very much indeed.'

At home, Beth and Juliet cobbled together a comforting casserole of braised steak, mushrooms and root vegetables. Harry took a detour to Harrington's to update Adam; George and Inspector Collins took statements from both John and Major Carlton and, after some time, left them all in peace.

In the early evening, after both John and his father had taken hot baths, both were made comfortable in the lounge with a warming brandy. James stoked the fire and added more logs. Beth switched on the tree lights and lit candles. The room looked welcoming and homely and its ambience helped both Carlton men to relax. The Major sat close to his son as he expressed his desire to be able to live his life again and make the right decisions.

'I made a huge error of judgement during that mission. I cannot blame my own father although he bullied me into joining up. I should have stood up to him. I wasn't a fighter. I should have joined the medical team, something to help the wounded rather than help to kill. I was a coward before I even reached the trenches.'

John squeezed his hand. 'No you weren't, Dad. That's the shock talking.'

'No John. It's the truth. I tried to be a good officer but I didn't have it in me. It ruined my life and made me choose options that I never thought I'd have to consider. I signed the authority for Franks to be shot. I killed Arthur Strong to save myself. And look at the misery it caused. Why they put me in charge of that mission, I've no idea. They must have seen I wasn't a leader.'

Juliet heaved a sigh. 'Because someone had to do it, Major Carlton. If it wasn't you, it would have been someone else. Yes, you should have stood up to your father. You should have admitted your failings as an officer before leading those men. You should have taken responsibility for your actions. But you didn't; and this is the culmination of those events. These things have a habit of turning on us and you will have to live with that. My friend and confidant, Mr Patel, refers to it as karma; a Buddhist expression. You may have heard of it.'

James had. He recalled Patel explaining karma to him some time previously: how one's actions determine one's fate in life. Provide random acts of kindness, he'd said, and you will receive that kindness back.

Major Carlton accepted another brandy

from Beth. He held his glass up. 'I want to thank all of you for what you did. I feel unworthy of such support. I've lost my dear wife as a result of decisions I made but Miss Billings cannot take away the wonderful memories I have of her. Thank you, Lord and Lady Harrington, Miss Brooks-Hunter. I value everything you did and I'm well aware of my failings in your eyes.'

30

James carried a portion of last year's Yule log through the main bar at the Half Moon. Bob Tanner and the Taverners launched into 'Good King Wenceslas' with several harmonies, a melodeon and a fiddle, whilst the beat on an Irish bodhran accompanied them. The villagers joined in enthusiastically, clapping and pounding on the tables while James placed the log on the already blazing hearth. Cheering and applause rang out before everyone settled down. Bob and the Taverners moved to the back of the pub and continued playing. James felt a nudge in his ribs.

'Oi, oi.'

'Bert, I was beginning to wonder if you'd disappeared for good.'

'No, mate, just finishing up on the Christmas deals. And people 'ave got more money these days so they're spending it.' He rubbed his hands together.

'That pays for the next few months.'

James motioned to Donovan to pull a pint for his old friend. Bert explained that he'd been up at the markets and had been able to get some goods from a contact who worked in Hamleys. Hamley's was one of the biggest toy shops in the world and James was sure that his friend would have made a tidy profit dealing with them. Bert held his pint glass up.

'Cheers. By the way, I've got that portable record player that Beth wanted. I've left it with the Merryweathers at the vicarage.'

James baulked. 'Good Lord, has she been ordering from you?'

Bert shrugged. 'They'll always be dealers like me, Jimmy-boy, you may as well make use of me.'

He groaned. 'I'll pop by and pick it up later.'

'G-good evening.' Stephen slapped him on the back.

'Ah, another stranger reappeared. Has the vicar at Loxfield returned?'

'H-he has, thank the Lord. I-I feel as if I'm m-missing out on your little mystery.'

'Hello James,' said Anne. 'Where's Beth?'

'Ensconced in the booth by the window with Charlie and George. Go and sit down. What're you having?'

With their orders in, they made their way to the booth and squeezed in and shared some concern over whether they would be able to eat comfortably.

'Where are Luke and Mark?' Beth asked Anne.

'With all the other children. Mr Chrichton is an absolute peach. He's arranged a games night for them so we can all attend this little gathering. They're playing pin the tail on the donkey, pass the parcel, oh all sorts of things. He has two of his staff helping as well. The children will enjoy that much more than sitting here with us.' She sipped her sherry and stared at James. 'I for one would like an update on the news. We've missed out on all of the excitement.'

James addressed George. 'Will Mandy go to prison?'

'She's being held in an institution. Difficult to get any sense out of her but, in her lucid moments, we've got it all down.'

'H-has everyone gone from y-your place?'

'Juliet returned to Cornwall yesterday. GJ and Catherine are staying with her to celebrate Christmas. John and his father have returned to the Major's house. He's thinking of moving.'

Bert huffed. 'Too ashamed to face everyone.'

Donovan Delaney placed two chairs at the end of the booth. James smiled and turned. Threading their way through the crowded pub were Harry and Oliver. Donovan's wife Kate hammered on a tin tray with a wooden spoon. The villagers hushed.

'Take your seats! Dinners are coming out now.'

Every available space was taken by those who wanted to share in this unique experience. The members of the WI, which included most of the women seated in the pub, had been allocated specific jobs for this Christmas feast. Anne and Beth peeled the sprouts; Helen Jackson cooked the numerous hams that Graham had supplied. Donovan took responsibility for roasting the chickens and Dorothy Forbes and Graham's wife,

Sarah, had peeled the potatoes and parsnips. The Snoop Sisters, not wishing to be outdone, had made the stuffing and gravy.

The anticipation was almost tangible. Kate dashed amongst the tables, lighting candles. Many of the women, including Beth and Anne, rushed out to the back of the pub to help bring out the meals. Bob Tanner sang 'We Wish You a Merry Christmas' and, as everyone joined in, the women distributed the food. In ten minutes, all the villagers had a substantial plate full chicken, roast potatoes, vegetables and gravy, in front of them. Stephen stood up to say a brief prayer and then the pub buzzed with chatter and laughter. They pulled crackers and read out their jokes and placed paper hats on their heads.

After catching up on the news, Oliver took a swig from his beer.

'So, Dad, when did you suspect Mandy? Was it quite early on?'

'At first, I found the whole thing baffling. I couldn't understand what the link was between Olivia Dupree and the

Carltons and, of course, there wasn't one. Mandy was not only quite mad but clever with it. Her mother collected those awful bottles and a number of them were from chemists' shops.'

'With the poison still in them?'

He explained that old bottles were just thrown out and Mandy's mother had unknowingly stocked her house full of the stuff. 'The poisoning of Olivia Dupree had been a test. There was no love lost between them. She'd more or less told us that at the start. Mandy had read up on doses and decided to give Olivia the night off.'

'But her real target was the Major?'

'Yes.' He outlined to the group how Mandy had found her grandfather's diary and the disturbing entries she'd read. The old man, on leaving the army, had continued writing a diary and eventually named William Carlton at the end of his ramblings. 'He was still scared Carlton would come after him so the diaries were never shown to anyone.'

'B-but it all g-got too much for him?'

'Never right when he came back from

France. The doctors sent him home because he had family; they thought he'd be better there but he just got worse and shot himself. His son bore the brunt of the depression and became affected by it. He decided to end it all and then his wife poisoned herself. A sad state of affairs all round.'

'S-so Mandy pretended to be E-Enid while she s-stalked the Major?'

'That's right. When the postmistress started asking questions, she gave her a name and a reason for being there.'

'I wonder,' said Anne as she sliced into her parsnip, 'if madness is hereditary.'

'Certainly seems like it,' Beth put in. 'But if you're surrounded by family who are a little unhinged, perhaps you can't help but be affected.'

James agreed. 'Thinking back, Beth and I both witnessed little mood swings here and there; some short temper, but you don't think it's anything more than that.'

George sipped his water, scowling at James' beer with envy. 'It's a wonder Carlton wasn't found to be a coward sooner.'

'Yes, he certainly played a perilous

game.' He cut into his chicken. 'Will he face charges for cowardice?'

George shrugged. 'I've no idea. I'd be surprised if he didn't have that commendation taken away.'

'And where did Enid disappear to?' asked Anne.

'She did exactly as she said she was going to. Walked out of her job and was happy to have annoyed Olivia by doing so,' replied James. 'She walked into the arms of her chap, Derek, and back to her parents in Devon. And, I think a dice with death softened Olivia. Bert?'

'That's right. I 'eard she's spending Christmas Day with her mum and dad.'

'Oh what a relief,' said Beth. 'Her parents must be thrilled.'

With their dinners finished, the villagers took it in turns to take their plates through to the back room. They scraped any leftovers into a huge bin that Graham would use to feed his pigs. Meanwhile, Kate was serving out portions of Christmas pudding. James, along with Philip and Stephen, joined them.

'Anything we can do to help?'

She wiped her hands on her apron and thrust a tray into his hands. 'Put those bowls of brandy butter, cream and custard on trays and set one of each on every table.'

They did as they were told. For the second time, Kate rattled a battered tray and ordered everyone to take their seats. Donovan stood on his chair with a bottle of brandy.

'We're to be thanking Lord Harrington's granny for this recipe.' As he spoke, several WI women came tripping out with Christmas puddings and spoons. They placed one on each table. 'You've a small brandy on the table and a box of matches. Don't be setting fire to my pub but I'll appreciate you setting fire to your own pudding.'

Beth leapt up. 'And don't forget there are some sixpences in the pudding. Don't break your teeth.'

As the flames lapped around the puddings, the villagers applauded. Charlie took a spoon and sliced into their table's dessert and served equal portions all around.

'I say, Charlie, you're not too upset about Mandy, are you?'

'I was to begin with but I sort of knew it wasn't going to work. Those sudden mood swings upset the kids and that made my mind up.'

Anne, who sat the other side of him, patted his hand. 'Someone will come along for you one day.'

He looked wistful. 'I'm all right most of the time. Don't you fret yourself about me.' He looked at Beth. 'You ready for your first stage appearance?'

Beth assured him she was as nervous as a fox being chased by the hounds. 'But we're sold out and the money is going to a good cause. And we have a special visitor.'

James explained about Private Fluff Irwin. 'I think he'd probably enjoy it more sitting with the children.'

'W-well, then, that's what w-we'll do.'

Beth snuggled up to him. 'I'm proud of you, James, but please don't confront a mad woman with a gun again. Promise me.'

He kissed her forehead. 'I promise.'

'A-and I'm pleased to s-say that, for once, I-I didn't get coshed,' Stephen said.

A chuckle rippled around the table.

Donovan shouted over the chatter. 'Happy Christmas everyone!'

The villagers raised their glasses. 'Happy Christmas!'

James sipped his Christmas ale and pecked Beth on the cheek. 'Merry Christmas, darling.'

THE END

Grandma Harrington's Mince Pie Filling and Gingerbread Slices

MINCE PIE FILLING

Mince pies originated centuries ago and contained thirteen ingredients to represent Christ and his apostles. Unlike today's mince, the old Georgian recipe actually contained meat!

1 cup minced beef

½ cup minced veal
½ cup brown sugar
1 cup raisins
1 cup currants
1 orange use zest and juice
1 lemon use zest and juice
¼ tsp ground cloves
¼ tsp ground nutmeg
pinch of black pepper
1 cup dates

Mix ingredients. Cover and let sit overnight. Place filling in pastry crusts. Glaze with egg yolk or milk and bake in the oven at 350F or gas mark 4 for 35–40 minutes.

GINGERBREAD SLICES

6oz butter
6oz caster sugar
3 eggs
3oz black treacle
8oz flour
1 tsp mixed spice
1 tsp ground ginger
Pinch of baking power
Pinch of cinnamon
1oz flaked almonds
3 tablespoons milk

Set the oven to 350F or gas mark 4.
Cream the butter and sugar and add the eggs, beating them in well.
Sift all the dry ingredients together and fold into the mixture with the treacle.
Fold in the almonds and milk.
Pour into an 8-inch tin.
Bake for 45 minutes.

We do hope that you have enjoyed reading this large print book.

Did you know that all of our titles are available for purchase?

We publish a wide range of high quality large print books including:
Romances, Mysteries, Classics
General Fiction
Non Fiction and Westerns

Special interest titles available in large print are:
The Little Oxford Dictionary
Music Book, Song Book
Hymn Book, Service Book

Also available from us courtesy of Oxford University Press:
Young Readers' Dictionary
(large print edition)
Young Readers' Thesaurus
(large print edition)

For further information or a free brochure, please contact us at:
Ulverscroft Large Print Books Ltd.,
The Green, Bradgate Road, Anstey,
Leicester, LE7 7FU, England.
Tel: (00 44) **0116 236 4325**
Fax: (00 44) **0116 234 0205**

LORD JAMES HARRINGTON AND THE CORNISH MYSTERY

Lynn Florkiewicz

While on holiday with his wife Beth in Cornwall, James learns that a local fisherman vanished during the recent opening procession of the Cornish Legends Festival. When more men disappear in broad daylight, he can't help but put his sleuthing hat on. If they were kidnapped, why is there no ransom demand? What are the flashing lights off the coastline? Who is the eccentric woman on the moors? Have the Cornish Legends really come to life? As James delves into the mystery, he realizes his questions come at a price . . .

REDEMPTION TRAIL

Victor Rousseau

Petty criminal Alfred Collins finds himself the victim of a conspiracy to frame him for murder. Sentenced to twenty years in prison, he manages to effect a daring escape, and assumes a new identity. Eventually he learns that the man who framed him has fled to work for a lumbering company. Consumed with the passion for revenge and the thought of being able to force a confession that would clear his name and free him from the life of a fugitive, Collins follows his trail into the Canadian wilderness . . .

LORD JAMES HARRINGTON AND THE AUTUMN MYSTERY

Lynn Florkiewicz

James and his wife Beth are helping with harvest festivities when they learn that escaped convict Locksmith Joe, a known killer, is in the area. Also, new arrivals Christie Cameron and his sister Jeannie refuse to integrate into the community and have upset a number of villagers. When Christie is found dead in his bedroom, clues suggest foul play, yet the room was locked from the inside. How did the killer get in? Was Locksmith Joe involved? Then a second death occurs, and James puts his sleuthing hat on . . .

THE PIEMAN'S LAST SONG

Tony Gleeson

The Tennessee Pieman was a beloved celebrity until he disappeared into seclusion near a small town. Now he's turned up murdered, his body discovered inside a garage on his ranch, and local police chief Wilma Acosta has assembled a bizarre list of likely suspects: employees who all seem to be harboring their own mysterious secrets. Despite her doubts about whether she's up to the task, if anybody can find the hidden killer among the perplexing cast of characters on hand, it will have to be the intrepid Wilma.

DRIVE EAST ON 66

Richard Wormser

Police Lieutenant Andy Bastian is hired to drive young teenager Ralph Bartlett from California to Kansas, traveling east on Route 66. Ralph's rich father has booked his brilliant but unstable son into a mental clinic for treatment, and wants the arrangement to be kept secret from the public. Accompanying them is Olga Beaumont, a psychiatrist who has been hired to care for Ralph. But before they've gone far, Andy realizes they're being followed. Then they discover that their car's been sabotaged, and narrowly escape death . . .